HOOFPRINTS

Also by Laura Crum

Cutter

*To Karen,
Hope you enjoy
this!*

HOOFPRINTS

LAURA CRUM

Laura Crum

ST. MARTIN'S PRESS ✿ NEW YORK

Library of Congress Cataloging-in-Publication Data

Crum, Laura.
    Hoofprints / by Laura Crum. — 1st ed.
        p.   cm.   -
    "A Thomas Dunne book."
    ISBN 0-312-13983-7
    1. Women veterinarians—California—Fiction.   I. Title.
PS3553.R76H66   1996
813'.54—dc20   95-40670
                                                     CIP

10 9 8 7 6 5 4 3 2

For Bill, my husband.

With thanks and love to my animals,
who lent their personalities to these stories.

Flanigan, Gunner, Burt, Pistol, Rebby, Plumber, and
Lester—the horses;

Joey, Brett, and Fergie—the dogs;

Sam, Bonner, and Gandalf—the cats.

Special thanks to Wally Evans, my partner on many of
these horses, and Barclay and Joan Brown, my always
supportive parents.

And finally, my most sincere thanks to Dick Francis,
who has entertained and inspired me more than any other
writer.

HOOFPRINTS

ONE

He didn't give me any warning. I ducked out of the way just in time to feel half a ton slam by and miss me by inches. The sorrel horse pulled back on the rope that tethered him to the post and fought and twisted like a trout on a line. Stressed beyond its limits, the rope snapped suddenly and the horse went crashing over backward. Landing with a thump that shook the ground, he thrashed on his back, red legs waving, hooves beating the air. He wasn't hurt, just dumb enough to have a hard time figuring out where his feet were. In a minute he scrambled up and ran off, dragging the inadequate piece of rope he'd broken. I shook my head in disgust. This was a hell of an overrated way to make eight dollars an hour.

It took me twenty minutes to catch the horse and finish doctoring him; I was cold enough to be mad by the time I was done. Seven o'clock on a foggy morning was not the ideal time to be treating, or trying to treat, an ill-broke backyard dink of a horse.

Washing the rest of the antiseptic salve off my hands, I told the sorrel gelding what a worthless piece of shit I thought he was and turned him loose to eat his breakfast. As I stuffed strands of my once neatly braided hair roughly back into place and shoved my numb hands deep into the pockets of my denim coat, I cursed myself for being a complete idiot. I didn't have to be here. I wasn't even being paid my miserable eight bucks an hour to be here. It was just pure stupidity on my part, my inability to say no to someone who seemed to need help.

The sorrel gelding belonged to a twelve-year-old girl. The girl lived with her divorced mother, who held down a full-time job as a checker in a grocery store. Neither one of them knew the first thing about horses. They had paid too much for the gelding, who was a half-breed Arabian with a bad attitude and no training. The girl rode him bareback on the beach every afternoon after school, and he went pretty much wherever and how fast he wanted to go. But she called him Flame and thought he was perfect, and he represented, both to the mother and the daughter, the idea of the life they wanted. He was their one luxury.

They had called me out to treat him a week ago for a deep, possibly crippling wire cut on a back leg. In their faces, and in the mother's immediate, tentative questions about the cost of the visit, I could see their fear. They could barely afford the horse at all; they couldn't afford a vet bill. They could also, it turned out, barely control the horse. When he objected, naturally enough, to my touching the painful cut on his back leg, he simply dragged the girl all around the field. I had sighed, fetched a knowledgeable assistant in the form of a helpful local horseman, doctored the horse, and accepted the twenty dollars they could stretch themselves to come up with for a sixty-dollar visit. I had also agreed to come out every day for a week and treat the cut so it didn't develop scar tissue and make the horse lame. For free, of course. It was no problem, I told them. I'd be glad to. Yeah, right.

You are really a sucker, Gail, I told myself as I got back in the pickup.

The dog lying on the floorboards lifted his head and wagged his stump of a tail at me. "Stupid horse, huh, Blue?" I rubbed the wedge-shaped head. "Be better off in a dog-food can."

I scratched the old dog behind the ears for a minute, comforted by his presence. Blue was a thirteen-year-old Queensland Heeler, what the AKC calls an Australian Cattle Dog. He looked like a stocky blue-gray coyote with a bobbed tail, and he was every bit as smart, stubborn, and independent as his distant cousin. I had reason to know; Blue had been my more or less constant companion since I was nineteen.

Shoving the heater up to full blast, I put the truck in gear and jolted down the narrow, rutted driveway. The fog was thick enough to make me turn my windshield wipers on about once a minute—a summer morning like every other summer morning in Santa Cruz.

Santa Cruz, my hometown, sprawls on the northern edge of the Monterey Bay, a half-moon-shaped bite out of the coast of California about sixty miles south of San Francisco. The city has grown big enough to ramble carelessly over the redwood-studded hills, but the heart of it lies in the flatland along the San Lorenzo River. My charity-case horse lived on the northern outskirts, which forced me to drive through town on my way to the next stop.

I crossed Pacific Avenue, the main street, staring down it with a kind of morbid fascination. Once a familiar, picturesque row of old-fashioned brick and masonry buildings, carefully restored, it was now an incongruous combination of a few surviving structures, some slickly modern brand-new buildings, and gaping empty lots filled with rubble. In effect it was not unlike post–World War II Berlin, but the cause wasn't enemy attack; a 7.1 earthquake had struck

3

Santa Cruz in October of 1989, and the town was still rebuilding.

I rumbled across the San Lorenzo River bridge and up the hill and smiled a little as I looked down on Beach Flats and the Boardwalk. The outlines of the roller coaster and the old Cocoanut Grove Casino were just visible through the fog. They seemed to carry with them a touch of the 1920s carnival air that had made Santa Cruz a fashionable beach-town resort, and nothing, not hell, high water, or earthquakes, could make them appear less than raffishly cheerful.

Warming my still-numb hands in turn against the heater vent, I followed East Cliff Drive, winding for a couple of miles through the small beachside communities of Seabright and Live Oak. Halfway between Live Oak and Capitola, I turned down Rose Avenue, going toward the bay.

Ed and Cindy Whitney's place was the last one on the street, on the tip of a spur of land that stuck out into Monterey Bay. Their front yard was a deck over a steep cliff dropping right down into the surf, and the view from their windows was usually spectacular.

This morning the view was a solid blank of gray. All the tourists here in town for a July vacation on the coast of California were probably sobbing in their hotel rooms. The fog would clear in the afternoon—it always did—but Santa Cruz summer mornings were disappointing for those who had imagined themselves in bikinis rather than down coats.

Cindy's little barn, rustically shingled to match her house and complete with a cupola on top, looked deserted. I couldn't see any signs of life, or human life, anyway. My patient, the cocoa-colored gelding who stood in the barn, hung his head over the half door of his stall and nickered.

Plumber, short for Plumb Smart, was a registered Quarter Horse, four years old, and one of my favorite patients.

4

Cindy had bought him two years ago, paid five thousand dollars for him as an unbroken colt, and invested several thousand more in a couple of years of professional training. I'd been his vet the whole time, seen him grow and change from a sweet, babyish youngster into one of the nicest working cow horses in the whole area, and I'd developed a special fondness for him.

Plumber was a "people" horse, friendly and interested in everything the humans around him were doing. Aptly named, his intelligence, combined with a cooperative spirit, had made him extremely teachable; Cindy and her trainer, Steve Shaw, had won several big contests on him already.

I knew all this because Cindy, a cheerful, talkative extrovert, had chattered happily to me about her horse every time I came out on a routine call, invited me to dinner and several parties at her home, and generally extended the client/veterinarian relationship to one of mild friendship.

I walked over to Plumber and patted his neck, and he bumped me with his nose. Calling, "Cindy," I looked around the empty barnyard in surprise. Cindy was usually waiting for me.

A search of the barn produced zero results. No Cindy in the feed room. No Cindy in the tack room, either, just bridles, saddles, blankets, brushes, and medicines scattered everywhere. A dusty old desk seemed the obvious place to leave messages, but all I saw was horse bric-a-brac and general junk—horseshoes, a mortar and pestle, an empty Coors can, half a dozen bottles of phenlybutazone (horse aspirin), and a couple of rolls of Vetrap (horse Band-Aids). I shuffled the stuff around but couldn't find a note.

Plumber neighed anxiously, hearing noise from the direction of the feed room. I stuck my head in his stall and saw that his manger was empty, which explained all the talking he was doing. Cindy must have overslept; she would never have left Plumber without his breakfast otherwise.

Reluctantly I walked to the house, hoping Cindy was up and dressed and wouldn't stumble to the door in a nightgown and bathrobe.

My knock echoed hollowly in the big wooden house which a real estate agent would have described as a mansion. More realistically, it was a large two-story house with a lot of character. Shingled all over, with a steep roof and many small windows, it had been built by a successful bootlegger during Prohibition, which gave it a kind of disreputable glamour.

I knocked again. Echoes of the wooden banging bounced off the fog, but nobody answered the door.

Back at the truck, I consulted my appointment book. There it was: "Cindy Whitney, 8:00 A.M., shots and worming." Plumber watched me and nickered again, and I glanced at the dashboard clock: 8:15. Cindy's horse was her main preoccupation in life, and she was never late or neglectful of anything that concerned him. I decided to wait fifteen minutes more and sat down in my truck.

Slow, cold quiet pressed in around me, as if it were part of the fog. I could just hear the muffled boom of the surf on the cliffs. Doves cooed in a clump of Monterey pines, the trees a black shape against gray. Reaching for the thermos on the seat beside me, I poured a cup of coffee; it steamed into the cold air as I cradled the cup, savoring the look and feel of it as much as the taste. Slowly, the muscles across my back began to relax, though I hadn't realized I was tense. Tension, it seemed, was an occupational hazard.

All my life I'd wanted to be a horse vet; it was only after I'd achieved my goal that I'd realized my dreams hadn't prepared me for the reality. Somehow I hadn't pictured how frantically busy I would be, or how stressed. Neither had I supposed that my starting salary, when I calculated it in terms of a wage, would work out to be about eight bucks an hour. It was my bad luck that I'd graduated from vet school at a time when there was a glut of young vets on the market; competition for available positions was intense and salaries were low. I'd been delighted and relieved when I was promptly hired by Dr. Jim Leonard, the resident horse specialist in my hometown. Little did I know that Jim would expect something akin to slave labor; the expensive fees I charged clients went to his coffers, not mine.

Sipping more coffee, I watched Plumber's face, the white star on his forehead giving him an aristocratic look as he stared at me over his stall door. "Where's breakfast?" his eyes asked.

I felt cheered just looking at him. Plumber, and horses like him, were what made veterinary work worthwhile. He was the exact opposite of the horse I'd worked on earlier; he wanted to help you, not hurt you. Like people, horses are individuals, and one of the disadvantages of this job was that you got some assholes—human and equine. But you got some Plumbers, too.

Stretching back into the truck seat, I contemplated without pleasure an extremely uncooperative mare due for a pregnancy check at the next call, and the side mirror caught my reflection—dark brown hair that looked black in the cold morning light and blue-green eyes, a legacy from my Irish ancestors. There were some faint lines at the corners of the eyes—not so much age as strain. I was only thirty-two, after all.

Not an easy thirty-two years, though. Both my parents had been killed in a car wreck when I was eighteen, claimed by Highway 17, a notorious stretch of road between Santa Cruz and San Jose. Grades and football games, boyfriends and parties, the trappings of an ordinary upbringing had all vanished in a night. Alone and unconnected, my pain had resolved into a determination to turn my childhood dream of becoming a veterinarian into reality. Since then all my energy had gone into building a new life for myself—one that appeared to be carving wrinkles in my face at a high rate.

Ah, well. The job was deeply interesting and absorbing, as I had always believed it would be, and I was practicing in my hometown, a stroke of good luck that I hadn't expected. On the whole, I wouldn't complain.

Plumber neighed hopefully, bringing me back to the present. My fifteen minutes were almost up and there was still no sign of Cindy, which was very odd. Cindy was a horse person, and to horse people, horses are the center of the universe. The ones I know think and talk mostly of their horses, with brief breaks for food, drink, and other minor necessities of life. To them, and Cindy was no exception, forgetting, or even being late with a horse's breakfast is in the neighborhood of a mortal sin.

The clock on the dashboard said 8:30; I finished my cup of coffee and screwed the top back on the thermos. Plumber nickered at me eagerly when I got out of the truck and went over to him. As I tried to pat his neck, he swung his head away from me and toward his empty manger. The message was plain. Quit trying to pet me, you dummy, and feed me.

Another quick scrutiny of the barn didn't reveal anything new. I was headed for my truck, but my feet slowed to a stop before I reached it. Like a drawing in a child's magazine, something was wrong with this picture.

A newspaper lay in the driveway, getting damp in the fog. Plumber, still hungry, watched me intently. On impulse, I walked around the corner of the garage.

Inside the open doorway, Cindy's white BMW and Ed's red Ferrari crowded together, leaving a narrow walkway to the back door of the house. A nerve was twanging inside of me as I knocked on the door. Getting no response, I turned the knob and felt it open under my hand. My "Cindy" shuddered off into the dim interior as I stepped through the doorway.

Narrow windows leaked the cold light of the foggy morning into the back hall. I followed it into the living room, yelling, "Cindy" again, and the sound seemed to go up in spirals, bouncing off the walls and finally hitting the cathedral ceiling.

Ed and Cindy's living room had always felt cozy and comfortable when I'd been in it before; a huge stone fireplace and chimney and natural-wood paneling gave it a rustic hunting lodge ambience. This morning, unlit, chilly, and smelling faintly of the cold ocean, it seemed dank and cavernous. Skirting a few scattered armchairs and couches and calling Cindy's name, I stuck my head in the kitchen.

Two bodies sprawled on the floor, utterly still. Blood, dark and slimy, blotched their clothes. The back of the body nearest me was covered with it. That heavy mane of white-blond hair, it had to be Cindy; next to her, I recognized Ed's white face staring upward. My God. Oh my God.

I stood frozen in place, staring helplessly. This wasn't real. This couldn't be. There was a strange rushing in my ears and I felt suddenly dizzy. Abruptly, I sat down and put my head between my knees. My ears roared; everything grew dark. You will not pass out, I commanded myself; you will not.

I sat there for what seemed like a long time, with my nose inches from the tile floor, oblivious of everything but the need not to faint. When the roaring in my ears receded, I lifted my head, keeping my face firmly averted from the bodies.

Okay, so far. Tentatively, I got to my feet. My legs felt shaky, but I stayed up. I took a hesitant step forward. Then step by careful step, I inched into the room until I was next to Cindy's body. One arm was stretched out toward my feet, palm up, as if imploring me to help. The back of her white T-shirt was a solid dark red stain. Next to her, Ed's chest showed two horrific dark holes surrounded by clots of blood.

My mind jumped chaotically. The silent room was grotesquely unreal, as if I were trapped in an old black-and-white science fiction movie. I forced myself to think. Gritting my teeth, I bent down and touched Cindy's arm, choosing the inside of the wrist, pressing the cold, rubbery flesh just long enough to be sure, to know that there was nothing I could do. Shuddering, I stepped around her, carefully avoiding the blood on the floor, and did the same for Ed. Then I walked across the room to the phone, noticing with surprise that my hand was steady as I punched the numbers.

The operator's voice was brisk. "Nine one one."

"I need police, sheriffs, whoever, to come to One two eight Rose Avenue." My own voice sounded absurdly calm—the voice I used to reassure clients who called in frantic emergencies at 2:00 A.M.

"And what is the nature of the problem?"

"The two people who live here have been murdered."

The words weren't right, or maybe there were no right words. Keeping my voice composed and my eyes on the kitchen counter, I answered some more questions and hung up the phone.

When I turned back toward the room, the dead bodies hit me like a punch in the solar plexus. I had seen death before, I had caused it myself, plenty of times, when I put animals out of their pain, but this violent human death was blindly, all too personally final. I stared at what had been Cindy and Ed. Their bodies sprawled on the floor, empty as bags of old clothes. A coppery sweet scent seemed to emanate from the dark bloody patches. Something rose in my throat and I jerked my eyes away. I wanted out of that room.

Half-walking, half-running on unsteady legs, I pushed through the house, sharply aware of all the rooms where he, she, whoever had done this, could be, might be, waiting. My heart was thudding as I reached the back door, my hands fumbling for the knob, and I yelped, scared out of whatever composure I had left, when a knock reverberated on the other side of the door, right at the level of my face.

The police—it had to be the police. Hands shaking, I pulled the door open, to find a man staring at me. *Not* the police. A man, with an odd look on his face that I couldn't fathom, standing in Ed and Cindy's garage. I took a step backward. "Who are you?" I demanded with all the iron I could muster.

He looked as surprised as I felt. His mouth dropped open, and he mumbled some words I couldn't catch. At least he didn't seem to pose an immediate threat; he was obviously as alarmed as I and was backing away. With a shock, I realized I recognized him.

Vacant round blue eyes, snub-nosed boyish face, tightly curled blond hair—he was one of the regular Santa Cruz street people; I called him "the Walker." Unlike most of them, he always looked clean, and I never saw him pushing a shopping cart full of cans or carrying armloads of junk. He just walked. I'd seen him dozens of times, all over town, walking and talking to himself.

Maybe the recognition on my face alarmed him. Suddenly, for no reason that I could see, he turned and ran out of the garage. I stood where I was as if frozen, replaying his expression in my mind. Startled—like a wild animal. He reminded me of surprising a buck in the woods. He had the same look—distant and wary, almost otherworldly, and in the split second before he knows you for a human, not unfriendly.

TWO

No one was in sight when I walked out of the garage. The Walker seemed to have vanished into thin air. Plumber neighed at me; a human being emerging from the house looked promising to him. I could hear sirens in the distance as I went into the feed room, got a flake of hay, and put it in his manger. By the time I walked back out of the barn the sirens were close, coming down Rose Avenue.

I stood by my truck as the two sheriff's cars pulled into the driveway. They'd turned off the noise, but the red lights were flashing and the four uniformed sheriff's officers got out of the cars fast. I half-expected them to pull their guns and yell, Freeze. Instead, the oldest one, a man with a square chin and some gray in his hair, walked up to me and said, "We were called out here on a possible homicide?"

It took a few minutes of explaining on my part and checking on theirs, but when they figured out it wasn't just a possible homicide but a definite double murder, they worked fast. In no time at all, it seemed, there were half a dozen cars in the driveway, and a full dozen men, in uniform and out of it, walking in and out of the house. That was all I got to see of police procedure, because I was kept politely but firmly from leaving my position out in the driveway. I was watched by a man who struck me as too young to be carrying a gun; he seemed to devote all his energy to holding his face and body as stiffly as possible.

"Is it all right if I call my office and cancel my appointments?" I asked him.

He swiveled a severe glance my way.

"I'm a vet. I can call in on the two-way radio in my truck."

"All right," he said, and positioned himself where he could hear my conversation with the office.

I canceled all my appointments for that day, not knowing what would happen. Then we waited.

Eventually another car pulled into the driveway and two plainclothes people got out. The short female figure looked familiar—blond hair in a wavy bob, neat olive green wool suit, an air of cool self-possession.

"Oh, no," I muttered.

The woman was Detective Jeri Ward, who had investigated the murder of my friend Casey Brooks last fall. I'd gotten involved in the investigation and Detective Ward had not been happy about it—not at all. In fact, I was pretty sure Detective Ward thought I was a first-class pain in the butt.

"Hello, Dr. McCarthy." Her greeting was carefully civil.

"Hello, Detective Ward."

"I hear you found some more bodies."

A sudden vivid picture of the bodies I'd found—Cindy and her husband—choked back any snappy reply I might have made.

"Would you care to come down and give us a statement?" It might be phrased as a request, but I knew perfectly well it wasn't. Without pausing for an answer she went on briskly: "I need to go inside and have a look at things. If you'll wait here, I'll be out in a minute."

Leaning on my pickup, I waited. The young sheriff's deputy watched me out of the corners of his eyes, keeping his face turned rigidly away. Time crawled. I got in the truck and rubbed Blue's head awhile, adjusted both windows so he'd have plenty of air, and told him I'd be back soon. He cocked an ear and curled up a little more comfortably. Blue was old and stiff enough that he preferred to sleep in the truck unless there was something interesting to do—attack a bigger, younger dog maybe.

As I watched various official-looking people arrive and leave from my vantage point in the driveway, I thought about the man I'd seen in Cindy's garage; what in the world had the Walker been doing there? Santa Cruz was a mecca for the homeless; they thronged the city itself, particularly Pacific Avenue and the downtown area, where they mingled indistinguishably with the students from the local university. Mild climate and the liberal atmosphere that had dominated Santa Cruz since the university was opened drew them, and they presented a problem that the city had, as yet, been unable to deal with very effectively. Shelters affiliated with churches and staffed by volunteers were still the main coping mechanism, though it was hard to see just what else could be usefully done to help that large proportion of street people affected with some type of mental illness—victims of the Reagan administration's wholesale shutdown of government care.

The Walker didn't really fit the street person mold, though. For one thing, he always looked clean-shaven and neatly dressed; for another, I usually saw him over in this area. Rose Avenue, where I stood, is on the outskirts of Capitola, a high-dollar little resort city on the beach, which fancies itself another Catalina and is as conservative in its leanings as Santa Cruz is liberal. Capitola is the hangout of upwardly mobile young stockbrokers and lawyers; it runs to expensive clothing stores, Yuppie bars, and pricey restaurants. The street people in general avoid Capitola—perhaps they find the atmosphere not to their taste—and the Walker was unique in that he was a regular feature here.

What *could* he have been doing in Cindy's garage, though, knocking on her door? Did she know him? Did Ed know him? Could he possibly have killed them? Somehow I didn't believe it. The expression in his eyes had not been that of a killer. It had been too innocent, too startled.

When Detective Ward reemerged from the house, a good half hour later, I'd had plenty of time to speculate on who might have killed Cindy and Ed, if the Walker hadn't. I can't say I thought of anything useful.

Jeri Ward ushered me briskly into the passenger seat of a dark green sheriff's car without a word. Once she was driving toward Santa Cruz, though, she seemed to unbend a trifle.

"Did you know them?" Her voice held a hesitant sympathy.

"A little. I've been over to their house for dinner, a couple of parties. Cindy was a client of mine." I felt reluctant to pose as a grief-stricken friend, as our relationship had been casual at best.

"Do you know anything about them?"

"Well, Ed was a Whitney. One of *the* Whitneys."

"As in Whitney-Kraus. That's what his paperwork suggested." She made a slight reflexive negative motion with her chin and was abruptly silent.

I could guess what she was thinking. Whitney-Kraus was one of the larger software firms in Scotts Valley, Santa Cruz County's miniature version of the Silicon Valley, and the Whitney family was one of Santa Cruz's wealthiest families. The phenomenon of their recently acquired millions was closely linked to the incredible population growth Santa Cruz County had experienced in the twenty or so years since I was a child. At that time the county was mostly rural, and Santa Cruz was a sleepy little resort city that came to life only in the summer, when a constant stream of tourists poured in from the San Francisco Bay Area bound for the beaches and Boardwalk.

Even during my high school years, though, the writing was on the wall, as the Santa Clara Valley became the heavily industrialized and even more heavily populated Silicon Valley. Santa Cruz, a mere twenty minutes away via that very torturously winding Highway 17 that had taken my parents' lives, became home to ever-increasing numbers of commuters. Developers had had a field day, and the Whitneys, major landowners in what was once the one-store town of Scotts Valley, had sold large portions of their land for housing tracts and commercial buildings and started their own highly successful computer software firm on the remaining piece. From their point of view it was doubtless a real Cinderella story. But there were lots of longtime locals like myself who were deeply saddened at the changes in the county; many of the fields and farms I remembered, including my childhood home, were now ugly suburban neighborhoods.

Jerking my mind away from the ever-sore subject of Santa Cruz's continual growth, I asked Detective Ward, "Do you think the Whitneys will make this difficult?"

She shrugged noncommittally; still, it was the most human gesture I'd seen her make yet.

"I think Ed was more or less estranged from his family," I offered tentatively. "He didn't work in the business; in fact, as far as I know, he didn't do anything but play."

She didn't reply, just fixed her eyes firmly on the road; I decided it was time to shut up. When we pulled into the parking lot of the county building and got out of the car, she asked me to come with her in a formal tone that made me think she regretted her departure from routine.

After I was established, more or less comfortably, in one of those neutral-looking waiting rooms, or conference rooms, with plastic chairs and industrial carpet, she left me. I had a paper cup of lousy coffee that a receptionist-type deputy had given me, and I sipped it. Patience, I told myself. In ten minutes, or close enough, the door was pushed open again and a short, fat, balding man in a suit came through it. Detective Ward was behind him. They seated themselves on the other side of the long table in the middle of the room, and Detective Ward put a tape recorder on the table and clicked it on.

The short man said, "I'm Detective Reeder. Detective Ward says she knows you. We need to ask you a few questions."

"Okay."

"Your name?"

"Gail McCarthy."

We went through my address, phone number, and occupation. Then he asked me, "What were you doing at One twenty-eight Rose Avenue?"

"I had an appointment with Cindy Whitney, to worm and give shots to her horse, Plumber."

"What time was the appointment for?"

"Eight o'clock."

We went through it all step by step. The short, fat detective was as impersonal as a machine. I explained how I had looked around the barn, knocked at the house, had a cup of coffee, and gone back to the house and looked in the garage.

"Why did you do that?" he wanted to know.

"I don't know," I said truthfully. "It didn't seem right. The paper was still in the driveway; the horse wasn't fed. I had a funny feeling about it. When I saw the cars in the garage . . ." I spread my hands and shrugged. "I can't say I guessed anything like the truth. I suppose I was afraid that

Cindy was sick or incapacitated in some way."

"What did you do next?"

"I went in the house." I paused, and the detective looked at me. "I ought to explain, I guess, that I knew Ed and Cindy socially as well as professionally. I'd been over to their house a couple of times."

The detective nodded. I told him how I found the bodies. He questioned me closely about where I had walked, what I had touched. I was able, I thought, to recount every step exactly.

"I called nine one one; then I left the house."

I hesitated. Only I could link the Walker to these murders, and I had an inward conviction, maybe unreasonable, that he hadn't done them. I wasn't sure who he was or where he came from—he didn't look as if he slept under a bridge—but in his constant walking and talking were the obvious signs of a mental disorder, and he, like many of the other street people, aroused my sympathy. Suppressing a feeling of guilt, I went on. "There was a man in the garage, knocking on the back door, when I opened it."

"Did you recognize him?"

"I've seen him walking around town before. He's got curly blond hair; in his thirties, I'd say. Sort of a young face. I'd know him if I saw him."

"All right. What did this man do?"

"He ran away. I said, 'Who are you?' and he looked at me and ran off." I wasn't sure if it was my imagination, but I thought Reeder grew more focused suddenly. His face stayed impassive, but something in his posture, maybe his eyes, reminded me of an Airedale spotting a mouse behind the feed sacks. Then it vanished.

Finishing my story with the arrival of the sheriff's cars, I sat quietly in my chair, wondering if I was done.

Detective Reeder looked down, then back up into my

face. I was getting to know his eyes. Brown, a little blood-shot, with pouchy bags under them, like fat men have.

"Did you know Cindy Whitney well?" His voice was neutral.

I tried to answer the question honestly. "Not really. I'd been around her maybe thirty times in all, counting professional calls and running in to her at her trainer's barn and at horse shows. We were friendly."

"What was she like?"

"Outgoing—her main interest was horses. Definitely an extrovert, very social. She and Ed gave a lot of parties; it's my impression they were a part of Santa Cruz society, whatever that means these days. Cindy and I weren't close. She liked me, I think, because I was young, single, and a horse vet; I was the type of person she liked to know. She would have said we were friends." Inside I felt a little uncomfortable, as though I had betrayed Cindy.

"What about the husband?"

"Ed. I knew him even less than I knew her. She was the one that had the horse; he wasn't involved with it. He could be kind of abrasive."

The detective pounced on this. His voice didn't change, and the tired-looking brown eyes stayed droopy, but I could feel his mind pouncing. "What do you mean by abrasive?"

"He liked you to know he had a lot of money."

Reeder kept his eyes on my face, and I could see I was expected to continue.

"I'm not sure how to put this. As I say, I didn't know him very well, but he seemed to be the typical spoiled rich kid who's busy trying to impress everyone all the time. He had the Ferrari, the beautiful blond wife, the extravagant lifestyle. He liked to mention he'd flown to Aspen last weekend in his best buddy's Learjet. That sort of thing. His attitude toward Cindy, too—sort of casual possession, as if she were an object he'd bought and paid for—it was irritating. I didn't find him an appealing person."

Reeder nodded impassively. "Do you know anyone who might have wished to harm them?"

"No."

"Think about it," the detective repeated. The pouches under his eyes tightened as he narrowed his focus at me. "Don't forget, they were murdered."

"I don't know of anyone who had a reason to kill Ed and Cindy Whitney. I liked Cindy; as far as I know, everyone else did, too. I didn't know them well enough to be aware of any enemies they might have had."

Reeder sat silently for a minute. "Where were you last night?"

"I saw two emergencies and got home around midnight. The last time I could prove where I was would be about eleven-forty, when I left the second case." I gave him the names and addresses of the people involved.

"You live alone?" he asked.

"Yes."

"Would any of your neighbors have seen you come in?"

"It's possible." I gave him their names and addresses.

"All right," he said. "That's all for now. You'll be in town this week, Dr. McCarthy?"

"Yes."

He nodded. "Thank you for your time."

Heaving himself up, he left the room. Fat body, ugly, crumpled suit. Detective Ward stood and watched him go, and I could swear there was resentment in her glance. Then she looked at me. Not warmth exactly, but some sort of unspoken shared comment seemed to pass between us. "We'll be in touch," was what she said.

THREE

A young deputy with a square face took me back to my truck and waited carefully to see that I drove away from the scene of the crime. They had the house roped off and all kinds of vehicles parked around it. They needn't have worried; I had no desire to stay and spectate.

I drove back to the office slowly, feeling disgusted with myself. It seemed to me I ought to have felt more grief over Cindy and Ed. We weren't close friends—I had told the fat detective the truth—but Cindy, at least, had been friendly and hospitable to me. Their lives had been cut short with a savage finality, and I found that inexplicably intertwined with my sorrow was an interest and excitement that made me ashamed. What is it that drives us to stare at traffic accidents—that draws us to horror? Some sort of relief that at least it isn't me, this time? The relish I felt at being in the center of such a drama was leaving a bad taste in my mouth.

I pulled into the office parking lot filled with a sense of chagrin at the failings of human nature—my own in particular. It didn't help any to realize that half of my excitement about the murders had been the thought of telling my story at the office. That's sick, I told myself, sick.

Blue spilled stiffly out of the truck when I opened the door, ready to water the familiar trees in the parking lot. Looking up into my face when he was done, he snorted softly and stumped off to lie in his favorite box stall. Blue knew my emotions better than I did, I sometimes thought. Right now he knew I was in a rotten mood, not conducive to scratching his ears.

Shaking my head at myself, I walked in through the back door of the office. The rubble on my desktop was about knee-deep; I shoved it around, thinking that if I was a good person, I'd catch up on some long-overdue paperwork. I'd left the back door open and the sunny summer day poured into the room behind me. It was noon and, as usual, the fog had cleared. A Santa Cruz summer afternoon—seventy-two degrees, and the nicest weather in the world. I stared out the door thoughtfully, wondering if paperwork was such a good idea after all.

As I watched, a truck drove in. It was an old red Ford pickup, faded-looking but clean. Bret Boncantini was driving it.

The red truck swung casually into one of the spots marked STAFF ONLY, and Bret got out deliberately, not hurrying, making a point of it. He held himself up, shoulders back, stomach in. Sunglasses masked his eyes, but I knew they would be moving from one thing to another, quickly, curiously. Checking it out, he would have said. The same old Bret.

I sat at my desk and Bret walked confidently in the back door—again marked STAFF ONLY. Bret was a great one for back doors. He looked at me and grinned. "You look like you're working hard."

I had to smile. Then I thought of Cindy, and the smile died quickly. Bret and Cindy had been friends.

Might as well get it over with. "Bret, Ed and Cindy Whitney were murdered—sometime last night, I guess."

"Are you serious?" Bret's voice reflected disbelief.

"I found them this morning. Shot—both of them."

"Jesus." He sat down slowly in an empty chair. "I was over there yesterday afternoon."

We stared at each other a moment. Bret was nothing if not quick. "I guess I'll have to go talk to the police."

"And you'd better do it right away."

He didn't say anything. He was gazing out the back door and his eyes weren't focused; they were watching something inside his mind. Sunlight made a sheen on the fringe of hair above his eyes.

Bret was something to look at. His smooth brown skin, brown hair streaked with blond, and square chin could have come out of an ad for California living. His eyes were green-brown, with lashes longer than most women's. They were laughing eyes, eyes that said, You and me, we understand things.

I'd known Bret since we were children; we'd grown up together as neighbors, and somehow our friendship, casual, undefined, and unlikely, had stood the test of time. Maybe because I was impervious to his sexual charms. Most women, however, weren't.

Cindy had been no exception. Bret was one of her favorites. She had met him somewhere—everybody had. Bret had become a fixture in the local horse world. He shod horses, rode colts from time to time, did spells of work for various horse trainers, always quitting in the end. He left town for long periods—he'd been gone for the last two months—and then reappeared. From what I understood, he'd been a blackjack dealer in Tahoe, a cowboy on a high-desert ranch in Nevada, and a logger up near Yosemite, among other things. Now and then he would drop a quick comment about where he'd been and what he'd done, but in general he was uncommunicative about his other lives. Bret lived in the here and now.

"I didn't know you were in town," I said.

"Got in yesterday," he answered automatically. He didn't volunteer anything more, and I could see his mind was still somewhere else.

It would have been typical of Bret to have gone to Cindy's house right away. He often visited her, and I understood that the kind of free and easy hospitality she delivered had suited him right down to the ground. In the same way, his instant, playful charm had suited her. They had had, I thought, a mutually beneficial relationship. Bret kept Cindy from getting bored, and Cindy provided Bret with lots of free meals and all the beer he wanted. For a drifter like Bret, these were the essentials.

People had speculated about Cindy and Bret—how close they were, whether there was more than flirtation between them, but I thought such speculations were misplaced. Bret's emotions were buried deep, not hanging on his sleeve where people could get a grip on them. At the most, I guessed that Bret had been mildly fond of Cindy; whether he'd slept with her was an open question, but he wouldn't suffer much grief over her—certainly not over Ed. Ed hadn't been crazy about Bret; I expected few husbands were. For his part, Bret had always been unwilling to act very impressed about Ed's money.

In fact, I realized I wasn't sure what Bret felt about the Whitneys; to be honest, I wasn't even sure what he felt about me. Bret was of the same nature as a big tiger tomcat who had come to live with me for six months while I was in college. Aloof and independent, he had charmed me when he felt like it with his big yellow eyes and his purrs, then moved out abruptly and finally; I never knew why. Had he used me; was he fond of me? Such questions seem ridiculous when asked of cats, but they applied to Bret.

"Where'd you stay last night?" I asked him, remembering that his last home in Santa Cruz had been with a long-departed girlfriend.

His attention snapped back from wherever it had been with a visible jerk. One finger tapped my desk.

"In my truck," he said at last.

"Not at Cindy's?" I said, suddenly filled with foreboding.

He looked at me intently and I knew I was on the track to that thing his unfocused eyes had been seeing. "No," he said. "But it was kind of strange why I didn't."

He glanced around the back room as if seeing it for the first time. The white counters covered with books, papers, medicines, and machines. The orderly mess. A female tech in a lab coat sat at the other end of a long counter, looking in a microscope. Bret studied her carefully, the speculative look he gave all women, before turning back to me.

"Let's go have lunch. Little Mexico?"

"Sure."

I had already checked out for the day. It was just a question of getting out of the office before someone called in and the receptionist came back and cornered me.

"Come on," I told him, "we'd better get if we're going."

Bret drove us to Little Mexico in his truck, the cab crowded with a rolled-up sleeping bag, three or four brown paper bags full of clothes, a couple of coats, and half a dozen empty beer cans. Everything smelled like Skoal—mint green tobacco—and unwashed clothes.

At the restaurant, he moved instantly to sit on the deck. It was sunny and almost hot out there, and we ate tortilla chips with a spicy salsa that had big chunks of peppers in it. Bret thought we ought to drink margaritas.

"Sitting on the deck, on an afternoon like this?" He gestured around.

"I want to be able to function the rest of the day."

"One," he held up a finger. "One liter."

We ordered the margaritas.

Leaning back in my chair, I watched his eyes drift around and felt a familiar half-annoyed amusement. They were the eyes of a burglar checking a house for valuables to steal; Bret was looking for women to hustle. He was perfectly capable of spotting one he liked, striking up a conversation with her, and trying to talk me into finding my own way back to the office. At times like that, I wondered what I was doing with him; his carefree irresponsibility often verged into irritating selfishness. To be fair, I supposed my dogged I've-gotta-make-a-living-attitude bored him to death. Common childhood memories probably didn't hurt, or maybe it was just old habits dying hard.

One thing was for sure; Bret never threatened my sense of independence. A secretive, private person himself, he shied away instantly at the merest hint that anyone might cling to him. Evasion of intimacy was his forte.

I took a sip of my margarita—icy, head-tightening cold. Little Mexico made the best margaritas in town, not sweet at all, with a faint background of lime and a kick like a mule. Resting my chin in my hand, I studied Bret's expression. Despite the fact that margaritas in the sunshine were one of his favorite things, his usual half-cocked grin was missing. "I can't prove where I was last night, Gail," he said slowly, not looking at me. "And when the police find out that I was at Cindy's yesterday, they're going to start wondering."

"Were you planning on spending the night at Cindy's?" I asked him, feeling a renewed sense of foreboding.

"I was thinking about it, but Ed threw me out." His eyes met mine across the table. "I don't like to say it, now that he's been killed, but the son of a bitch got in some kind of jealous fit and told me to get out."

He sucked his margarita and stared off into the trees along Soquel Creek, and I knew he wasn't seeing the ducks floating on the water. "It was funny how he did it, though. I could have sworn it was all an act, that he wasn't really mad. He wanted me out of there all right, but I don't think he was really jealous. It doesn't make sense. I've been friends with Cindy for years, and he doesn't say a word. We know we don't like each other, but so what? I don't think anybody really liked that asshole, anyway. I come back to town after two months of being gone and he's suddenly jealous? Give me a break. No, it was something else, some other reason he wanted me out of there, and he made this big scene so I wouldn't stay."

Bret's eyes swung back to me with an uncharacteristic expression in them—worry. "I called you, but you weren't home. I couldn't think of anybody else where I could just drive in and ask to sleep on their floor, not right at the moment, so I pulled Big Red down this road I know. I've stayed there before. I just slept in the cab. It's a good thing I'm short." He grinned. "The question is, Are the police gonna believe all that, or are they gonna think I hung around and shot Ed and Cindy out of 'jealous rage'?" He shook his head. "I still can't believe they're dead."

I told him about finding the bodies and he expressed shock and fascinated interest. I'd gotten, I thought cynically, the audience I'd wanted. It was probably a natural human reaction—to distance the horror, make it less personal and threatening, but it still didn't seem right to me. Ed and Cindy were dead, and Bret and I were ordering enchiladas for lunch.

I told Bret about seeing the Walker in the garage and asked him, "Do you know anything about that guy?"

Bret grinned reflexively, his initial response to most questions. "Yeah," he said after a moment, "he was kind of a project of Cindy's. His name's Terry something. He walks around town—every day. You see him everywhere. Guy must be incredibly fit."

"I've seen him."

"So, anyway, I guess he walked by Cindy's every morning about the same time, when she was usually with the horse. She got the idea of trying to tame him, sort of—the guy." Bret flashed his eyes at me in an aren't-women-crazy look. "It sounds funny, but she told me he reminded her of a wild animal. She'd say hi to him all the time and eventually he'd say hi back and then he got where he'd come pet the horse, and the last morning I was over there before I left town, he actually came in the kitchen for a cup of coffee. He didn't talk much, at least not so's you'd understand, and he looked pretty skittish, but he obviously liked Cindy."

"Would he ever have hurt her, do you think?"

"How would I know? The guy had problems, that's for sure. Cindy told me he was a schizophrenic; lived in some board-and-care place over by the harbor—had a state check, you know. She didn't really know much about him; she just sort of took to him the way you'd take to a stray dog, I think."

A sense of remorse rushed over me at his words. Cindy, whom I had spoken of so lightly to the cops, over whose death I hadn't really grieved, had been kind enough to be sympathetic to the Walker. I'd never even bothered to say hi to him.

The waitress brought out our enchiladas at that point and conversation ceased.

When we were done I said, "Now we're going to the sheriff's office."

"Later."

"Nope, now. I'm going with you. You need to get this done, Bret."

He shrugged. "Have it your way."

He looked stubbornly reluctant when we pulled into the

parking lot of the county building, an ugly multistoried gray cube of a structure on Ocean Street—a part of Santa Cruz I seldom saw. The street is one long row of fast-food restaurants, convenience stores, gas stations, and cheap motels—a tourist's route to the beach. Jammed with visiting cars in the summer, tawdry and depressing always, it's an area I avoid when I can.

They took Bret to the same room where they'd taken me. Sitting in an uncomfortable chair in a hall that echoed with the tapping feet of sheriff's deputies, I studied the green spotted linoleum, possibly the ugliest linoleum I'd ever seen. The cold white light from the fluorescent bulbs did nothing to improve it.

After awhile I stopped studying the linoleum and started studying the faces of the deputies who walked by. Mostly men, mostly young. One dark-haired and mustached type gave me a hi-pretty-lady smile. I smiled back—friendly but not inviting. That was my intent, anyway.

Time passed—slowly. There was a clock on the wall, put there, no doubt, to infuriate anyone waiting.

A door opened across the hall, and I looked up, eager for any diversion. A woman appeared in the doorway, followed by Detective Ward, who was politely holding the door open. The lady getting this courteous treatment was dressed in a black-and-white glen plaid business suit that was more than a match for Detective Ward's olive green outfit, and her shoulder-length blond-streaked hair fell in expensive-looking layers about her face. It was a face that could have been attractive—mid- to late-thirties, pleasant, regular features—if it wasn't for the sharp, autocratic expression it wore. Her voice, which carried easily to where I was sitting, was as icy and authoritative as her face. "Detective Ward, I expect you to conduct this investigation along professional lines, certainly; but you will not pull any police procedure crap on me. My lawyer will be clear on that."

Jeri Ward's face was unperturbed and patient, but her body language was stiff. "Ms. Whitney, I, we, the sheriff's department, are not trying to 'pull' anything. We're trying to find out the facts."

"I'll have my lawyer speak to you."

The woman stalked off with a staccato tapping of high heels on linoleum, watched by me and everyone else in the hall. She didn't seem the least bit disconcerted. Her head was high on a long neck, her carriage confident, her emotions well under control. Everything about her said money, from the smooth waves of her hair down to what were no doubt Italian pumps on her feet. It didn't take a lot of brains to guess who she was. Ms. Whitney. One of Ed Whitney's relatives. One of *the* Whitneys.

Detective Ward was staring after her, too, her face deceptively quiet. I could guess what five-letter word was in her mind. She noticed me after a minute and walked over to my chair.

"Dr. McCarthy." She greeted me politely but distantly, and she looked, I thought, just a touch bedeviled. Her normally polished appearance seemed marred, ever so slightly, in comparison with the formidable Ms. Whitney, and her always-composed face held a trace of strain.

"Hello, Detective Ward."

"Did John Reeder call you back in?" she asked.

"No, a friend of mine came by to see me and I found out he'd been over at Ed and Cindy's yesterday. We decided he should come by here."

She seemed to withdraw slightly. "Your friend—is he being questioned right now?"

"I don't know. I assume so."

She was silent, and I wondered what to say. I wanted to ask about the woman but wasn't sure it was the thing to do. In the end, I decided to keep my mouth shut. Easier not to stick my foot in it that way.

Detective Ward focused back on me. "I'd like to see your friend before he leaves; I think I'll just check the interview room. If you think of anything about this case I should know, give me a call."

It was the friendliest tone I'd ever heard from her, and I risked a smile. "I'll do that."

"Thanks." She turned away abruptly and marched off down the corridor, leaving me to wonder if she really had ventured a smile in my direction or if it was just my imagination.

I waited almost an hour before Bret came back from the interview room, my stores of patience wearing thinner every minute. Detective Reeder was with him, bloodshot brown eyes as impassive as ever. Bret walked up to me quickly. "Come on, let's get out of here."

On the way back to the truck Bret recounted his interview sketchily, dodging, in his adroit way, all my questions. Once again, his mind seemed to be elsewhere. When we got to my office, he said he had to "see some people about some work." It was all vague, but he wanted to come sleep at my house. I didn't argue; Bret had done this before for brief periods, and usually he was no trouble. He left with a quick wave, Big Red booming away in the distinctive fashion of a truck with a broken muffler. Bret was in a hurry.

I called Blue and got in my own truck slowly. Home would be empty and silent, and I felt the need of someone to talk to. Lonny Peterson, my boyfriend, steady date, main squeeze—whatever you want to call it—was out of town on business and wouldn't be back till tomorrow night. No use thinking of him.

All in all, it took me only a minute. He might not provide conversation exactly, but I wanted to see Gunner. I pointed the truck toward Soquel.

FOUR

Gunner and I both lived on Old San Jose Road, in an area south of Santa Cruz known as Soquel, a sheltered inland valley that is more rural and gets less fog than Santa Cruz itself—two of my principal reasons for choosing it. Old San Jose Road follows Soquel Creek up toward the distant blue ridgeline of the Santa Cruz Mountains, winding through narrow canyons full of redwoods and emerging into sunny meadows. Gunner lived at Kristin Griffith's place, in just such a meadow, at the end of a long driveway with a white-board fenced pasture running down one side of it. Kristin's horse, a dark brown gelding she called Rebby, raised his head to look at me as I drove in, then kicked up his heels and ran off across his field in an excess of joie de vivre.

I smiled as I watched him. Rebby was a "running" Quarter Horse, bred for the track; he had a lean, breedy head and the long, flat-muscled, rangy look of a Thoroughbred. He also had big, soft, friendly eyes like an overgrown retriever, and he loved to be petted. Rebby was another "people" horse.

Pulling into Kristin's barnyard, I parked my truck near

the fence and Gunner came out of his shed and nickered. Gunner was my horse, a four-year-old Quarter Horse gelding by Mr. Gunsmoke out of an own daughter of King Fritz—breeding which, in the cow-horse world, made him royalty. Buying a horse like that would have been way beyond my means; Gunner had been given to me a year ago when he severed the suspensory tendons in his left front leg. His owner had been unwilling to wait out the yearlong period of enforced rest and inactivity that was necessary if the tendons were to have a chance of healing. I'd taken the colt, boarded him with Kristin Griffith, and waited.

Luck had favored me. Gunner was a sound horse today, completely recovered from his injury, and for the last month I'd been riding him as often as I could. The rides were short—twenty minutes or so of light walk-trot-lope exercise in Kris's arena—because the horse needed to be legged up slowly and because I never had any time.

Today, I thought, we'll go an hour. It was only four o'clock, and the summer afternoon and evening stretched well until eight. For once, I didn't need to be in a hurry.

I caught Gunner without any trouble; he was a friendly horse who met you at the corral gate, anxious to do something, anything. Leading him to the barn and tying him up, I brushed his shiny red coat and combed his long black mane and tail, savoring the warmth and the nice horsey smell of him.

A bay with three white socks, a big white blaze, and one blue eye and one brown one, Gunner had distinctive markings by anybody's standards. His blaze and two-colored eyes gave him a clownish look that fit his personality; Gunner, I'd discovered, was playful as a child.

He bumped my arm with his nose when I brushed his face, and I held out my hand, knowing what he wanted. Nosing and licking my palm, he begged for beer, his favorite treat.

"Sorry, buddy, no beer today," I told him as I slung the saddle pad up on his back. Next the saddle, a heavy roping saddle I'd borrowed from Lonny, who was a team roper. I was developing impressive biceps lifting it on and off.

I cinched the saddle up loosely, then slipped the halter off and held the bit up to Gunner's mouth, which he opened obligingly. Pulling the headstall over his ears, I fastened the throatlatch and patted him on the shoulder. "Ready, pal?"

Another bump with the nose was his only answer.

Taking it to be an affirmative, I led him down to the arena, tightened the cinch, and climbed on. The first time I'd done this I'd held my breath and taken a good grip of the saddle horn, prepared for anything. Gunner had had ninety days of professional training before he'd been hurt, so I knew he was ridable, but I hadn't really known how he would behave.

Lonny'd been with me and had offered to ride the colt himself, but I'd refused. Gunner was my horse, and I wanted to be the first one on him. Still, my knuckles were pretty white as I clutched the saddle horn and urged him to take his first few steps with me on his back.

As it turned out, there was no problem. Gunner was green but willing, and we'd gotten along just fine. Lonny watched our whole session, and when I'd put the colt up, he'd grinned at me. "That horse won't hurt you, at least not on purpose," he said. "He's got a real good eye. He'll do whatever you ask him to, if he knows how."

And so it was proving. As I hoisted myself up on Gunner's back this afternoon—I still hadn't developed a very graceful mounting style—I felt no fear, only pleasant anticipation of our interaction.

Letting him move out at an easy walk, I took in the late-afternoon sunlight slanting between the redwoods down by the creek and heaved a deep sigh. Finally, for the first time

34

since that awful moment when I'd seen the bodies, I felt a sense of peace.

I rode Gunner for the hour I'd intended, more or less, mostly at the walk and trot, with a couple of brief bouts of loping. I kept a hand on the saddle horn the whole time; on another horse, I wouldn't have—it's not considered good style—but Gunner had a quirk that made it necessary; he was a spook.

I'd discovered this on our third ride; a little piece of paper had blown into the arena, and you would have thought it was a horse-eating monster, judging by his reaction. He'd leapt away from this terrifying creature, clearing, I swear, thirty feet in a single bound. Only my grip on the saddle horn saved me; I'd clutched automatically and kept myself from landing on the ground by the skin of my teeth.

After his one enormous jump, Gunner had stood still, trembling and staring at the paper, his heart beating in great thudding thumps that moved my legs. I'd assembled my scattered wits, straightened myself in the saddle and urged him forward, and with some trepidation, he'd complied.

Since then I'd learned that this was his pattern. He'd see something he didn't like and make one jump—that was it. He never tried to run away or buck. If you could last through the initial leap, you were fine. The trouble was, his jumps were astounding—sudden, violent twenty-foot-plus swerves I could never get used to. Thus I rode with a hand on the horn.

Urging Gunner into a lope for a final couple of laps, I enjoyed the easy rocking motion of the horse underneath me. I'd had a horse for a few years when I was a teenager, and I rode well enough to exercise Gunner and get him legged up, but this was about the extent of what I was currently able to do. Gunner was bred to be a working cowhorse and I wanted him to achieve his potential; when he was fit and ready Lonny planned to take him and train him to be a rope horse.

The thought of Lonny made me smile, and I allowed myself to picture him as I cooled Gunner out at the walk. At forty-seven, Lonny was no one's idea of a handsome young stud; his sandy hair was thinning on top and the slight roll over his belt and the sag under his jaw revealed his age. But the long muscles down his back were strong, and eight months into a "relationship," I felt the same powerful sexual attraction to him as I had from the beginning.

Why, I asked myself, why this man?

It was his eyes that drew me originally, I decided. Kind eyes, framed by habitual smile lines, eyes that laughed easily. That and the affectionate rapport he seemed to have with his horses. And he was a big man, and I like big men. And his intelligence. And the way he respected my intelligence. And his sense of humor. And the very male aura he exuded. And, and, and. I laughed out loud.

There were dozens of reasons and I was finding more every day. Tomorrow night, I thought. Tomorrow night we'll be together.

Patting Gunner's neck, slightly damp with sweat, I swung off of him and told him, "You just wait. You've had it easy for a long while; pretty soon you'll have to work. Lonny's gonna turn you into a rope horse."

In another month he'd be ready. If I could get him ridden regularly in the meantime. Leading him to the barn, I unsaddled him and brushed him. I was just putting him in his corral when I heard a "Hi, Gail."

I turned with a smile and greeted Kristin Griffith, the owner of this barn, a client and a friend. She was in her mid-thirties, a slim, spare whip of a woman who trained and competed successfully in endurance riding—to my way of thinking, a very tough sport. Kris had won the Tevis Cup several years ago, a legendary hundred-mile race, and she was riding this weekend, I remembered, in a fifty-miler up on the north coast.

At the moment she looked elegant, her short, no-nonsense blond hair brushed high off her forehead and her slender frame shown off in a white silk blouse tucked into close-fitting black pants. Her face, bare of makeup and decorated only by attractively tinted glasses, was unremarkable except for the impression of force and intelligence that immediately caught your eye.

"Don't you look nice," I told her, feeling suddenly aware of my faded, dirt-smudged Wrangler jeans and crumpled chambray shirt—go-to-work clothes for me. Well, they'd started out clean, I reassured myself.

"Rick's taking me out to dinner." Kris grinned. "How's Gunner?"

"He's doing fine. He's completely sound, as far as I can tell."

"That's good." Kris gave me another wide smile. "I just wanted you to know, I won't forget his dinner. I'm feeding when I get back, so's not to get hay all over my good clothes."

"No problem."

Kris looked over her shoulder as the little gold Porsche in the driveway beeped authoritatively. "Rick's in a hurry; I'd better go."

She hustled off, and I watched her jump in the Porsche and zip off down the driveway, wondering where Rick was taking her to dinner. Somewhere expensive, no doubt, and upscale. Rick liked to show off the fact that he had bucks.

An engineer for a high-tech munitions firm in the Silicon Valley, Rick Griffith was handsome, self-assured, and polite, and I couldn't understand what Kris saw in him. He had a way of subtly flaunting his trappings of power—car, suit, briefcase—that got on my nerves, and I resented the sense I had that he expected to dominate any situation or conversation. Particularly with a woman.

Come on, Gail, I chided myself, don't be so touchy. You're probably just jealous.

Well, was I? Kris had this five-acre ranchette I'd have given my eyeteeth for, a seven-year-old daughter who was one of the nicest kids in the world, the freedom not to work, and the money to pursue her sport to the limits. She had all this courtesy of Rick, a man with whom I wouldn't have lasted a day. To put it simply, I don't like men who assume they have the right to tell me what to think and how to live. Not at any price.

My mind pictured Lonny again, and I smiled, almost involuntarily. Lonny had no inclination to tell me what to do. Taking it all in all, I didn't really think I was jealous of Kris.

Gunner stretched his nose through the corral rails at me, and I leaned toward him and blew gently into his nostrils. He blew back, his breath warm and sweet. I'd watched horses greet each other this way many times, and I'd found that they would greet a human they were friendly with in the same fashion.

"See you later, fella," I told him as I straightened up to go. He watched me with his ears forward, the very picture of what a horse should be, and my heart warmed.

I called Blue and got back into the pickup, reflecting that horses are more than a sport to those of us who love them; they are a way of life. They seem to personify an elemental harmony, to provide a continual response to all that was ugly, sordid, and depressing in the modern world. I drove down Kris's driveway, feeling wiped clean of the dark taint of murder, free of the urge to retell my story as if it were some TV docudrama. Instead, I thought of Cindy and how much she'd loved Plumber, and slowly, the tears I hadn't shed filled my eyes.

FIVE

A mile down the road, I pulled into my own driveway. I lived on the edge of Soquel Creek, too, but my little cabin was a long ways from Kris Griffith's ranchette. Tiny, sided with half rounds so it looked like a miniature log cabin, my house was crowded onto a steep minuscule lot between the road and the creek, with lots of redwoods and firs towering up above. I had painted it reddish brown with dark green trim to match its surroundings, and filled the small flower bed in front with salmon-colored impatiens. It wasn't fancy, but it did look like a home.

Unlocking the front door, I followed Blue into the living room, which was in more or less original condition, though I had all kinds of plans for remodeling—someday. At the moment, just making the house payment was stretching me. I'd learned to live with phony wood paneling—dark and dingy—and old-fashioned floor tiles, speckled brown and white and cracked and chipped in a dozen places. My one extravagance—a large wool dhurrie rug patterned in shades of brown and tan—covered most of the ugly floor. I had a few pieces of antique furniture my parents had left me. The rest consisted of director's chairs, a battered couch, and some assorted, unwanted relics. Everything covered with a thin coat of Blue's hair.

At least there was cold chardonnay in the refrigerator. I poured myself a glass and settled on the couch, stepping carefully over Blue. He was half-asleep already, curled up next to the spot where he knew I would sit.

The wine tasted good. I put my feet up on a threadbare footstool and stared out the old casement window into the tangle of green branches and steep hillside that fringed Soquel Creek. My mind wandered, touching briefly on Gunner, going over the appointments I had missed, brushing once again on Lonny. I sipped the wine slowly, turning the wineglass in my hand and watching the evening sunlight on the pines and redwoods.

Inevitably my thoughts returned to those bodies. How empty they'd been, minus the spark that had made them human and alive. I thought of Cindy as I had known her, her frothy white-blond hair framing her animated, fair-skinned face, her voice going a mile a minute, chattering and laughing. What horrible chance had brought her to that end?

I shivered. If the Walker hadn't killed them, and I simply didn't believe he had, then who? And why?

Some dark twist unknown to me, in her life, in his life— there must be a motive. "The four L's—love, lust, lucre, and loathing. And the strongest of these is love." I remembered reading that in a P. D. James novel.

Had someone loved, hated, desired Ed or Cindy that much? Or had someone simply coveted the money they undeniably had? It struck me that the first question would be: Who inherits?

Half an hour later, I was still staring and thinking when I heard a car pull in. Blue got up and woofed softly. I had left the door unlocked and Bret gave it a brief preliminary knock and walked into the room. Blue quit barking right away and limped up to Bret, wagging his little stump of a tail.

"Hey, old man." Bret knelt down and made a big fuss over the dog, rubbing his head and muzzle, scratching his back. Blue flattened his ears and wiggled, for all the world as if he were a big dumb Labrador instead of an ornery Blue Heeler. Bret was one of Blue's favorite people—a member of the select group he allowed to pet him. Most folk were in the other category; their attempts to placate him resulted only in subdued growls.

After he finished rubbing the old dog, Bret got slowly to his feet. "So, Gail, what's the deal?"

I shrugged. Bret grinned his goofy grin. If he'd been wearing a hat, he would have pushed it way back on his head—an attitude that went with the grin.

"Know where I've been?"

"No, but I can guess."

"I been drivin' truck."

"You've been doing what?"

"Drivin' truck. You know . . ." He straightened his back, put his hands on an imaginary steering wheel, cocked his foot for the throttle. His eyes got the steely look of a man guiding an eighteen-wheeler down the highway at 2:00 A.M. He nodded gravely. "Drivin' truck."

Abruptly he abandoned the pose. "Drivin' Big Red truck." He laughed. "You got any beer in this house?"

He was already at the refrigerator, looking inside. I could hear him getting a beer out. He came back in the room, carrying two. "Have a beer, Gail; they're on the house."

"You're already about a dozen ahead of me."

"Don't let it daunt you. Never be daunted. I read that somewhere. Hemingway. I read it in Hemingway." He looked pleased with himself for remembering. "Seriously, Gail, the thing to do is drive truck."

I shook my head. "The thing to do is have dinner. Where've you been drinking?"

Bret grinned his half-cocked grin. "The Back Door. I saw Bob down there. You remember Bob. Asked him what he's been doing. He said, 'Drivin' truck,' " Bret mimicked a serious macho tone. Then he laughed. "The dumb son of a bitch drives a Goodwill truck around town, picking up clothes from people's backyards. Drivin' truck." Bret shook his head, still laughing.

I knew the Bob he was talking about. Another perennial hanger-on in the local horse world, he was one of those people who is an expert on everything. He tended toward black leather jackets, cowboy hats with long feathers in the band, and snakeskin boots. Most people I knew went out of their way to avoid him. It was like Bret to sit and drink with him; Bret got some kind of a kick out of difficult people.

"Let's go eat," I said.

"How we gonna get there?"

"I know, I know; we're gonna drive truck."

He laughed. "That's right. Now you're getting it. Drivin' truck."

I drove truck down to Carpo's—a favorite institution in Soquel. It features Santa Cruz-style fast food, which means that though you wait at the counter and scramble for a table, as you would at any burger joint, the food and drink would not shame a moderate French restaurant, at a price that's still competitive with the burger joint. Carpo's was a regular evening stop for me, as I didn't like to cook unless I had time to enjoy the process and the results, and it was a rare evening that I got home early enough for that.

I found a parking place in the always-crowded lot and was following Bret through the swinging doors when someone, pushing their way out, grabbed my arm and said, "Gail." Focusing on the face, I recognized Gina Gianelli, one of my clients, along with a man I couldn't immediately place.

Shouting, "Calamari with pasta and veggies," after Bret, who was disappearing into the throng around the cash registers, I turned to Gina. She was in her early forties, a weathered-looking woman who trained and competed on her own horses in reined cowhorse classes—very successfully. Gina was one of the few amateurs who could beat the pros.

The man with her looked familiar—middle forties, overweight, and paunchy with it; his olive-skinned coarse-featured face had a brutish, forceful confidence that struck a chord. In a second I had it. Tony Ramiro, a well-known cowhorse trainer, a man I'd met once—when he'd stiffed me for my fee.

Something about the proprietary hand he had on Gina's shoulder sent an obvious signal. Shit, I thought. What was old Tony doing here? He trained near Sacramento, from what I remembered when I was trying to track him down to send him a bill. And what was Gina doing with the skunk?

She was clearly dressed to impress; I'd never before seen her out of battered work clothes (much like my own), and her pressed jeans, polished boots, clingy sweater, and over-emphasized makeup were a new departure, as far as I was aware. Her short dark hair, with the gray just beginning to show, had been freshly permed into a fluffy mop and the whole effect was unfamiliar and (I thought) unappealing. But the story was an old one and easily readable—Gina and Tony were now an item.

Gina was performing introductions, unaware that Tony and I had met, and I wondered if I ought to bring up the hundred dollars he owed me for the emergency call to treat a bowed tendon on one of his show horses—at the Santa Cruz County Fair, almost a year ago. Tony was watching me as though he recognized me, all right, and wished he hadn't. Oh well, no use embarrassing Gina; I could take it up with him later.

"We've met," was what I said, and Gina, unaware of our mutual silent hostility, went on. "Gail, I read in the evening paper that you found Ed and Cindy Whitney."

"That's right." In a split second, all my tangled feelings about discussing the murders rushed back, and I realized that far from being over, my predicament was just beginning. I'd never thought about the papers; if they'd printed my name in connection with such a shocking crime, I'd be asked about it for the next month at least.

Recalling that I had several times seen Gina with Cindy at horse shows and had always assumed they were friends, I started, awkwardly, to say how sorry I was, but Gina cut me off.

"It's terrible. It shouldn't happen to anyone." She sounded sincere, but not sorrowful, and if she was feeling any grief it didn't show. Her eyes were fixed on mine and she said, "I need to talk to you."

I looked at her, puzzled. "Okay."

"Not now." She glanced at Tony, who was ostentatiously pretending not to listen and looking impatient. "We're on our way to a movie. Tomorrow. I've got a horse I want you to look at. I'll call in the morning and make an appointment."

"Well, okay, fine."

At my words, Tony made a restless movement and Gina unlocked her eyes from mine with a visible jolt. "We'll be late," she said. "We'd better go." He put an arm around her and shepherded her briskly toward the parking lot; I stared after them, wondering what was behind her odd intensity, and, for the second time, what in the hell she was doing with him. I would have said she had better judgment.

* * *

Back inside the restaurant, I found Bret ensconced at a corner table, watching girls. Amazingly, he'd remembered to order and apparently had paid for my dinner. Gratefully I dug into it, suddenly aware that I was starving. As I munched, tuning out Bret's comments about the girls who walked by, I puzzled over Gina Gianelli and Tony Ramiro, and Gina's strange behavior. I hadn't come up with any bright explanations, and was only halfway through my dinner when my pager went off.

Bret looked up from his Italian sausage sandwich. "What's the deal?"

"I'm on call tonight." Taking a couple more hasty bites, I got up. "I'll be right back."

Outside at the phone booth, I called the answering service. The woman who answered told me that Steve Shaw had a horse with some heat and swelling in its leg and needed me. She started to give me directions. "That's okay," I told her. "I know how to get there."

Back at the table, I told Bret, "Eat up. We've got to go see a horse."

He looked at me over his beer. "See a man about a horse? Not a bad idea. I'd better do that."

He got up and walked steadily, if a little carefully, toward the bathroom. Shaking my head, I finished my dinner. When Bret got back, I handed him what was left of his sandwich, wrapped in a napkin. "Come on, we've got to go."

He reached for the beer. "You don't need that," I told him. "You've had plenty. Come on."

I hustled him into the truck and headed back up Old San Jose Road toward Steve Shaw's horse-training operation, a big old barn a mile outside of Soquel that all the locals called the Larkin place. Steve called it Riverview Stables and was trying to establish it as the classy boarding and training barn in the area. He specialized in Western pleasure and reined cowhorses; he'd been Cindy Whitney's trainer and he was considered *the* expert on Western-type show horses in these parts. He was also wonderfully handsome and lethally charming, a combination that appealed to many women, including me, I had to admit.

We drove down the hill that sloped to the barn, and even in the last light of the summer day, I could see the signs of lots of money being spent. The pastures were fenced with brand-new pipe fencing, there were neat, colorful flower beds around the barnyard, and the barn had a fresh coat of paint. Business was clearly booming.

Bret's eyes took in the scenery. "This is Steve's place," he said in a disgusted tone. "He's a real piece of work."

Steve Shaw was one of the few men I'd met who could outdo Bret in the looks department, and I grinned. "You're just jealous."

"I don't even want to see the little twerp." At six foot or so, Steve was considerably taller than Bret.

"Well, stay in the truck. I've got to see him." I climbed out of the truck, hoping Bret would stay, but I should have known better. He slithered right out after me, looking around at the big barn with its covered arena.

"Pretty nice place he's got. I used to shoe a few horses here, once upon a time. Steve and I don't get along real well, though." That was obvious.

I heard a door open in the house that stood on one side of the barnyard and Steve's voice called, "Come on in; I'm on the phone."

Bret and I walked in that direction. Four-square, stucco, from the fifties—the house was practical, solid, and painted a boring beige that was entirely in character, with a neat lawn bordered by flower beds. The front door was open, and we walked in.

Inside, Steve Shaw's house was equally conventional— white walls and ceiling, wall-to-wall beige carpet—and decorated like a typical trainer's home, with pieces of fancy tack and paintings of horses on the walls. There were lots of framed photos of a smiling Steve accepting a trophy, and even more photos of Steve looking quietly composed aboard various shiny horses. Bret gave them a disgusted look.

Leather-covered couches dominated the living room; a brick fireplace, a wet bar, and an expensive looking entertainment center—TV, stereo, VCR, and so on—covered the length of one wall. I settled myself on a couch. Bret stood over by the fireplace. We could hear Steve's light voice from the other room, assuring someone that there was "no problem, no problem at all."

A few seconds later, he mouthed some regulation closing phrases, sounding as if he was placating a nervous client, and a moment after that he stepped into the room.

As always, I was struck by his physical presence. Steve Shaw lit up any room he entered as though someone had thrown the switch on an incandescent bulb. Dark hair with a premature sprinkling of silver, astonishingly blue eyes, smooth tanned skin, and a lean, hard body didn't hurt, but it was more than that. His smile when he greeted me conveyed genuine interest and appreciation, and despite the fact that I knew charm was his stock-in-trade, I felt, well, charmed.

"Hi, Gail. Thanks for coming out. I've got a mare with a lot of heat and swelling in her leg. She's supposed to show at Salinas this weekend, so I thought you'd better have a look."

The warmth in his eyes as he gazed at me kept to the pleasant side of flirtatious, and I smiled back as I answered him matter of factly, "No problem. I'll see what I can do."

Steve noticed Bret at this point, who was still standing by the fireplace, sulking. They nodded coolly at each other—perhaps Steve, too, was conscious of Bret as competition—

and Steve turned back to me. "I've got the mare's leg wrapped in ice packs; I just changed them ten minutes ago, so there's no rush. Can I get you a drink or something?"

I was about to decline when Bret spoke from behind me, "Sure. I'll have Jack Daniel's and soda in a tall glass. If you have it."

Steve's mouth tightened up, but he nodded civilly. "How about you, Gail?"

"The same, thanks."

He went to the bar at the other end of the room to get the drinks, walking like a dancer or a gymnast. In his Ralph Lauren polo shirt, casually untucked over khaki chinos, with his dark good looks and easy manners, he took all the shine out of Bret, who leaned against the hearth, his thumbs hooked in the pockets of his old and dirty Wrangler jeans, as sullen as a cowboy who's mistakenly entered the "wrong" sort of San Francisco bar. I felt as if I were caught between a greyhound and a Queensland—both bristling and showing their teeth.

Steve came back with our drinks and handed them out, sitting down on the couch with me, close enough to be friendly, not so close he invaded my space. "Gail, I read that you found Ed and Cindy Whitney; that must have been terrible."

"It was pretty bad," I admitted.

"I still can't believe it. I've got Plumber at the barn here, since the police didn't know what to do with him. They found my name in Cindy's address book and called me, and I went down and picked him up."

"That's good," I said, watching Bret take a long swallow of his fresh drink.

"It was the least I could do. I've known Ed and Cindy for ages. Plumber's just like one of my own horses."

"What's going to happen to the poor little guy?"

"In the long term, I don't know. He's entered in the hackamore class at Salinas this Saturday, paid up and everything, and I got in touch with Cindy's lawyers and they said to go ahead and show him. I know that's what Cindy would have wanted. I guess anything he wins will just be part of her estate."

"Do you know who inherits the horse?" I asked, thinking of Plumber, what a good-natured, friendly colt he was, a lot like Gunner, hoping he would end up with a good home.

"I've got no idea." Steve appeared to be thinking along the same lines I was. "I sure hope he goes to the right place." Shaking his head, he added somberly, "It just seems terrible. Ed and Cindy were great people."

"You knew them pretty well, didn't you?" I asked him.

"Oh, very well. We were all really good friends." He looked rueful. "Of course, the police wanted to know if I was particularly good friends with Cindy."

I bet they did, I thought to myself. Handsome Steve Shaw was a husband's nightmare. From what I understood, half of his female clients were in love with him.

Steve was still talking. "I told them it wasn't like that. We were all just close friends. I'm going to miss her," he said sadly. "She was a lot of fun."

That was a pretty good epitaph for Cindy, and one that she would have liked.

"And Ed, too," Steve was saying. "I don't think people understood Ed very well. Ed was a really genuine person."

Now, that was debatable, I added in my mind. Bret looked nauseated. He'd finished his drink, I noticed, and curled his lip at Steve. "Ed was an asshole."

Steve glanced over at him. "He was a friend of mine," he said briefly and, with smooth civility, changed the subject. "Still shoeing?"

Bret shrugged.

"My shoer left town last week, and all my horses are due. I could give you a couple of days of work, if you're interested."

Bret shrugged again. I felt mildly surprised that Steve would consider using Bret; he was a capable shoer, but notoriously unreliable, and he and Steve were clearly not on the same wavelength.

"Thirty dollars still your rate?" Steve asked.

"Uh-huh."

"Start tomorrow. I've got twenty horses that need doing."

Steve was brisk, and I thought I could guess his reasoning. Bret did a good-enough job, and thirty dollars was half of what horseshoers in Santa Cruz County were currently charging. When you were talking about twenty horses, it added up.

"All right." Bret still sounded sullen, but again, from his end, too, economics were probably the bottom line. I suspected Bret was broke.

Steve stood up and looked at me. "Do you want to have a look at that mare?"

"Sure."

"Go ahead and make yourself another drink." That got tossed at Bret over Steve's shoulder.

Bret grinned. "Don't mind if I do." Then in a stage whisper to me, "Never be daunted."

"I'm sorry to get you out after dinner, Gail." Steve was walking toward the door. "I know you've had a rough day."

I murmured agreement.

"Did you just drop by to visit Cindy and go in and find them dead?" Steve half-shuddered.

"Cindy called me out to see Plumber," I told him. "It was almost an accident that I found them at all. I sat out at the barn and waited for her for a while, and at the last minute, I tried the house. It was a pretty bad shock," I admitted.

Steve put a hand on my shoulder lightly, and I felt grateful for the sympathy as well as the absence of grisly questions.

We walked side by side through the summer night—cool, with the wet edge of fog—into his big barn, a covered arena with a row of stalls down each side and a huge hay shed at the back. Steve flicked a switch and one row of stalls lit up. We started down the lighted breezeway, Steve glancing into each stall in a horseman's automatic routine check.

I stopped when I saw Plumber, munching hay contentedly in the third stall down. Leaning over the half door, I reached a hand out to touch his shoulder. "How're you doing, buddy?"

Steve stopped with me and we both stared appreciatively at the colt. Plumber was a horse that took your eye; it was hard to say exactly why. At fifteen hands, he was medium-sized for a Quarter Horse, he had good but not outstanding confirmation, and his breedy head was attractive, but not at all halter horse "cute." His color was unusual—light brown—the color of coffee with cream in it, or freshly made cocoa. Still, unusual or not, it wasn't a flashy color, and Plumber had no fancy chromelike white markings, only a tiny star in the center of his forehead. No, it was nothing external; it was the expression on his face—friendly, curious, intelligent—that said, this is a good horse.

Echoing my thoughts, Steve sighed. "He's a good one. The whole time I've trained him he's been just like a smart dog, right there with you, wanting to do what you ask. I'll be sorry to lose him."

"Well, maybe you won't."

"Who knows." Steve glanced at me curiously. "You know, one thing I wondered about. Was Cindy buting this horse?"

Remembering the bottles I'd seen on her desk, I told him,

"Not that I know of. I saw quite a few bottles of bute in the tack room when I was looking for her, and it seemed kind of odd to me. She wasn't the type to just start giving her horse painkillers without having a vet check him first."

"I wouldn't have thought so either." Steve looked reflective. "I guess if something's wrong with him it'll show up. Well, that mare's down here," he added, turning away.

I followed him to a stall where a buckskin mare stood, one foot cocked in a relaxed way, her head down and her eyes half-closed. Her left front leg was carefully wrapped in cumbersome ice packs, but she didn't seem to be in any distress.

Steve walked in the stall with her and began unwrapping the leg, his fingers deft and competent. Bending down next to him, I caught the tang of his aftershave and was briefly conscious of a sense of intimacy. I put it out of my mind automatically; many of my veterinary calls involved moments like this one with overtones of linked physical closeness. The quiet barn, the gentle sigh of the mare's breath, Steve's soothing voice as he murmured to her—these were the ingredients of an awareness I'd learned to thrust away as inappropriate.

I could feel Steve's eyes on me, his face close to mine as we both crouched in the shavings, but I kept my own attention firmly on the mare's leg as I ran my hand up and down her tendon. There was swelling all right, quite a bit of it, but through the puffiness I could feel the tendon itself, and it felt smooth and firm, uninjured.

"I'm not one hundred percent sure," I said slowly, "but I think she's just nicked the tendon sheath. Is she lame?"

"No, not at all."

"Just keep icing it on and off, maybe three times a day for the next couple of days. If she stays sound, you ought to be able to use her this weekend, even if it's swollen. I'd ice her right before and after I showed her, and keep her wrapped."

Steve smiled in relief. "That's great." He seemed about to say something else when we both heard footsteps in the barn aisle. Abruptly his face tightened up. "That must be Amber. This mare belongs to her."

Oh shit, I thought but didn't say. Amber St. Claire had the dubious honor of being my least-favorite client—a prize example of that type who calls the vet out to look at every little scratch and complains constantly at the size of her bill. The whole office down at Santa Cruz Equine Practice regarded her as a royal pain in the ass, and even Jim, my boss, capitalistic money grubber that he was, would probably have dispensed with her business if it wasn't for the fact that she was so incredibly rich.

Amber was the daughter of Reg St. Claire, a legendary figure in Santa Cruz County, one of our earliest millionaire transplants from the San Francisco Bay Area. He'd moved to the Santa Cruz Mountains to retire and raise Quarter Horses; Amber, his only daughter, had grown up on his glamorous Rancho Robles, inheriting it when he died. She was in her forties now, had never lifted a finger to do any sort of work, at least none that I knew of, had been married and divorced three times, and continued to raise horses—from a distance.

Reg St. Claire had been an avid horseman; Amber, so far as I could tell, had no particular liking for the equine species; she even seemed a little afraid of them. But she continued to breed Quarter Horses, employing a crew of at least half a dozen to do all the actual work, and she usually kept a couple of show horses in training. Currently with Steve Shaw. Rumor had it that she was angling to make him husband number four.

Banishing all traces of the oh-shit I felt as her footsteps approached, I schooled my face to a noncommittal expression of polite civility and glanced at Steve. His own face was as casually bland as mine, concealing what emotions I had no idea.

Amber walked into the stall with us as confidently as a queen making a royal entrance, preceded by a wave of perfume strong enough to overcome the rich, horsey smell of the barn. I felt like wrinkling my nose but refrained; it wouldn't have been politically smart. Amber was our single biggest account.

"Hi there." The smile she gave Steve was full wattage; she turned a much milder version on me. "Hello, Gail." Back to Steve immediately. "So, how is she?"

He explained what the mare had done, how he'd treated her and what I'd said; Amber listened with her head cocked to one side, drinking in every word that came from his mouth. Her expertly tinted auburn hair, worn in a smooth, shining wedge, somehow failed to clash with her vivid red lipstick and fingernails, or the suede coat the color of fallen leaves. There was no denying Amber had style, of a sort, though I thought she looked out of place in a box stall. I also thought the adoring gaze she fastened on Steve Shaw overdone, and a little too girlish on the face of a forty-something woman.

"Do you think she'll be okay?" she asked him anxiously, though I noticed she'd never once looked at the horse.

"Gail thinks so." Steve's eyes met mine briefly, and I caught the quick ironic sparkle before I looked away.

Amber seemed uninterested in my opinions, and laid a hand possessively on his arm. "Will we be able to show her at Salinas?"

"You bet." Steve looked down at her, his smile radiating blue-eyed charm.

Seeing that I clearly wasn't needed, I sketched a slight wave and said, "I'd better be going."

Amber ignored me; Steve smiled with his usual warmth.

"Come on over and watch me show Plumber this weekend if you have time, Gail. At the Salinas Rodeo Grounds. Saturday morning. You'd enjoy it."

I saw Amber frown, and a little devil nudged me. "I'd love to, Steve. See you there."

As I stepped out of the box stall and started down the aisle, I could hear her voice from behind me saying pettishly, "What did you invite *her* for?" I grinned. Amber might like to think she owned Steve, but she clearly wasn't too confident of him. And I more than suspected old Steve had had a lot of practice evading matrimonial lures.

Still, Amber's brand new fire-engine red Mercedes convertible was parked outside the barn; maybe Steve could see his way clear to being a kept husband—Mercedes and all.

Spotting Bret sitting in my truck, I hurried over and got in before he could change his mind and jump out.

"Why'd you leave me in there?" Bret's voice was more than slightly slurred.

"I had to look at the horse," I pointed out.

"Goddamn Steve." Bret shook his head as I drove up the hill. "Wants me to shoe his horses. I know what he does. I charge him thirty dollars and he charges his people sixty. Pockets the extra. That's why he's so rich."

"I doubt that." I forbore to point out that such ill-gotten gains would hardly provide Steve with a royal income.

"Sure he does." Bret brightened up at the thought of Steve's larceny and rattled on the rest of the way home about his imagined sexual preferences and his failures in the truck-driving category.

I tuned him out as much as I could. Bret was about twenty ahead of me at this point; Hemingway or no Hemingway, I was definitely daunted.

SIX

When we got back to my house, Bret staggered in and flopped on the couch. He looked around my tiny living room with slightly glazed eyes and said, "You aren't quite in the same class as Steve, old buddy."

"Take it or leave it, pal."

He stretched out on the couch, already half-asleep. "I'll take it, I'll take it," he muttered.

I smiled, walked into the kitchen and got some almond-praline ice cream out of the freezer. Dishing it into a bowl, I looked at the clock. Nine-thirty. With any luck, I was home for the evening. The ice cream was cold and sweet and satisfying. Bad for my health and figure, but soothing to my tired brain. I settled myself at the kitchen table with a Dick Francis mystery.

I had been sitting at the table an hour, alternately reading and eating ice cream, when my pager went off. I looked at it in disgust. "Shit."

Picking up the phone, I called the answering service.

"There's an emergency in Bonny Doon," the woman

said. "Some horse has a severe colic. He's down and thrashing." She repeated the words carefully.

"Who's the client?"

"He said his name was Mark Houseman. The address is Twenty-one twenty Pine Flat Road."

"How do I get there?" Both name and address were new to me, and I wasn't very familiar with the Bonny Doon area. I took down directions. Up the coast, right on Bonny Doon Road, right again on Pine Flat Road where the road forks at a bar called The Lost Weekend. Two miles, on the left, a metal gate painted yellow. The numbers were on a post by the gate.

"What's the phone number?"

"He said he doesn't have a phone. He was calling from the neighbor's house."

"Okay," I said resignedly. This sounded like another backyard horse case. Worse yet, a backyard horse back up in the wilds of the Santa Cruz Mountains. There were some pretty odd little places buried up there in the redwoods. With some even odder people living on them.

I left the house quietly so as not to wake Bret. It was a wasted effort, I was sure. Bret was snoring so loudly he would have wakened himself if he hadn't been so deeply under. Blue slept on the floor next to him, and I stepped carefully over the old dog, not waking him, either. In his younger days, I never could have sneaked by him like that, but old age had made him increasingly deaf.

Headed down Old San Jose Road once again, I ran my fingers through my bangs and thought longingly of bed. Nighttime emergencies were the rule, not the exception; horses, like people, seem prone to having their disasters in the dark. When I was on call I expected to have my evening interrupted at least once, if not more often; it was a rare night that I wasn't paged at all. I crossed my fingers that the calls wouldn't be too far away and that they'd be of an easily solved nature—which wasn't the case here. Bonny Doon was a good hour's drive, and colic was unpredictable. A generic term for any type of digestive disturbance in a horse, colic cases ran the gamut from horses with minor bouts of gas that would be fine when I got there to those with life-threatening problems that would involve me in an all-night battle to save them. You could never tell.

Bonny Doon is north of Santa Cruz, an area of the mountains more than an actual town. In the daylight it's beautiful, full of redwoods and great open fields of grass with long vistas to the ocean in the distance. At night, the mountain roads curved and twisted secretively between the black shapes of silent trees, and I saw few cars, the scattered lights of an occasional dwelling.

I found The Lost Weekend without any difficulty but had to retrace my route a couple of times looking for the yellow gate. It was set back a little way from the road and the yellow paint was old and had mostly peeled and chipped off. Not an easy thing to spot on a dark night.

The gate was shut. I pulled in and got out of the truck. There was a chain with a lock, but it was hanging loose. There was also a faded sign that said, PLEASE CLOSE GATE. I opened it, drove in, and pushed it shut. Ahead of me, a set of faint tire tracks ran off across a field. I could only see about ten feet in the glare of the headlights; the fog had come in and swirled around the truck, cold and thick, blocking out the world.

I bumped slowly across the field, following a poor excuse for a road. Eventually a mass of black loomed up in front of me, blacker than the foggy darkness. Trees, I judged, a big clump of trees. At the same time, the headlights showed another gate. This one was wooden, a sliding rail gate. I got out and slid the rails to one side, then drove through.

Fifty yards farther, a building showed up in the headlights. It was dark and silent—no lights on. I stopped the truck and cursed inwardly, hoping this wasn't going to be one of those real "mountain man" situations, where people were living without electricity on a whim of some kind. I got my flashlight out of the glove compartment and got out of the truck.

The small flashlight beam didn't show much. I walked up to the building, which proved to be a cabin; it had windows, anyway. Around the corner, I found a door. It was locked, but there was a note on it with an arrow that pointed away from the direction I'd come. It said, "Am out at the barn. Mark Houseman," in neat square printing.

At least I was at the right place. I held the flashlight up, trying to see where I was supposed to go. It looked as though I was underneath some big redwood trees. When I swung the beam from side to side, I could see a few huge trunks. Their earthy, bittersweet smell rose above the cold, wet, ocean smell of the fog.

Stepping forward into the night in the direction the arrow pointed, I went a hundred feet when another building bulked up in front of me. Again there were no lights and no noise. I stopped and stood still. This morning a routine call had turned into a murder case. Maybe it had upset me. All I knew was this silent, empty barnyard seemed odd.

I was used to midnight emergencies; I was accustomed to driving up to strangers' homes alone, to unknown faces filled with panic, to animals in life-or-death situations, their owners almost irrational with distress. My nerves were proof against all that, but something about the eerie still-ness here was bothering me.

Eventually, I walked forward. The normal thing would have been to call out "Hello," or "This is the vet," but somehow I didn't want to do that. I walked quietly toward the dark building and felt myself straining to hear any sound in the night around me.

The barn was big and high-roofed, with a silo tower at one end of it. I could tell that much with my flashlight. There was a black hole in the middle—the doorway. Stepping inside, I swung the flashlight around. The beam picked out a couple of wooden pens, but they were falling apart. There was no sign of a horse or any human being, and the barn had a musty, long-dead smell. I didn't think there had been any animals in it for a while.

Staring at the empty pens, I felt annoyed and a little nervous. It wasn't a mistake. The note on the cabin door proved that. Somebody wanted me out here. But why, and where were they? I swung the flashlight around the barn again. I saw a few rusty pieces of old haying equipment, a few gaps in the board wall, a stack of firewood in the corner. A bright new nail glinted in the light at my feet. Automatically I bent to pick it up. Nails on the floor of a barn, even an apparently empty barn, went against my instincts; nails are horse cripplers.

That nail saved my life. As I bent over, the silent darkness was blown apart with a loud, angry boom. I dove for the door, not thinking, reacting on my nerves. Something told me that the gun and whoever held it were very close to me.

I landed scrambling, got to my feet, and ran into the night in the direction of my truck. There was another crashing boom behind me. I dodged to one side of a tree and ducked around a branch, trying desperately to see where I was going in the jerking beam of the flashlight.

Another shot cracked just as I saw the black bulk of the cabin ahead of me. I dove hard to get behind it and heard a crunch as my flashlight went out. "Shit," I gasped, struggling to my feet and running blindly toward where I thought my truck was. Where it had to be. Somewhere in the darkness.

I ran toward where I remembered it and it materialized out of the night. Thanking God it was a white truck and not a black one, I threw open the door which, mercifully, I hadn't locked, reached for the key which was still in the ignition, and threw the thing into gear as I started it.

I spun a wild circle in front of the cabin, the headlights cutting a crazy path through the dark. I thought I saw a human figure standing by the building in the fog, but I didn't hesitate to find out. I heard another crack and asked the engine for everything she had. I shot through the wooden gate with a roar and bounced across the field as fast as she would take it. I probably set the world's speed record for opening a gate and getting back into the truck.

When I was finally on the public road, doing a good brisk fifty miles an hour away from the deserted cabin, my heart started to slow down a little. Not much, but a little. I saw that my hands were trembling on the steering wheel. Shock, I noted clinically.

The Lost Weekend showed ahead of me in the headlights. What I need, I told myself, is a drink. I pulled into the parking lot and headed for the bar.

Inside it was warm and lighted and cozy. The five men sitting on the bar stools turned their heads to look at me. Giving them a wide smile entirely inappropriate for a strange woman entering a bar full of men, I parked myself on an empty bar stool. At this point, I was so glad to see some normal, civilized people that I would have been happy to get any kind of ridiculous come-on. I was beginning to be afraid Bonny Doon was populated entirely by fog, redwoods, and murderers, with maybe a few ghosts thrown in.

The bartender got up and limped in my direction. He had gray hair, a gray beard, a battered cowboy hat, and an old vest. He gave me a friendly smile. "What'll you have?"

"Jack Daniel's and soda in a tall glass," I said automatically.

He fixed the drink and brought it over. When I paid him, I asked, "Do you know a place about two miles down the road, metal gate painted yellow, Twenty-one twenty Pine Flat Road?"

"Sure." He looked at me curiously. "Fred Johnson's place that was. He died a year ago."

"Anybody living there now name of Houseman?"

He shook his head. "Nope. It's shut up tight. Estate's in some kind of litigation. All his kids fighting over who gets it, I imagine. None of 'em were any damn good." His bright, curious eyes looked into mine. "Why?"

I sighed. "I'm a vet. Somebody called me out there for a sick horse. Nobody was there. Practical joke, I guess."

The old man shook his head again. "Gate locked?"

"No."

"Should have been."

We looked at each other. I already knew I was not going to tell the good old boys at The Lost Weekend about the shooting. Finishing my drink, I thanked the bartender for his help. He looked disappointed when I turned to go; he'd sensed something was up.

I got back in the truck and headed toward home, feeling confused and deeply tired. Someone had shot at me and I had no idea who or why. My story didn't make sense, even to me; what in the world would the cops think? In any case, exhaustion was rapidly growing to be the predominant feeling. Tomorrow, I decided, I'd deal with it tomorrow.

SEVEN

I stood in the flat dirt parking lot behind the office at 8:00 A.M. the next morning and watched a sorrel gelding trot away from me. The strong ropy muscles in his hindquarters propelled him evenly and powerfully. All four white-socked legs hit the ground in a steady one-two one-two beat. He was sound as far as I could see. This was a shame because he was supposed to be lame in the left hind.

The owner, an older woman with a lined face, gave me a frustrated smile. "He's not showing it, is he? I swear he's been lame in that leg."

I smiled back. At least this wasn't one of those deals where I couldn't see a lameness that the owner could. A lot of my reputation as a decent horse vet rested on my ability to diagnose lameness. Accurately. Mistakes weren't tolerated very well by the clients.

I ran my hand down the gelding's left hind leg, and he jerked it up suddenly. Keeping my hand firmly on his fetlock, I talked to him soothingly: "Take it easy, you big baby; I'm not going to hurt you."

Horses might look like large, powerful creatures, aggressive and threatening, but inside themselves most are something small and timid—a rabbit, maybe. This horse was being uncooperative because he was afraid of me, not because he wanted to hurt me.

When the gelding relaxed a little, I pulled his leg up and held it tightly flexed for the two minutes required for the spavin test, then told the owner to trot him away from me. He went off with a noticeably short step. We repeated the test a couple of times and got the same result. Bringing out the X-ray machine, I took pictures of his left hock, developed them, and told the woman her horse had bone spavin.

"Is it bad?" She looked at me anxiously.

"It's not that bad. It's like having arthritis. Do you have any bute?"

She shook her head.

Handing her a bottle of the white tablets, I said, "Bute—phenylbutazone, really—is a painkiller we use with horses more or less the way people use aspirin on themselves. Grind two pills up and put them in his feed night and morning for a week, to get the pain and inflammation out, and then just give him two pills the night before and the morning of the day you want to use him. He'll probably do fine. This isn't a bad lameness to have if you've got to have a lameness."

She smiled in relief. I talked to her a little longer, reassuring her, and then went back inside the office, looking for Jim.

He was sitting at his desk, phone cradled next to his ear, rooting through his papers with one hand. He glanced up when he saw me. "That was a bad deal about the Whitneys."

"Yeah, it was."

"I hear you're right in the middle of it," he added. He kept looking for whatever it was he was looking for as we talked. That was typical of him. Jim, in his mid-forties, was such a tireless, intense workaholic that he made me feel lazy no matter what I did. His short, stocky frame always reminded me of a compact dynamo, bristling with energy, and only the fact that he really was a virtual genius as a veterinarian made it possible for me to tolerate his complete disregard for me as a person. To Jim, a junior vet was part of his equipment, a necessary tool. His sole interest in me revolved around how well I got the job done. He paid me the lowest acceptable wage and worked me the highest possible number of hours, but he was generous with advice and knowledge, and I'd learned more in two years than I would ever have guessed was possible.

"I need to go down to the sheriff's office this morning," I told him bluntly. Blunt was the only useful approach with Jim.

It stopped his paper shuffling. He looked back up at me. "Damn it, Gail, you've got a full day of appointments booked and so do I."

"I'm sorry, Jim. I've got to go down there." I felt reluctant to tell him why. The whole idea of being shot at in a barn in Bonny Doon sounded melodramatic standing in the office at eight in the morning. Ridiculous, even.

Jim looked at me curiously. I stayed quiet. He shrugged. "Okay. If you've got to, you've got to. I'll change the schedule around. Get back here as soon as you can."

The words were barely out of his mouth before his attention went sharply back to the form he'd found. As I left the office I could hear his voice reassuring his caller that he'd be out right away, first thing.

Turning the collar of my coat up as I got in the pickup and started it, I stared at the gray sky outside the windows. Summer weather in Santa Cruz is pretty repetitive—fog in the mornings and sunny afternoons. The cold mornings sometimes gave me a dismal feeling, and the thought of the sheriff's office was not cheering.

Driving toward town, I rehearsed what I'd say. I had thought about it while I got ready for work with Bret snoring on the couch, and revised it all the way down to the office. It still sounded like an unlikely story, and I wasn't exactly eager to tell it.

I stopped at the deli on Soquel Avenue, more to delay myself than out of any real hunger, and bought a breakfast burrito. It tasted great but leaked badly, and by the time I got to the county building I'd narrowly missed two cars in my frantic attempts not to get melted cheese all over the front of my T-shirt. Eating and driving is not smart, I told myself, not for the first time.

The front hall of the sheriff's office seemed to be filled with people hurrying to somewhere, and the place had that cold institutional atmosphere I associated with high schools and hospitals. I walked to the front desk.

There was a woman behind it this morning. Short brown hair, tortoiseshell glasses, neat appearance, wearing the same expression of professional sternness that Jeri Ward wore. Maybe they learned it at the Police Academy: I'm not a person; I'm a cop. I supposed they needed to feel that way to do the job.

I asked for Detective Ward and was told she was out for an hour. Too long to wait. I asked for Detective Reeder, and the woman escorted me to the same uncomfortably sterile interview room that I'd sat in yesterday morning. I asked for and got another paper cup of lousy coffee. At least it was hot. I sipped it and stared at the stained ceiling tiles; it looked like they had a leak. I'd memorized every inch of the ceiling, the floor, and the nondescript furniture by the time Detective Reeder came in. He must have kept me waiting a good half hour.

Detective Reeder was as sloppy as ever. Crumpled suit, stain on his shirtfront—no attempt at professionalism here. I gave a mental shrug. My jeans and bright turquoise

T-shirt probably didn't look too professional to him, either.

"Dr. McCarthy," he said. It was both a noncommittal greeting and a question.

"Detective Reeder," I answered, trying to remember my rehearsed speech. Maybe taking the bull by the horns was the best approach. "I was shot at last night," I said baldly.

Detective Reeder didn't blink. People being shot at were his line of work.

I told the story of the barn on Pine Flat Road with few interruptions. When I was done, Reeder stared silently at me. His face was completely devoid of expression. There was no way to tell what he was thinking, but I had a suspicion it was along the lines of whether I was some kind of deranged personality who was making up stories in order to stay in the spotlight. I gave another mental shrug. Any attempt to defend what I'd said would only make me look foolish. Staring silently back at the detective, I willed my face to stay as impassive as his.

He broke first. "Dr. McCarthy, is there any reason why someone would try to kill you?"

"None that I know of."

"Is there a reason why you didn't inform us of this incident immediately?"

I shook my head. "It was late and I was tired. I just didn't feel up to it."

"You realize you've made our job more difficult?"

I decided there was no good answer to that so I didn't make one.

The baggy brown eyes fixed themselves on me. "Do you know of any way this incident could be connected with Mr. and Mrs. Whitney's murder?"

I sighed. "I guess that's the point, isn't it? That's what it came down to, when I thought about it. Do I know something the murderer thinks is dangerous?" I looked back at the detective. "I've wracked my brain, and I don't know what it would be. But I guess that's the only logical explanation."

Detective Reeder nodded and looked for a split second as though maybe he believed me after all. I realized, with a sudden jolt, another obvious explanation that must have occurred to him. If I'd murdered Ed and Cindy, maybe I'd cook up a story like this in order to direct suspicion away from myself. That sounded logical, even to me.

"All right, Dr. McCarthy. If you think of anything that could help us with this investigation, please let me know. In the meantime, I'd appreciate it if you'd go with one of our people to this barn where you were shot at." His voice was carefully not skeptical, but the skepticism was there, I thought.

"Okay," I said.

"If you'd wait here . . ." Detective Reeder got up and stumped out of the room. I settled back down to wait. Without any coffee, this time.

Ten minutes later Detective Ward walked into the room. She was looking a little less dressed for success than usual, I noticed; her wheat-colored linen jacket was paired with denim jeans and casual loafers—the jeans were close-fitted and artfully faded, jeans that said high fashion, big-city style as clearly as my own Wranglers said I-work-with-livestock, but they were jeans nonetheless.

"Dr. McCarthy," she greeted me.

"Gail," I said on impulse.

She didn't respond, but I had the impression she was pleased.

"John Reeder says you told him you were shot at last night."

I noted Detective Reeder's mention of my story allowed room for doubt, and I smiled. "I don't think he believes me."

Her mouth curved in the faintest upward direction. "Let's go have a look."

Escorting me to a sheriff's car in the yard, she drove us out into downtown Santa Cruz. I told her where we were going and settled myself into the passenger side of the seat, watching the drab little shops along Mission Street give way to the wide fields of artichokes and brussels sprouts, rough, hilly pastures, and cold gray ocean vistas of the north coast. Once we were moving along, I looked over in her direction. Since her eyes were on the road, I allowed myself to stare a little.

On close examination, Jeri Ward had an oddly nondescript face, somewhat at variance with the golden blond hair worn in a wavy jaw-length bob—a style that implied a forties-style glamour. Her features were regular and unremarkable, the skin fair, the nose a little snub, eyebrows neither light nor dark, eyes that color somewhere between blue, gray, and green. What struck you was her sense of tight inner poise, a complete composure that hid her real self entirely, exposing only a carefully controlled veneer.

As if she could hear my thoughts, she glanced in my direction inquiringly, and I dropped my eyes. "So, how's the investigation going?" I asked, hoping to distract her attention from my too-obvious staring.

She gave an infinitesimal shrug. "Well, we haven't arrested anyone yet."

"I saw the woman at your office yesterday—Ms. Whitney. One of Ed's relations, I guess." I said it neutrally, not wanting to sound inappropriately nosy, but she responded naturally enough.

"Ms. Anne Whitney. Ed Whitney's sister, his only sibling, which makes her his next of kin, since both his parents are dead, and his sole heir."

"Oh."

"Exactly. She inherits a couple of million dollars, more or less, in a trust fund—an income of about a hundred thousand a year—and that property on Rose Avenue free and clear. That's what we got from his lawyer this morning."

"Was it news to the sister that she inherits?"

"We don't know. In a case like this, the first thing we do is notify the next of kin. Ed Whitney had his sister listed in the emergency numbers, right by the phone, so we called her and asked her to come down to the office. When I asked her the usual questions about where she was at the time, she got furious. Wanted to know why I was wasting time suspecting her instead of tracking down the 'real killer.' " Jeri Ward's mouth twitched. "It's a fairly common reaction, more common than you'd maybe guess. Certain types of people can't or won't allow themselves to feel sadness; they express it in anger."

This was the longest, most revealing speech she'd ever made to me, and I ventured a personal comment in return. "Not much fun for you."

"No. She's been asked to come back down this afternoon—since we talked to the lawyer and found out she's the heir; I can imagine how she'll feel about that."

I nodded. "How about Cindy's relatives. Do they inherit anything?"

She glanced over at me. "We still don't know who Cindy Whitney's relatives are. There isn't a piece of paper anywhere that identifies her as anything other than Cindy Whitney, Ed Whitney's wife. And her will simply says that she leaves everything to Ed and his heirs. We're trying to find her family, with no success so far."

"That's odd. I don't remember ever hearing her say anything about her family or her childhood, but then, there wasn't any reason why she would." I looked back at Jeri; I was starting to think of her as Jeri. "Do you have any ideas about who killed them?"

Her face grew guarded. "Nothing definite," was all she said.

Getting the message that she didn't want to talk about the investigation anymore, I lapsed back into silence, pondering what she'd told me and wondering what had prompted such unusually forthcoming behavior.

The north coast slipped along outside the windows, blanketed in cold gray fog, but when we turned inland and headed up toward Bonny Doon, the sun broke through. The ominous dark redwoods of the night before looked green and welcoming in the morning light. I directed Jeri to the yellow gate at 2120 Pine Flat Road, and we both got out of the car.

Up here, the air was already warm and I could smell the tanbark smell of the redwoods and the dusty dry grass of July. Beyond the gate the little field I'd driven across last night showed two bare ruts running through a blaze of golden wild oats. It was quiet. Crickets chirped. A harmless country scene.

Walking over to the gate, I studied it. It was an old gate and hung crookedly, so that it swung shut by itself. I certainly hadn't bothered to close it last night. It was shut now, with the chain hanging loose as I had first found it. The chain itself was old and rusty, except in one place where broken links showed bright silver metal.

Jeri was watching me. Now she came over and looked at the chain, too.

"Bolt cutters," I said.

"And recently, it looks like." She raised her eyes to mine. "Show me what happened last night, as accurately as you can."

"Reconstruct the crime, you mean?"

She smiled. "As we say in the business."

"Let's see. The gate was just like this, as far as I can remember. I opened it, drove through and shut it, and drove across the field." I gestured at the ruts in the grass.

Pushing the gate open while she drove through, I hurried its slow closing and got back in the car. Then we drove across the field and through the sliding rail gate, open as I'd left it, to the deserted cabin in the redwood grove.

The big trees were majestic in the sunlight, the little cabin sleepy and quiet. Nobody around. It was cool and still damp in the deep shade under the redwoods; green ferns and delicate leafy vines clustered everywhere.

We walked to the cabin and around the corner to the door. As I'd more than half-expected, the note was gone. Something was there, though. A shiny nail head showed in the varnished wood. A tiny edge of white paper was still stuck beneath it.

"That's where the note was. It read, 'Am out at the barn. Mark Houseman,' with an arrow pointing this way." I gestured across the grove.

"Okay, and then you did what?" Her eyes were intent.

We were walking through the redwood grove now, with me telling her my movements and ideas of the night before as closely as I could remember them. In the daylight, the little grove was amazing. The trees were gigantic, the base of their trunks ten feet and more in diameter, rising up like dark red-brown pillars in a cathedral. The green branches made a canopy far above. There was a peculiar stillness underneath them, and my voice hushed to a whisper as we walked.

I looked over at her.

"They're great, aren't they?" She was staring up at the trees.

"Yeah, they are."

There was a minute of quiet while redwood needles

crunched softly underfoot; the sun sparkled through the branches like light through stained-glass windows. I felt for the first time as though I might grow to like this woman.

We walked out to the barn in silence. In the daylight it was obvious that the building was more of an antique than a functional barn. There were as many gaps as there were boards, and half the roof was off. The silo tower leaned crookedly. I followed last night's steps and walked through the empty doorway.

The barn was deserted. There were the tumbledown pens, the rusting haying equipment, the stack of firewood, the same musty smell. I looked over at Jeri.

"This is where I stood last night. I swung my flashlight around." I pointed to my right. "Whoever shot at me stood somewhere over there."

She walked to the corner of the barn and I watched her bend down to study the dusty ground. She looked at it in silence for a while and then looked back at me. "Could you come over here?"

I walked over to her and we studied the ground together. It was bare and smooth, with a pattern of faint wavy lines. I looked back toward the doorway. Our sets of footprints ran across the dirt, neat and distinct. Without a word, we both walked back to the doorway. There were no footprints in the barn besides our own.

"My footprints from last night should be here."

"Yes."

Staring at the faintly patterned dirt, something clicked in my mind. "I know that trick," I said slowly. "We used to do that when we were kids. Playing Indian. You get a branch and brush the ground to hide your footprints. That's what it looks like." I glanced around the doorway and saw the handy switch of redwood branch, right where it had no doubt been dropped. "Look," I told her.

I brushed the ground where we had walked with the

branch. When I was done the footprints were gone and the dirt showed the same tracing of thin wavy lines.

Jeri didn't say anything. I walked back to the doorway.

"This is where I was standing when I bent to pick up a nail. Whoever shot at me stood over in that corner, behind the stack of wood, while I was standing here, lit up by my own flashlight. It was a sure shot, if he could shoot at all. Except that I bent over to pick up a nail." I shook my head. "Chance." It was deeply disturbing to think that without his or her bad luck, my body could be lying in the dirt where we were standing.

Jeri watched me quietly. When the silence grew, she nodded and gave a final assessing look at the barn. "We'll check for spent shells," she said, "but anyone who'd brush away the footprints would probably pick those up. I'll have a couple of the crime-scene boys come up here this afternoon, dust for fingerprints, and look around, but I don't have much hope."

We both turned and started back through the redwood grove. Under the trees, she stopped, staring upward to their distant green crowns. Then she turned her head to me. "Your story looks a little odd, you know."

I'd been thinking the same thing. "I know. I know. There isn't much here to support it. I could easily have made it all up. And you don't have to tell me—I already thought of a few good reasons why I might have."

"On the other hand," she said, "there's nothing here to make me think it couldn't have happened as you described it. Why? That's the question."

I didn't have an answer.

We spent a few minutes peering through the cabin windows. It was obviously deserted, with dustcovers draping the furniture and the look of a place that hadn't been disturbed in a long time. Jeri checked the door to make sure it was locked and studied the nail on the door. I mentioned that it was one thing in support of my story. Jeri didn't comment.

We made the drive back along the coast without talking, and I felt a trace of that tension you feel when you go out for the first time and wonder, at the end of the evening, if he does or doesn't want to kiss you. When we were back at the county building, Jeri met my eyes. "Thanks, Gail," she said awkwardly. "If you think of anything else that could help, let me know."

Still wondering what had prompted this new current of friendliness, I nodded. "I will."

She hesitated, seemed about to say something more, and then raised her eyebrows briefly. "I'd like to solve this case."

EIGHT

When I got back to the office, Gina Gianelli was waiting for me in the parking lot. She had a gray horse tied to her trailer and an anxious look on her face; in a flash I remembered our odd conversation of the night before—subsequent events had driven it out of my mind.

"Hi, Gina," I greeted her. "Sorry to keep you waiting."

"That's okay. The girl at the desk said they didn't know when you'd be back. I told them I'd wait."

"So what have we got here?" I asked her, looking at the horse.

"He's a bridle horse, a good one. Tony found him for me; he belongs to some friends of his and they're selling him to me cheap. I just want to get him vetted."

I winced inwardly. Vet checks were not my favorite activity, especially not on performance horses who would be used hard and needed to stay sound. I had the impulse to flunk the horse without even looking at him.

Stifling the chickenhearted thought, I walked over to the animal in question. He was standing quietly by the trailer, a gray gelding with a compact appearance and a plain head. Gina untied him and I got down to the business of feeling his legs, looking in his mouth and eyes, and listening to his heart. All routine.

His legs had plenty of knots and bumps and showed the signs of a hard life. That wasn't surprising. Bridle horses take a pounding, physically, particularly their legs and feet. I couldn't find anything that definitely looked like it might cripple him.

His teeth showed him to be eleven years old, as he was supposed to be, and it appeared he could see out of both his eyes. His heart rate was strong and even, his lungs clean. No problems there. I sighed.

"Okay, let's jog him in some circles," I told Gina.

This was the difficult part. What clients really wanted to know when they paid for a prepurchase exam was—will this horse stay sound for a reasonable period of time? Say two years. The trouble was there was no way to answer that question. I could tell, most of the time, if the horse was sound today, and I could tell, some of the time, if the horse was liable to go lame in the near future. But tell if he'd stay sound for a few years? There were no guarantees.

The worse aspect of this was a veterinarian's nightmare. Pass a horse with no obvious problem, have him come up dead lame in a week with something incurable like navicular disease—a degeneration of a small bone in the foot—and face a furious client who's convinced you should have seen it. Sometimes you should have. Other times it's something nobody could have seen. Either way, you look like a fool. The only safe way to handle prepurchase exams was to flunk every horse that came along. That way you'd never be blamed. On the other hand, people might catch on after awhile.

Gina trotted the gray gelding in circles to the right and

the left and my heart lifted a little. The horse looked sound. I flexed all his joints, did the spavin test, jogged him some more, and he still looked sound.

I turned to Gina. "Do you want me to shoot some pictures?"

"Yep. For five thousand dollars, it's worth it."

I gave a low whistle. "Five thousand. That's cheap?"

"Cheap for a good bridle horse."

I shot the X rays, put them in the developer, and went back outside. Gina was standing there holding the horse's lead rope and looking uncomfortable. I patted the gelding's shoulder.

"What's the real difference between a bridle horse, like this guy, and a cutting horse, like my friend Casey Brooks used to train?" I asked her.

Gina's face relaxed instantly. "A bridle horse is a reined cowhorse; it's a style of working cattle that was developed here in California by the vaqueros. We train them to be real 'broke in the face'—it's like having power steering. It takes years; we start them out in the snaffle bit, then move on to the hackamore, then at six years old or so, a horse is put in a full-on bridle with a bit. A good bridle horse will spin a hole in the ground or slide a mile at the lightest touch of the reins."

"So how are cutting horses different?"

"Cutting comes from Texas—cowboys back there didn't get their horses broke this way at all; they just put a bit in their mouth and started them working cattle. Cutting horses work the cow on their own; you don't steer them. Reined cow horses—bridle horses, hackamore horses— work a cow under your direction. That's the main difference."

Gina's face was animated as she talked and she looked a lot more like the Gina I was used to. Her lined and weathered skin, faded blue eyes, and graying hair showed all the signs of a life spent out in the sun and wind on the back of a horse, but normally, she had a vitality—a life force, if you will—that made her, to my eyes anyway, very appealing.

Abruptly her face shut down. "Gail, I need to ask you something."

"Ask away."

"It's about Cindy. I don't know what to do, who to tell."

I picked my words carefully. "Gina, if you know something important, you should tell the sheriff's department."

"That's just the problem." She looked down, then back at me. "Tony doesn't want me to."

Oh ho, I thought, so it was Tony who was the problem. Gina seemed unwilling or unable to tell me what was on her mind; she pushed a few strands of improbable corkscrew curls off her forehead and stared at the gray gelding as if he might hold the answer. The newly hectic curls, brilliant blue eye shadow on her lids, and tightly fitted and ruffled lavender blouse all gave silent testimony to Tony's current influence on her life. Why, I wondered again, had she gotten involved with that jerk.

Now, Gail, I answered myself, maybe she was lonely. Weren't you lonely before you got involved with Lonny? A little sometimes, I had to admit. But never so much that I would have traded my independence for the company of just any man. And absolutely never for a coyote like Tony.

Gina finally turned her eyes back to me. "Can I tell you this in confidence?"

Now it was my turn to ponder. "Within reason," I said at last. "I mean, if you know who killed Cindy and Ed Whitney and you want me to keep it a secret, I won't." Particularly if it was Tony, I added to myself.

"No, no, it's nothing like that," Gina reassured me, but she still looked unhappy. "It's just that Cindy called me, the day before . . . the day before she was killed, I guess."

My instincts were prickling. "What did she say?"

"Not very much, really. But she was upset. She said she might not be able to make it to the show at Salinas, and she asked me if I'd be willing to show Plumber in the nonpro hackamore class for her."

"And?"

"I said I would, since I'll be over there to show my mare in the bridle-horse class, anyway." Gina looked down. "But I had to call her back and tell her I couldn't."

"Why was that?"

She still wouldn't meet my eyes. "Tony didn't want me to. He's showing a hackamore horse this year and his horse and Cindy's horse are running neck and neck for the year-end championship. He didn't want me to help Cindy."

Sounded like Tony Ramiro—true to form. "Is Tony living around here now?" I asked curiously.

"He's living with me," Gina said, almost defensively, though with a kind of shy pride, too. "He moved his horse-training operation to my place a month ago."

"Oh." I tried not to look as nonplussed as I felt. After all, maybe Tony and Gina were simply in love; it happens to the best and the worst of us. But somehow I couldn't shake the notion that Tony was always looking out for number one, and Gina was neither glamorously beautiful nor fabulously rich. Her place, an old dairy she'd inherited from her Swiss-Italian father, was an adequate spot for a person to train a few horses as a hobby, but it certainly wasn't fixed up as a fancy training barn. Gina herself made a living driving a school bus; she was hardly in a position to support Tony in luxury. Still, Gina's small ranch was probably paid for; if Tony had fallen on hard times this might be the best deal he could arrange.

Gina was talking slowly, her eyes still averted from my face. "I know I ought to tell the sheriff's department about that phone call, Gail, but Tony doesn't want me to. He didn't want me to tell even you; we fought about it last night, after we ran into you."

"Why?"

"He's got this crazy idea the cops will suspect him," Gina admitted miserably, "because of the year-end awards competition between the horse he's showing and Cindy's horse."

"That doesn't seem like much of a motive to kill two people; I don't see what he's afraid of."

"He couldn't have killed them, anyway. He was with me that night and all the next morning. He has an alibi."

"So why's he worried?"

"I don't know. I don't understand it. He just says he wants me to stay out of it and to keep my mouth shut."

My mind was clicking like a laser printer. If Tony truly had fallen on hard times as a trainer, maybe he really needed this year-end award to reestablish his reputation. Maybe that was a motive, who could say? But, and this was the interesting part, Tony had known Gina wanted to talk to me, had known it *before* I got shot at. Tony had a motive, of sorts, for shooting at me.

"Was Tony home last night?" I asked Gina, idly, I hoped.

"No. Like I told you, we got in a big fight, never made it to the movie, and I took a cab home. I haven't seen him since."

"He didn't come home at all, then?"

"No." Gina looked completely miserable now, her bright makeup garish on her anxious face. "Gail, I don't know what to do. I *know* Tony didn't kill the Whitneys, but I ought to go down and talk to the sheriffs, and I'm afraid he'll leave me if I do. Maybe he already has."

"Do you want me to tell the sheriffs for you?"

Gina looked half-panic-stricken, half-relieved. "I don't

know. Can it wait one day? Let me see if he comes home; let me talk to him."

"All right," I agreed. "One day. And then one of us has to tell them."

She nodded affirmatively, seeming a little more relaxed at having made a decision.

"I better go get those X rays," I told her.

The X rays, when I got them out, proved inconclusive. I showed them to Gina and explained. "His navicular bones have a lot of changes; see these little shadows on them. Those are signs of bone deterioration. A horse with changes in his bones like this could easily be lame. Every horse is different, though. Since this one is sound now, it's a hard call to make. Some horses have X rays that look a lot worse than this and yet they stay sound. Others look a lot better and go lame."

Gina sighed. "It figures. Now I don't know what to do about this, either. What do *you* think?"

I shook my head. "There's no way I can make a guess on whether he'll stay sound unless you can show me some X rays from a year or so ago. Then we could see if the disease was progressing."

"Under the circumstances, I don't really like to ask. His owners are friends of Tony's; they told me he was sound. They don't even know I'm vetting him."

"Okay. Well, maybe I'll talk to Jim. He's had a lot more experience than I have. I'll show him these X rays and tell him about the horse when he gets in."

"Thanks, Gail. We'll talk about that other deal tomorrow, I promise."

Gina led the horse back to the trailer and tied him up, then came walking back over to me, carrying her checkbook. I started to tell her the cost of the exam when motion in the corner of my eye caught at me. I looked back. The gray horse was trotting away from the trailer, ears forward, moving like he meant to go somewhere. There was no lead rope on his halter.

I didn't stop to wonder how he'd gotten loose. I just ran for the gate, knowing before I started that I wouldn't beat him. He was out in the paved front parking lot when I made the gate, and he broke into a lope and headed for the road. I yelled, "Whoa" desperately. He didn't even cock an ear. The heavy midday traffic whizzed up and down Soquel Avenue and the gray horse charged out into it.

Miraculously no one was coming. There was no screech, no crash. The horse galloped down the middle of the street, headed for the freeway, his hooves clattering on the pavement. I chased after him, running as fast as I could, not quite believing it was all happening. This five-thousand-dollar horse couldn't be out here among all these deadly solid cars. He couldn't.

He was. I had to catch him. He was way ahead of me now, up by the stoplight. No one had hit him yet, but it was just a matter of time. I ran, legs pumping, heart pounding.

People stared from their cars, faces full of shock and apprehension. No one in Santa Cruz was used to horses on a main street. Up at the intersection the cars had come to a stop. The horse skittered to a stop, too, his head up, his eyes big. Nothing looked familiar to him—no grass, no other horses. Only these shiny, noisy machines all around him. He didn't like it.

I was closer to him now. I slowed down, said, "Whoa" as firmly as I knew how. He looked at me; the whoa was familiar. A human on two legs, walking toward him with authority, that was familiar. He put his head down and walked to meet me, and I could have sworn there was relief in his eyes; I know there was plenty in mine.

Taking hold of his halter, I led him up on the sidewalk

and started back for the office, waving a grateful hand at the cars. My heart was pounding as though it wanted to jump out of my chest.

A shaken Gina met me halfway back. Her face was pale and she had a hard time thanking me. It wasn't lack of gratitude; she was having a hard time talking. She clipped the lead rope back on the halter and we both stared at it.

"I don't know how it came off," she said.

I wondered if her anxiety level over Tony was so high she'd simply forgotten to clip the rope on correctly in the first place, then decided it didn't much matter at this point.

Back in the parking lot, I helped her load the horse and watched her pull out while my heart slowed down. Then I went in the office to check my schedule.

The first thing on the list made me say, "Uh-oh" out loud. It was a horse I'd seen earlier that week, a twenty-six-year-old horse that belonged to a woman who'd owned him since she was sixteen and he was seven. She'd turned him out to pasture with some friends who didn't know much about horses, and the old horse had gotten to be skin and bones without their realizing it. When his owner had gone to see him she'd been aghast and brought him home, but shortly after that he'd gotten a respiratory disease. I'd been to see him and given her the appropriate antibiotics and instructions, but it didn't look good, and I'd told her so. Old horses had a tendency to get pneumonia under those circumstances, and if they were as run-down as this one they tended to die of it.

I went on out and got in the truck, checking to make sure I had the necessary drugs to put the horse down. Giving a horse the green needle, as it had been called in vet school, always filled me with a mix of sadness and anger, even when it was obviously the only thing to do. I hate to lose a patient; it was both a personal defeat and a reinforcement of the underlying futility of my profession. It was my job to preserve life, and I always battled fiercely to do so, but neither I nor anyone else could succeed in an ultimate sense.

Teresa Kelly was waiting for me out at her barn, and I could tell by one look at her face that the news wasn't good. It was obvious she'd been crying. She had bright red hair and a round, chubby face with lots of freckles and she looked terrible, her skin dead white, with the freckles standing out like sores, her eyes red-rimmed and bloodshot. I felt a rush of sympathy for her. I knew that I was going to feel pretty bad when Blue's time was up, or Gunner's.

Teresa shook her head when I got out of the truck. "He's a lot worse, Gail. I probably should have called you a couple of days ago, but I kept hoping he'd get better. I know what you're going to say when you see him."

I looked at her and looked down, wishing I could find the right thing to say. This type of situation was hard, and unfortunately common in the veterinary trade. I felt a lot of empathy with people when they were grief-stricken over their animals, but I also knew I couldn't let my emotions run away with me. If I took every animal I lost too deeply to heart, the job would rapidly become so stressful I wouldn't be able to do it.

"Let's go have a look at him," I told Teresa gently.

She led me to a clean stall at the back of the old shed that served as a barn. The horse was there, lying on his chest in a bed of crisp shavings. I could hear the labored wheeze of his breathing from the door.

I checked him over carefully as a matter of routine, but I knew what was wrong with him. He was painfully thin, his spine standing up in a row of sharp ridges, his hipbones and ribs jutting out. The old brown eyes under their sunken hollows looked at me calmly. This horse had seen enough to take anything in his stride.

I stood up and saw Teresa was crying. Shit. This was going to be difficult. "I'm sorry, Teresa." I tried to say it as kindly as I could. "He's got pneumonia and he looks like he's going downhill fast. I think the best thing to do is put him down."

She nodded, not speaking, and walked over to pet the horse. He pushed his face up against her and she rubbed his ears. It was clearly a routine they had.

Tears were running down her face, but when she spoke her voice was under control. "I just feel so bad, like it's my fault he got so thin and run-down and all. I meant to do him a favor, turning him out to pasture, and it's ended so badly." She looked at her horse while she talked, gently rubbing his ears. "I've had him a long time. He's always been a good horse."

The old horse bumped his head against her again and her voice caught in her throat. She gave him a final pat and stood up. "Okay, Gail, I know it's the right thing to do."

"It might be easier if you don't watch."

She looked at me and then at the horse and reached down to stroke his ears again. "All right," she said. "Will you pet him while you do it?"

"Yeah, I will."

She turned away, her face still wet with tears. I took the syringe out of my pocket, where I had put it earlier, just in case, and bent to the old horse to make the injection in his jugular vein. I rubbed his ears and spoke to him as Teresa had done and was relieved when he died easily, folding over on his side. The shot killed quickly, but some horses reacted more violently in the first instant of its effect than others. I'd seen one flip over backward.

When I walked out of the shed, Teresa was waiting for me, her face more composed. She gave me a questioning look and I said, "He died real peacefully."

She nodded in relief and, obviously making an effort to change the subject, said, "I heard you found Ed and Cindy Whitney, Gail. That must have been hard on you."

"It was pretty bad."

Teresa went on talking as we walked out to my truck. "My husband's a deputy sheriff and he says they're getting ready to arrest one of those street people. I guess they found him at the house and he ran away."

I shook my head with a sense of shock. That would be the Walker. "What do they have on him?" I asked her.

"Mike said he's been arrested for assaulting people. He hasn't got an alibi and I guess they think he had some kind of obsession about Cindy. Anyway, his fingerprints were in the kitchen."

"Was he supposed to have a gun?"

Teresa shrugged. "I don't know. But Mike said there were half a dozen guns hidden in that house. A gun in every drawer, he said. I guess the guy must have picked one up." She sighed. "This has been a bad week. First hearing about Cindy and now poor old Toby."

"Did you know Cindy well?"

She shook her head. "No. She was friendly, though. I saw her at a couple of horse shows. It just seems so terrible." Teresa's eyes were filling. "Thanks, Gail," she whispered.

I knew it was time for me to leave. She probably wanted to be alone to cry. Stifling my desire to ask her more questions about the Whitneys' murder, I got in my truck.

"Okay, Teresa. I'm sorry about Toby," I added awkwardly.

She gave me a faint smile. "Thanks. I know it was the only thing to do."

I could see her walking back to the barn in my rearview mirror. Her head was bent forward. Poor Teresa. I felt bad for her and a little bit bad for myself. Situations like this were the hardest part of being a vet.

NINE

I spent the rest of the day looking at horses. A mare with a messy uterine infection turned out to be a smelly job that took me an hour. Next I stitched up a stallion who'd climbed on top of a pipe corral fence in an overeager attempt to get to a mare in heat. He had a gaping hole in one side that looked worse than it was. I stitched it up neatly, put a drain in it, and told the man who owned him that he'd be as good as new in a couple of weeks.

After that I saw three horses that were lame for various reasons, none of them serious, and one mild colic case. I didn't get home until 5:30 and I was due to meet Lonny at 6:00. The sun was low in the western sky, and the evening fog put a cold edge in the air as I pulled into my driveway. There was a car parked there. Not Bret's old red pickup, but a little white convertible Volkswagen Bug. I recognized the car.

The girl who went with the car was sitting on my porch, obviously waiting. Her name was Lynnie. I had met her at one of Cindy Whitney's parties, and she had a barrel racing horse named Tucker that I treated occasionally. Bret had dated her some last winter. All in all, I'd spent enough time around Lynnie to know I didn't care if I ever spent any more. I didn't dislike her exactly, but she was a type I tended to avoid.

Lynnie was a pretty girl; that was her definition and her whole intent in life. In her twenties, with wildly kinked hair, tanned skin, and huge brown eyes, she had a face that was usually animated, with lots of sparkle in the eyes and a big smile. The only trouble, I discovered, was that all that sparkle wasn't wit or intelligence or even charm, but just a kind of forced gaiety, a routine she'd learned the way she'd learned to do her hair and put on her makeup.

She smiled at me now, but the smile was automatic. I didn't think Lynnie liked me any better than I liked her. I wasn't her type, though I doubt she would have put it that way. She would probably have said that I wasn't any fun.

"Hi, Gail." I detected a lack of interest in her greeting and wondered again what she was here for. She didn't leave me waiting. "Where's Bret?"

Ah hah. Somehow or other, Lynnie had discovered Bret was back in town and staying with me. I didn't bother to ask how. Lynnie probably had her ways.

"I don't know where he is," I answered truthfully.

Lynnie gave me a suspicious look, but I didn't volunteer any more information. Not just because I didn't have it but also because I made it a rule never to interfere with Bret and his women.

Lynnie's look changed from suspicious to curious. "I read in the papers that you found Ed and Cindy Whitney. Do you think it was a hit?"

"A hit?"

"You know, like a professional hit man. Because of what Ed sold."

"Because of what Ed sold?" I parroted, feeling stupid.

"I thought you knew. You were over there all the time."

"Actually, I'm not sure what you're talking about. You mean Ed was selling drugs?"

Lynnie shrugged one shoulder. "Everybody bought it from Ed."

"What's 'it'?"

"Coke." Lynnie was looking at me as if I had just fallen off the turnip truck, but I didn't really care. A light was beginning to dawn somewhere inside my brain. Ed *had* offered me some cocaine once, when I was over at their house for a party; I'd declined and thought no more of it. It had seemed all of a piece with the fancy car and sophisticated, rich playboy attitude he put on. It had never occurred to me that he sold it on a regular basis.

"I didn't know he sold it," I said slowly. "I don't buy it."

"Well, he did. He always had lots of it, and it was always good stuff, too. That's why I thought maybe it was a hit. Everybody says the Mafia's behind all the drugs." She got up off my porch in a graceful tangle of long tanned legs. "Tell Bret I came by, will you?"

"Sure. You want him to call you?"

She was already turning away. One shoulder flipped casually. "Whatever."

She got in her car and the white Bug made a U-turn in my driveway, spraying a little gravel in my direction. I saw her license plate zipping away from me—FOXI LYN. I grimaced; I'd always hated that license plate.

Blue was still in the truck and he yipped pointedly at me now. I let him out, and he shuffled toward the stairs, telling me by his demeanor that he was ready to water some trees. I waited for him, hunching my shoulders against the chill of the fog and thinking hard.

What Lynnie had said about Ed surprised me, even shocked me. It seemed unbelievable, given the Whitneys' young and rich high-society image, but why would Lynnie bother to lie? I wondered if the sheriff's department had heard about this. If Ed had been a drug dealer, it might well be something to do with drugs that had caused these murders.

If I could stumble over this, the cops would too, I told myself. After all, I wasn't Sherlock Holmes or anything.

Blue looked at me and then into the trees and growled, as though at an intruder. I looked where he was staring and couldn't see anything. Gnats played in a single remaining beam of sunlight; squirrels chattered in the redwood trees, squawking like birds. The breeze stirred the branches along the creek, a cold, foggy breath. I listened; the dog listened. Nothing. You're getting nervous, I told myself.

Well, maybe I had a right. After all, I'd discovered two dead bodies and been shot at the day before.

When I let Blue back in the house I found a note on the table. It said, "Shoeing down at Steve Shaw's, Bret," in printing that resembled chicken scratch.

I glanced at the clock: 5:45. I had time, I thought, barely. It should only take me five minutes to change myself from a bone-tired vet to a femme fatale.

Peering into my closet, I studied my wardrobe of "dress-up" clothes. It wasn't extensive, since I lived the vast majority of my life in jeans, and was founded primarily on a simple concept: black pants. I had four pairs of black pants, ranging from dressy to casual, in a variety of fabrics suitable for winter or summer. Tonight I selected the most casual—stretchy leggings. I put on black lace trouser socks, shoved my feet into my all-purpose black shoes—slender suede flats—and the bottom half was done. For the top I picked a thigh-length dusty rose sweater with a deeply scooped neckline edged in scalloped stitches—something warm enough to be comfortable as well as elegant on a foggy evening. A string of freshwater pearls and my hair pulled high in two black combs and I was complete.

91

Scrambling back up my ladder "stairway," I scratched Blue on the back and told him to be a good dog and stay off the couch (not likely), grabbed a little black suede bag and stuffed my wallet in it, then dashed out to the truck. I had about five spare minutes, if I hurried.

Three minutes later, I pulled into Steve Shaw's barnyard. Steve's fancy dually pickup was absent, but Bret was very much in evidence. He was standing by a hitching rail in front of the big barn, holding a rasp in one hand, obviously in the process of shoeing the paint horse tied to the rail. He wasn't actually shoeing, though; he was talking to a girl.

She was young, in her late teens, with long yellow-blond hair, shy blue eyes, and a pretty, childish face. Probably one of Steve Shaw's many female clients, one who had managed to take her eyes off the trainer long enough to notice the horseshoer. She smiled at Bret like a puppy who hopes you'll throw a stick—half-playful, half-anxious. He was laughing back at her in a teasing way, his eyes lit up with fun. When I walked in their direction she looked embarrassed, said, "Well, see you later" awkwardly, and hurried away.

"She's too young for you," I said softly as he watched her departing rear view.

He gave me a sudden straight look. "Think I don't know that?" Then the cockeyed grin was back in place. "But just look at that butt."

I smiled. He didn't fool me. Bret was always careful that the victims of his charm were up to his weight. The girl was in no danger from him.

He turned his grin in my direction. "You don't look so bad yourself. Going out on the town?"

"You bet." My mind jumped back to the problem at hand. "I need to ask you something."

"So ask away."

"Did Ed Whitney sell a lot of cocaine?"

Bret's green-brown eyes were clear and blank, like a cat. "Why is it important, now that he's dead?"

"Of course it's important," I snapped in exasperation. "It might be the reason they were killed."

"So why are you so interested?"

I sighed. Bret could be aggravating. I'd learned over the years that despite his carefree image he was a secretive, private person; getting information he didn't want to give was about as difficult as forcing Blue to do what he didn't want to do. Maybe shock would do it.

"Somebody shot at me last night," I told him. "I have no idea who or why, but the only thing that makes any kind of sense to me is that it's connected to my finding the bodies. I still don't have a clue what the connection is, but Lynnie came by this evening looking for you and informed me that Ed was a drug dealer, which I didn't know. I guess what I'm trying to do here is find out anything I can that might explain who killed them."

"Did it ever occur to you it might be smarter to lay low and keep out of it?"

"I'd sort of like to know why I got shot at."

"Maybe getting shot at was an accident."

"It wasn't an accident." I told him the story of the barn on Pine Flat Road. It seemed to impress him a little.

"Shit, Gail." Bret looked at me a long time. The paint horse shifted restlessly and he patted its shoulder absently. "I'd leave it alone if I were you," he said finally. "Why cause more trouble?"

"Come on, Bret. I don't like people shooting at me. For all I know, whoever did it will have another go. I want to find out everything I can."

Bret leaned on the hitching rail, tapping the rasp against his palm, his expression that of a wary animal. "Yeah, Ed used to sell a lot of coke," he said at last. "Cindy told me."

I waited.

He picked his words slowly. "I don't think very many people knew this, so I wasn't going to spread it around, but Cindy used to be a working girl."

"A working girl?"

"Working girl is what they call it." He looked at me. "The ones who do it."

"Okay. So I'm naïve. It's the last thing I'd ever have guessed about Cindy." Cindy had been unmistakably part of the local Yuppie group. With her white BMW, her expensive show horse, and her fancy house on the cliff, she seemed completely removed from anything as sordid as turning tricks. I couldn't imagine her in a run-down massage parlor.

Bret nodded. "I know. I wouldn't have guessed, either. She told me one night when she was drunk. She made me promise to keep it a secret. Her name was Diamond." He shook his head. "Diamond. She told me she met Ed because he supplied the house she worked in with coke. She said he had some kind of a thing about whores—thought the idea was a turn-on." Bret shook his head some more. "Can you believe it? They started dating and then she moved into Ed's apartment with him. He used to drive her to work every evening and kiss her good-bye at the door."

We both studied on that for a while. "Anyway, I guess they decided to get respectable and got married and bought that house. Cindy had a horse like she'd always wanted. She was pretty happy about it. I think she would have liked to forget her old life. But she couldn't exactly, because Ed was still selling coke."

"I don't get it. Why would Ed Whitney sell cocaine? I thought he had money from some big family trust fund."

"That's another thing most people don't know. Cindy told me that the trust fund money didn't kick in till he turned twenty-five, which was six months ago. Up until then, all his money came from . . . uh, sales."

"Whoa. This is definitely stuff the cops should know."

Bret shrugged. "I figured they'd find it out for themselves. I also figured it was better to stay out of the whole thing."

"Well, apparently they haven't found it out yet. From what I heard they're planning to arrest that poor guy I saw in the garage."

"Maybe he did it."

"I just don't think so. Besides, I feel guilty, like it's my fault they suspect him at all."

Bret shrugged again. "Maybe you could find out where the guy was the night you were shot at. That would tell you something."

"That's not a bad idea. You'd think it would be the first thing the sheriffs would check out, though."

Bret watched me closely. "Are you planning to go down there and tell them all this stuff?"

"Well, yeah, I am."

"Keep me out of it, huh? I thought about it yesterday, before I talked to the cops, and I decided I'd better just keep my mouth shut."

I nodded, remembering his abstracted expression at the office and at lunch.

"It'll look pretty funny to that detective. Why I didn't talk, I mean."

"Yeah, okay. I won't mention you. I've got to go. Got a hot date." I slapped him lightly on the shoulder and turned away. When I looked back, he was bent over, picking up the paint horse's foot. In his dirty jeans and layers of battered sweatshirts, he looked like a derelict, and I could definitely see he wouldn't have a lot of credibility with the sheriff's department. Everything about Bret would seem suspicious from their point of view.

TEN

I was only ten minutes late at Lonny's. He lived in Aptos, a semirural community in the hills just south of Soquel; like Soquel, the Aptos area is thick with one- to ten-acre ranchettes, the homes of people who hold down fairly high-paying urban jobs. Lonny's place was just such a three-acre ranchette, but Lonny himself was somewhat of an exception to the "gentleman farmer" rule. He'd made his living and eventually his fortune running a pack station in the Sierra Nevada mountains; at forty-seven, he was semiretired, with a younger partner to manage his business. He checked in once a month or so during the summer (the only season when a mountain pack station can operate), which was where he'd been for the last week.

As I turned in his driveway, I glanced automatically at his two horses, Burt and Pistol, checking to see that they looked healthy and content. They watched my truck curiously, aware that it wasn't Lonny's, two sets of ears pricked sharply forward. I smiled at them, knowing them well enough to see them as individual personalities, not just two big quarter horse geldings. Lonny'd been giving me team roping lessons on Burt, the bay, who was a real character, with a habit of pinning his ears back grumpily at the slightest provocation—a grouchy mannerism that belied a good heart. Pistol I knew less well. A roan with a flaxen mane and tail and a bald face, he was standoffish, carefully well-mannered, and one of the best heel horses in the state of California.

Driving up the hill past the horses, then through a tunnel of oak trees, I pulled up in front of Lonny's house with my usual sense of appreciative pleasure. Hidden from the road by its screen of oaks, the house was unique—a round house, a decagon, wainscoted in brick, with lots of big windows, a shake roof like a hat, and a cupola on top. Lonny had built it himself, and it was as carefully and interestingly detailed inside as out.

I got out of my truck and Lonny appeared in the doorway, a wide smile splitting his rough-featured face in two. Without a thought I stepped forward into his outstretched arms, feeling his big solid body pressed against me, connecting to what felt like an electrical current of warmth and affection.

"Hi. How are you?" He murmured into my hair.

"Okay. How about you?" My own speech was similarly muffled, being directed at his shoulder. At six two, Lonny was tall enough to make my five seven seem short.

After a minute we stepped back, giving each other appraising glances. "What's this I hear about you finding some bodies?" Lonny was always direct.

"It's a long story. Make me a drink and I'll tell you about it."

"Come on in."

He assembled vodka tonics while I curled myself on the Navajo-patterned couch in his living room. The room matched the couch—terra-cotta tile floor, natural pine walls, a sand-colored easy chair. Giant windows stretched up to the eaves, bringing the trees inside.

Handing me my drink, Lonny settled himself on the couch next to me. "So tell me your long story."

I told, going through the shock and horror of finding Ed and Cindy, seeing the Walker in the garage, and my subsequent questioning. "And that's not the half of it."

"So what else?"

Off I launched once again into the story of the barn on Pine Flat Road. Lonny's face grew still as I spoke and his eyes were somber. "Someone shot at you?"

"Yes. More than once, too. It wasn't an accident."

"My God."

"I know. And the strange thing is, I really have no idea who or why. It seems impossible that it's not connected to the Whitneys' murders—after all, both things happened on the same day. On the other hand, I can't see what in the world the connection would be. And," I looked into his eyes, voicing the thought I hadn't allowed myself to dwell on, "I'm scared."

"I don't blame you."

"I keep looking over my shoulder, especially when I'm alone, and I get this creepy feeling someone's watching me." I shivered, remembering that odd prickle of nerves down my spine when I'd walked Blue. "The worst part, for me, is I just don't know why. Why in the world would I be a threat? And there's more."

I told him about Gina Gianelli and Tony Ramiro, about the fact that the sheriffs seemed ready to arrest the Walker, and about Lynnie's and Bret's strange story concerning Ed and Cindy. "It sounds incredible, given what I knew about them, but I believe it. Bret wouldn't have any reason to lie."

"Bret, huh?" Lonny's mouth curled in an expression both humorous and exasperated. Lonny knew Bret slightly, had used him as a shoer once or twice, and seemed to regard my friendship with him as odd but unthreatening. "I don't know as I'd take what Bret says too seriously."

"No," I agreed, "except Bret didn't want to tell me all this; I more or less pried it out of him."

"Humph."

"I need to go down and talk to Jeri Ward," I finished up, "but I think I'll wait until I have a chance to talk to Gina tomorrow. She promised she'd either go to the sheriff's department herself about that phone call, or let me tell them, and I need to know which it's going to be."

"Gail," Lonny's voice was serious, "are you planning on getting involved in this?"

"Not exactly. I'm involved already, whether I like it or not. I found the bodies; I got shot at. Nothing I can do about that. Are you telling me I shouldn't get any more involved?"

"I'm not telling you anything." Lonny grinned. "I know better. What I'm saying is, I'm worried. The last time you got involved in investigating something you almost got killed."

I sighed. "I know, and I don't have a death wish or anything. Getting shot at and not knowing why really bothers me. But I can't think of any better way to make that fear go away than to make sure that whoever murdered Ed and Cindy is caught. Then maybe I'd understand why that person shot at me, and maybe I'd feel safe again. Assuming it was the same person who shot at me.

"There's another thing, too." I met Lonny's eyes. "This may sound corny, but I don't think the Walker guy did it. Call it instinct or whatever you want, but I think he was just startled when I answered that door instead of Cindy, and he ran because he didn't know me. I don't believe he had any idea they'd been murdered."

"Why does the sheriff's department suspect him, then?"

"I'm not really sure." It struck me that Jeri Ward had been deliberately evasive on the subject of the Walker. "At any rate, I'm uncomfortable with the idea that I'm the one who cast all this suspicion on him."

Lonny put an arm around my shoulders. "Don't worry about it. You did the right thing."

"I know." I snuggled into the curve of his body. "So how come it feels wrong?"

"Beats me," he sighed, "but I know the feeling."

We were silent for a minute and I knew he was thinking of Sara. Sara, his estranged wife, for whom he had done everything he could think of to make it right—and it had still come out wrong. Sara was the biggest thorn in our otherwise-satisfying relationship. Lonny couldn't make up his mind to divorce her, thus ridding himself of half his assets, which included this house and his business, and I couldn't seem to really adjust to the notion that he was still legally married.

Sara herself seemed reasonably indifferent to the whole issue; I'd never met her, but apparently she lived with a doctor somewhere in Santa Cruz, accepted a monthly payment from Lonny, and seemed uninterested in changing the status quo. All in all it was a bearable, if not ideal, situation, but Lonny and I still had occasional brawls over it, whether fueled by his guilt or my jealousy I wasn't sure.

Tugging my mind firmly away from the subject of Sara, I asked Lonny, "Did you know Ed and Cindy Whitney at all?"

"I don't think so. The names don't ring a bell. I take it they were horse people."

"Sort of. Cindy was. Ed was rich. That was his be-all and end-all in life, as far as I could tell. To be frank, I didn't like him."

"Did you like her?"

"Yes. Mostly. She was a friendly, happy, talkative person, and she really loved her horse. I liked the horse, too; that helped. The one thing I had a problem with was her being with him, if you see what I mean. He didn't treat her very respectfully, and I have a hard time with women who let their men push them around."

"Unlike you?" Lonny grinned.

"Yes. Unlike me. As you know."

"Don't I." He hugged me again. "And I like you this way."

"I know you do." I kissed him lightly on the cheek. "I'm not sure why you turned out so well, but you're a distinct improvement on most of your sex."

He smiled at that. "In some ways, maybe. Not in others."

I kissed him again, knowing what he was thinking. "It's not a beauty contest, you know."

"Good thing."

After that things proceeded in stages, very satisfactorily, to the bedroom. Several hours later I was lying on my side, dozing, Lonny's arm around me.

Lonny's big pinkish beige cat, Sam, was hunkered down on the pillow next to me, staring deeply into my eyes and purring like a diesel engine. Ever once in awhile he'd reach out and touch my face with his paw, very gently.

"Go away, Sam," I told him.

He squinted his amber-orange eyes shut in a smile and purred louder.

I sighed. My clothes were scattered around the room and my hair was a tousled mess. I didn't feel up to repreparing myself for dinner out, but I was starving.

Lonny seemed to read my thoughts. "So what are we going to do about dinner?" he asked drowsily.

"Got any food? I'll cook."

"I went shopping on the way home. Place is stocked."

"Okay." I climbed out of bed somewhat reluctantly, driven by my stomach. Eyeing my sweater and pearls, I asked Lonny, "Mind if I borrow one of your old shirts?"

"Take your pick."

"Thanks. I'm a messy cook."

"I know. Every time you cook and I clean up, I think I should have picked differently."

"Don't worry about it," I laughed. "You can clean up in the morning. You just lie there and relax while I slave away."

I padded into the kitchen barefoot, wearing an ancient pink oxford-cloth shirt of Lonny's over my stretch pants, thinking that if I were pregnant, I'd fit the old male chauvinist description of the perfect woman to a T. Funny thing was, I didn't care. Being barefoot and in the kitchen felt pretty good. I wasn't so sure about pregnant.

We had chicken curry and chardonnay—an excellent curry, if I say so myself. The kitchen looked like a war zone and Lonny's shirt had yellow blotches down the front, but what the hell.

As we rolled back into bed together, to sleep this time, I wondered drowsily if maybe pregnant would be okay—with this man, anyway.

ELEVEN

My first call the next morning was down by the ocean—a Shetland pony with a severe colic. The pony was only a little bigger than a St. Bernard dog and as appealing as a stuffed animal—chocolate brown, with a fluffy cream-colored mane and tail. He was a mess right now, though, covered with dirt from constant rolling.

This was a bad sign. Horses with colic want to lie down and roll to ease the pain in their bellies. The trouble is that frantic rolling can cause the intestines to flip over and form a twist, like a hose with a kink. Nothing can get past the twist, and without an operation to remove it, the horse will inevitably die. Colic is relatively common in horses and by far the most frequent cause of death.

I checked the pony carefully. His pulse rate was up and there weren't any gut sounds. Not good. I took a sample of fluid from his abdominal cavity and found it was clear and pale, a sign that his gut hadn't ruptured yet. I couldn't tell if he had a twist or not, couldn't feel any major impaction.

The woman who owned him stood holding him patiently, her face tired and concerned. A small girl half-hid behind her, watching the pony anxiously. Head down, eyelids drooping, the little animal shivered in the cold, wet morning air. The painkilling shot I had given him had taken away his acute distress, but he was still miserable.

I studied his owner. She was a stranger to me, but judging by her appearance and the fairly run-down corral where she kept the pony, I didn't think she had a lot of money. The few questions she'd asked me earlier had revealed she wasn't very knowledgeable about horses. I began a slow, careful explanation of what colic was and the risks involved. "If he has a twist," I finished up, "the only way to save him will be to operate on him, and that means you'll have to haul him to the veterinary surgery center near Sacramento and be willing to spend at least twenty-five hundred dollars. That's what it will cost just to have them operate, even if they can't save him."

The woman shook her head. "I don't have that kind of money." Her eyes fixed on mine, as if asking for forgiveness. "I want to do the right thing for him, but I can't afford that."

"I know. I understand your position. This pony may not have a twist, so we'll give him painkillers and I'll put some oil and fluids in him and come back later this afternoon to see how he is. It's possible he'll get better on his own. If he doesn't, and it looks like he does have a surgical problem, we can talk then about whether to put him down."

The woman looked at the pony sadly. "Poor little guy. He's a great kid's pony. I wish I did have the money to spend on him."

Rubbing the pony's forehead gently, I told the woman to blanket him if she could and not to let him roll, then promised I'd be back that afternoon to check on him.

I got in my truck, hoping the pony would be lucky and make it, but unsure what his chances were. As I pulled onto East Cliff Drive, the sight of a slim sailboat breasting the choppy gray water of the yacht harbor channel caught my eye. The harbor. Bret had said the Walker lived near the harbor. I had an hour before I was due at my next call; it ought to be enough.

The first pay phone I saw was right down by the water, next to the loading dock. I fed it a quarter, breathing in the salt air and the wet wood and varnish smell of the boats. The fog was cold and damp around me, bellied down on the coast for another morning. Gray ocean, gray sky. My finger hovered over the phone buttons.

Terry something, Bret had said, a board-and-care down by the harbor. It wasn't much to go on, but it would have to do. I called the Mental Health Unit at Dominican, the local hospital, and asked for the names and phone numbers of any board-and-care facilities for schizophrenic patients down by the harbor. They gave me two. The first one, called Start, was it.

When I asked to speak to Terry, the female voice on the other end of the line said cautiously, "Is this the sheriff's department?"

"No, I'm a friend." I hesitated, wondering what to say. "Maybe it would be best if I came by." I got directions from the woman, who sounded distinctly reserved about my visit. She probably thought I was a reporter.

I drove the few blocks to 6380 Murray, an older two-story house behind a vine-covered wall, and parked the truck at the curb, cracking the windows for the dog and locking the doors. Though with Blue in the truck, locking it up probably wasn't necessary. Old he might be, but Blue still guarded the truck zealously—one of the ways his ornery, stubborn cow-dog personality came in handy.

Looking around curiously, I approached the Start house. The wooden gate in the wall was unlatched and I pushed it open and crossed a ragged, unwatered lawn to knock at the peeling front door of a turn-of-the-century Victorian. The building was painted white with dark green trim; that was the original intent, anyway; at this point the paint was mostly a memory.

The door was opened by a woman in her fifties with light brown frizzy hair and no makeup, wearing a long, swirling Guatemalan skirt and a matching embroidered blouse, her woolly sock-clad feet stuck into Birkenstock sandals. The sixties look. Still alive and well in Santa Cruz in the nineties, thanks largely to the influence of the university, UC Santa Cruz—one of the most liberally oriented campuses in California.

This woman did not have the glazed, inhaled-too-much-pot-lately expression many of the sixties types did, though. Her brown eyes were aggressive, intelligent, and not particularly friendly, and I sensed she was the voice on the phone and had quickly identified me as her caller.

"Yes?" she said inquiringly.

"I just called you, asking for Terry." I paused, still unsure what to say.

The woman waited, watched me, said nothing.

When in doubt, try the truth. "My name is Gail McCarthy; I'm the vet who found Ed and Cindy Whitney's bodies and saw Terry in the garage. I'd like to talk to him."

"Why?"

I locked eyes with the lady. "Because I don't think he did it. I need to ask him some questions."

The woman raised a hand to push her fuzzy hair farther off her brow, and her manner softened a touch. "Terry's in pretty bad shape." She studied me a little more and then held the door open. "Why don't you come into my office for a minute."

I followed her down a dark hall, got a glimpse of a worn but comfortable-looking room with four people in it watching a TV, and was ushered into a small room with a window facing the fog-shrouded yacht harbor. I could just see the spiky rows of masts, black scarecrows in the gray, but I imagined it would be a cheerful view in the sunshine.

Three file cabinets, a desk, and three chairs crammed all the available space in the room. My escort shut the door, squeezed past a file cabinet, and sat down at her desk. "I'm Glenda Thorne," she said. "My husband and I run this place. Have a seat."

I chose a chair and edged into it. Glenda Thorne stared at me thoughtfully. "Is there any particular reason why you feel that Terry is innocent?"

"Instinct, I guess. And it would help if I could get the answer to a question."

"You'd better try your question on me. I don't think you'll get any answers out of Terry." Her manner was blunt, but despite, or perhaps because of it, I had the notion I could trust her.

"I need to know where Terry was the night before last, between ten and midnight," I said, with a directness to match her own.

"You mean the night of the murders? I've already gone over that with the sheriff's department. Over and over it." She rolled her eyes. "I don't know where he was. We don't keep our clients locked up. Terry went out that evening—he often does—and I don't know when he came back. He's always very quiet."

"Not that night. The next night. The night after the bodies were found."

"The *next* night." Her eyes opened wide and then narrowed, but she answered readily enough. "I do know that, yes. He was here."

"Are you sure?"

"Yes, I'm sure. The sheriff's picked him up and questioned him that day. Apparently they recognized him from your description. Ralph, my husband, and I were called down to be questioned and to take Terry home. He, Terry, was a mess. He realized they thought he had something to do with these murders, and he was completely terrified. Since we brought him home, he hasn't left his room. He lies on the bed or sits in the chair and talks to himself. We checked on him two or three times that night, because we were worried about him."

"There's no way he could have been gone for several hours, then?"

"No. It's impossible."

I sighed. "Then he didn't shoot at me," I said, more or less to myself.

Glenda Thorne caught it, though. "Shoot at you? The next night?"

"Someone did, yes."

"Well, it wasn't Terry." She said it decisively and gave me an angry look. "He didn't shoot those other people, either, no matter what anybody says. Do you know anything about schizophrenia?"

I shook my head. "No."

"Schizophrenics," she went on, "Terry in particular, hear voices in their minds, voices that sound as real to them as external voices such as yours and mine. These internal voices sometimes, in fact often, convey messages of warning. In the past, Terry's voices have told him that such and such a person was a 'bad man' and that he should defend himself from him. He's been arrested a few times for striking out at people. The sheriff's department is referring to that as a record of violent assault."

Glenda Thorne snorted. "Terry never hurt anybody. No one ever even had a bruise. Not to mention he hasn't hit anyone since he got out of the hospital two years ago. They got his medication adjusted a little better, he's been living here and we make sure he takes his meds, and he's been fine." Her eyes met mine. "Terry would never, ever have shot those two people. I know him. He's a good person, despite the odd behaviors his disease gives him."

"That's the impression of him I have," I told her. "I see him walking around town a lot; I just had this feeling about him. I call him the Walker to myself."

Glenda smiled for the first time in our conversation. "Yes. He walks. It's his therapy. He worked that out for himself; he stays happier and more relaxed when he gets lots of exercise." She shook her head. "It's terrible for him to sit in his room all day, the way he's doing."

"Can I talk to him?" I asked, moved by an urge to let Terry know that I didn't think he'd done anything wrong.

"You can try, but I don't think it will work. I'll take you up to his room."

She led me up some stairs and down a hallway and knocked on a door at the end. I noticed that though everything was old and a little shabby, it was also clean. No one answered her knock. Knocking again, she called out, "Terry, it's Glenda. I'm coming in."

Motioning at me to stay where I was, she opened the door and went into the room. She was gone for a minute, then reemerged in the doorway and held the door open so I could step inside.

The Walker, Terry, sat in a chair in the corner of a room that held only a single bed, a dresser, and the chair he was in. The chair was next to a window that looked, as Glenda Thorne's had, out at the yacht harbor, but Terry had turned the chair so it faced the wall, not the window, and he was staring straight ahead, mumbling softly to himself.

His curly blond hair and oddly childlike face were the same as I remembered them from glimpses of him around town, but the man himself appeared completely different. The Walker had seemed alert and interested in his surroundings, a little shy, and if not precisely happy, not unhappy, either. The huddled figure in the chair had features that were blurred with some deep, fearful emotion, and he didn't seem aware of the room or us or anything around him at all.

"Terry, this is Gail. She came to see you. She's your friend."

Glenda spoke gently, touching Terry on the shoulder, but he never looked at her. He faced the wall, body hunched in a defensive curl, eyes blank. He mumbled—an endless, unintelligible monologue. He reminded me of a wild cat one of my clients had trapped and was trying to tame. It had crouched in a cage in the corner of her barn, deliberately facing the wall, terrified and resistant, unwilling or unable to trust, sure through bitter experience that all humans intended it harm.

"Terry," I said, wondering if any words could possibly help. "I know you didn't hurt Cindy."

At the mention of Cindy's name, he turned his head slightly and shot me a glance. The monologue stopped briefly and then resumed. I could hear Cindy's name, somewhat slurred, repeated, along with other words I couldn't catch.

"I know you didn't hurt her," I said again, not knowing what else to say.

Glenda touched my arm and we went back out, down the hall, far enough away that our voices wouldn't be heard.

"You see what he's like. He's terrified. And that detective wants us to bring him back down for more questioning tomorrow." She shook her head. "This is tearing him apart."

"I understand. I'm going to see one of the detectives today. I'll talk to her, but I'm not sure it will do any good."

"I'm not sure what would do any good, now." She looked down, her plain face sad. "But thank you for trying."

Escorting me to the door, she let me out, and I walked back to the truck with a sinking feeling in my heart. Blue was sleeping on the seat and sat up when I got in. I put my arm around him and rubbed his chest, and he licked my ear.

The depth of human misery I had caused by linking Terry to this crime dismayed me. I wondered if he would ever be the same again. With my rational mind, I knew I shouldn't blame myself, but my emotions were tangled. I felt responsible, at least in part, for Terry's despair, and I felt sure, even surer than I had been, that he was innocent. I wanted to do something about it.

TWELVE

I spent my lunch hour playing detective. My eleven o'clock appointment was in Watsonville, the agriculturally oriented city that dominates south Santa Cruz County and is as different from Santa Cruz as the hippiesque denizens of UCSC are from the mostly Latino farmworkers who earn their living in the fertile Pajaro Valley. Watsonville is a sometimes volatile mix of a minority of old-money, old-fashioned Republican landowners and the large Mexican-American community that forms the voting majority and has just recently started to assert its power.

My appointment was with one of the old-money types and involved diagnosing a lameness on a Peruvian Paso yearling—always difficult, as Pasos have such different gaits from other horses. I usually had a hard enough time figuring out if a Paso was lame at all, let alone in which foot. This Paso had a nail in his right front, which took care of the diagnosis. After opening the puncture so it would drain and wrapping the foot, I gave the owner instructions on antibiotics, painkillers, and rewrapping, and got done by noon, which left me an hour for lunch or sleuth work. I chose sleuthing and drove straight to Aromas, a small community in the hills just south of Watsonville. Gina Gianelli's twenty-acre dairy-converted-to-horse-ranch was on the outskirts of Aromas, and I had an unscheduled call to make.

As I bumped down the narrow gravel road that circled the apple orchard at the front of her property, I tried to decide what to say to Gina. If she didn't want to tell the sheriff's department anything, how was I going to deal with that? Play it by ear, I thought. See what it feels like.

I had a hard time believing Gina Gianelli could have had anything to do with the murders, mostly because I liked her. But Tony Ramiro, now that was a different story altogether. The trouble was, I simply could not believe that even Tony would murder someone in order to capture a year-end award. Not to mention Gina had said Tony had an alibi. Still, no doubt Gina was willing to lie about that. She had struck me as totally infatuated with Tony.

As I rounded the corner of the orchard and saw Gina's arena up ahead, with Gina and someone else—no doubt Tony—in it, both horseback, I felt a sense of trepidation. This could turn out to be an unpleasant scene if Tony was present. Well, tough shit, I told myself. We're talking about murder here. If Tony doesn't like it, so what?

It was Tony all right. His paunchy, baggy body was unmistakable, equally the trademark black felt cowboy hat. He was riding a gray horse, running him down the arena and sliding him to a stop, and the horse looked spectacular, light and controlled in the bridle, stopping with his hocks almost on the ground, leaving long eleven-shaped tracks in the dirt behind him. One thing about old Tony, he could ride a horse. I stared at the gray gelding in admiration and suddenly recognized him.

This was the horse who had gotten loose at the office, the horse I'd caught out on Soquel Avenue. The horse, I realized a split second later, with the odd X rays, that I'd been going to ask Jim about. I *had* left a note on Jim's desk, along with the X rays, but I'd completely forgotten to find out what he thought; I'd been too absorbed in the question of the Whitneys' murders.

Damn. Gina was sure to ask about the horse; I felt like a fool for forgetting. Not to mention irresponsible. I wasn't a private detective, after all; I was a horse vet. And Gina wasn't a suspect; she was a client.

Parking the truck, I got out and walked over to the arena. Gina gave me a friendly smile and rode the palomino mare she was on in my direction, but Tony beat her to the punch. He'd watched to see who got out of the pickup, too, and was headed toward me with a look of belligerent hostility on his jowly face.

He pulled the gray gelding up at fence and said, "I don't want you coming around here bothering Gina."

"I'm not bothering Gina," I said firmly. "I'm here to talk to her about the horse she brought in yesterday."

"Horse? What horse?" Tony's black eyes snapped over to Gina, who looked nervously apologetic.

"Oh, I just thought I'd have that gray horse vetted."

"Vetted? What the hell do you mean 'vetted'? This horse came from Stan Cameron—one of my best friends. You're gonna *vet* a horse Stan sends you?"

"Well, I thought it wouldn't hurt." Gina sounded sheepish, but even I had heard of Stan Cameron—a horse trainer known to one and all as a double-dealing coyote.

"Goddamn it, Gina, once in awhile you ought to listen to what I tell you." Tony wheeled the gray horse and rode off, slamming out the arena gate and leading the horse to the barn with a pronounced stalk that was probably supposed to represent angry, hurt feelings, but looked more like the waddle of a sulky duck.

114

I breathed a sigh of relief when he was gone, but Gina looked more nervous and unhappy than ever.

"He's been so difficult lately," she half-whispered to me, though Tony was clearly out of earshot.

I had to bite my tongue to keep from saying, so get rid of the son of a bitch, a comment I was sure would not be appreciated.

Looking into Gina's worried blue eyes, her well-wrinkled face once again heavily decorated with makeup, I felt deeply sorry for her and yet angry at her, too. Why did she put up with this shit? Gina was a tremendous hand on a horse—one of the best I knew. She owned her land, held down a responsible job, paid her bills, and was normally a friendly, funny, well-liked woman who derived tremendous satisfaction from her success showing bridle horses. What in the world had made her trade in such a pleasant life for the company of Tony Ramiro?

Loneliness, I supposed, thinking once again that it still wasn't a good bargain. It seemed to me that Gina, or I, for that matter, would be better off lonely than with this look of anxious insecurity in the eyes.

It's hard to judge other folks, though, and you probably shouldn't do it at all. Not being in Gina's shoes, I couldn't know what drove her, or maybe I just couldn't see Tony's good points. He must have some. They sure weren't obvious to me.

"Gina, I'm sorry," I said, "I haven't talked to Jim about that horse's X rays yet. I really came out here to ask you what you were going to do about talking to the sheriff's department."

Gina's expression went from anxious to miserable. "I don't know. Tony's furious with me already for not keeping my mouth shut."

"How about this. You tell me every word of that phone

conversation and I'll call a detective I know. I'll ask her not to bother you unless she thinks it's important, and to be discreet if she does call you."

"Do you think that will work?"

"Who knows. It's the best I can think of."

"All right." Gina looked decisive, a bit like the old Gina—for a split second. "Go ahead. I'll deal with Tony."

"So what did Cindy say?"

"Not very much. She sounded worried and upset, and she said she might not be able to make the show at Salinas and asked if I would show Plumber for her. I didn't ask her what was wrong; it didn't seem like any of my business. I just said sure, and then after I hung up Tony asked me what all that was about and I told him and he had a fit about it. So I called her back and told her I couldn't. She sounded as if she'd been crying, and I felt bad about backing out, so I got off the phone as quick as I could. I really have no idea what she was upset about. Really."

Gina sounded convincing, but I wondered. "Are you showing at Salinas?" I asked her.

"Yes. Tomorrow. Dolly here"—she patted the palomino mare—"is entered in the nonpro bridle horse class."

Tomorrow was Saturday, I realized, the day Steve Shaw had said he was showing Plumber. "So would Cindy have showed tomorrow, too?"

"Yep. First is the nonpro hackamore, which is what Cindy would have been in, then the open hackamore, where Tony's gelding is running against Plumber and Steve Shaw; then comes the nonpro bridle horse class, then the open bridle horse class."

"What time will it start?"

"About eight o'clock. They run it along with the slack. In the small arena on the track in front of the grandstand."

"That's right." The stock horse show in Salinas, I remembered, was run in conjunction with the Salinas Rodeo, one of the biggest rodeos in California. It was so large that the hundreds of contestants who entered could not all compete during the performance—not without making it six or seven hours long. Thus the slack, which occurred early in the morning, when all the contestants ran except those who'd been selected to be up in the show during the afternoon. I'd been to watch the slack before; it was much quieter and less crowded than watching the rodeo, and it was also free.

Apparently the bridle horses and hackamore horses would be running at the same time as the slack. Steve Shaw and Plumber, Tony and Gina would all be competing tomorrow morning. In a split second I decided.

"I'll be there," I told Gina. "I've never watched a reined cow horse show before; I'd enjoy it. Besides, Steve invited me." I grinned, remembering Amber's pique.

Gina seemed to be thinking along the same lines. "You'd better watch out Amber St. Claire doesn't claw your eyes out; she's got the hots for Steve."

"So I gathered."

"Amber can't stand anybody Steve seems to like. Anybody female that is. She hated Cindy."

"I can believe it. Enough to kill her?"

Gina shook her head ruefully. "I can't believe even Amber would do that." She sounded as if she'd have liked to believe it. "Though a nastier little cat never walked the earth than Amber St. Claire," she added.

I agreed with that assessment but thought I'd better not say so. "Well, I need to get back to work," I told Gina. "I'll talk to that detective today and do my best to keep you out of trouble. I'll talk to Jim about those X rays, too."

"Okay. Thanks, Gail."

"You bet. See you tomorrow."

Gina waved a friendly good-bye and went back to loping her mare. As I drove down her driveway I thought, not for the first or last time, that the number of genuinely good strong women who were undone by their longing for a relationship, any relationship—with a man—was probably legion. Gina was merely one of many. And I hoped, I quite desperately hoped, that no matter what trials old age or solitude might visit upon me, I would never be among that number.

THIRTEEN

The rest of the day was business as usual; I ran around in a constant hurry, looking at horses. I checked on the pony and was relieved to find he was better. Telling the woman to call me if he took a bad turn, I dashed off to see an expensive jumping horse whose cough had suddenly escalated into the flu. The whole afternoon was like that. Frantic. In fact, it rapidly turned out to be "one of those days."

Before it was over I had to put down an endurance horse who'd gotten caught in a fence and virtually torn his leg off, tell a woman I really liked that her team roping horse had ringbone, an incurable lameness that tends to get progressively worse, and stitch together a foal whose hindquarters had been severely lacerated by the family dog. My last call was to a smiling, ignorant middle-aged man who had allowed his backyard horse to go untreated so long that a sole abscess, normally a minor complaint, had virtually rotted the horse's foot away. I tried unsuccessfully to convince the man that the only thing that would help his horse at this point was thorough and relatively expensive treatment, but I ran up against a blank wall.

"I imagine it'll get better" and "I can't spend that kind of money," were his only responses. I looked with frustration at the swimming pool in the backyard and then at the horse, holding his painful foot so that it didn't touch the ground, and drove away filled with anger and a feeling of helplessness.

Nothing I could do, sometimes. No way to force that man to treat his horse properly. Oh, I could call the humane society. But time and experience had taught me that that course of action often did more harm than good. The humane society, in their bumbling bureaucratic way, seemed incapable of making individual judgments and would often abide by some rule that indicated they must impound or euthanize an animal, even when said animal could only be usefully helped in some other way.

No, I wouldn't call the humane society in this case. It was possible that the horse would recover on his own. I'd seen it happen often enough. But the man's indifference to his horse's suffering—that was a cancer of the spirit that nothing could cure.

I banged my hand on the steering wheel and yelled "damn" out loud. Blue looked up at me curiously, making me feel stupid.

"I don't know what to do, buddy," I told him. "Sometimes I hate this job."

Glancing at the dashboard clock, I noted that it was 5:30. The county building was on my way home, more or less. Maybe, just maybe, I could catch Jeri Ward before she went home and end my day by doing something useful.

My stomach growled a protest, but I took the Ocean Street off-ramp and drove down to the sheriff's department. A young crew-cut deputy informed me, after a moment's hesitation, that Detective Ward was not available.

I pondered the idea of talking to Detective Reeder, always assuming he was available, and rejected it. I simply wasn't in the mood to be grilled by the man.

"Tell Detective Ward Gail McCarthy was by to see her," I said, and turned to go.

Jeri Ward's "Gail" stopped me with my hand on the door.

"I saw you here at the desk," she said briefly. "I'm on my way out. Can I help you?"

"Well, it's a long story. Several long stories, really."

She glanced at a slim gold watch on her wrist. "I really do have to go." A second's hesitation. "Would you want to ride along with me? It should take about an hour."

My turn to hesitate. I was starving. But then, I'd come here to talk to her. "Sure," I said.

I didn't ask her where we were going as we walked out to the sheriff's car, and she didn't volunteer any information. Once we were moving down the road, I launched off into the story of Gina Gianelli and Tony Ramiro and Cindy's phone call to Gina, as it struck me as the most innocuous and least difficult of the subjects I wanted to bring up.

Jeri listened quietly. When I was done, she said, "I'll have to talk to her."

"I was afraid you might say that. Do your best to be discreet, if you can."

"I'll try, but I can't promise anything. I may need to talk to him, too."

I pictured Tony's outrage at that possibility and grinned despite myself. "Poor Gina. He'll give her hell for that."

Jeri Ward's mouth twitched ever so slightly; I had the impression she had little sympathy for women who allowed their men to give them hell. I'd have been willing to bet my life savings that she herself was single and uninvolved. There was something in her cool self-containment that seemed to say, touch-me-not, a sense of almost asexual aloofness, though she wasn't an unattractive woman.

Of course I could be wrong, I reminded myself. She could

121

be very different when she was off-duty. But I was still willing to bet there was no man in her life, though it wasn't a question I was liable to get an answer to anytime soon.

We were pulling off the freeway onto the Pasatiempo exit ramp, and my mind swung off Jeri's private life and back to the problem at hand.

"Where are we going?" I asked her.

"Thirty-six Pasatiempo Drive."

It was a classy address. Pasatiempo is a country club community. A lot of older homes, all of them big, laid out around a golf course that rivals Pebble Beach. In Santa Cruz County, a Pasatiempo address meant money.

"Can I ask why we're going there?"

"I've got an appointment with Cindy Whitney's father."

"Oh. So you found out who Cindy's parents are."

She nodded. "It's kind of a funny story. We never did find any paperwork to identify her. But today, after an article that included their pictures was run in the newspaper, a man called in and said he was her father. He was real cagey about the whole thing, didn't want to talk to us or come down to the office or anything. I more or less forced him into this interview."

"Oh." I took that in, wondering how it connected to everything else I'd heard. "How are you doing with Ed's relatives?" I added, curious as to how much information she'd feel comfortable giving me.

Jeri grimaced. "You mean Ms. Anne Whitney?"

"Sure. Wouldn't she be your number-one suspect? Two million plus seems like a motive to me."

"It's a motive all right," she answered. "The trouble is, she's also got an alibi. Medical evidence says that Ed and Cindy Whitney were murdered between six P.M. and midnight, at the latest. Anne Whitney was at a company party during the whole of that time. Dozens of people saw her.

They also saw her uncle and two cousins. Prominently on display. The whole Whitney family has an alibi."

"How convenient."

"Oh, that isn't lost on us, believe me. She has the money to hire someone to do her killing for her—no two ways about it. That's part of the problem. Her lawyer says her finances are in excellent shape; she might enjoy another couple of million, but she didn't have any pressing need for it. Two million isn't as much of a motive for her as it might appear to be."

Jeri peered out through the car window as she spoke. The evening fog was coming in and gray plumes twined between the dark Monterey pines and oaks that lined the narrow curves of Pasatiempo Drive, making visibility difficult. Big substantial houses, most of them set well back from the road, hid behind walls and hedges, giving an impression of prosperous secrecy. We were about at the fourth tee when I spotted the number 36 on a side hill, half-concealed by a clump of wild lilac. Jeri turned up a short, steep driveway that ended in front of a house you couldn't see from the road.

You couldn't see much of the house when you were parked right in front of it. A high hedge of bamboo reached to the eaves, and a brick front porch with a light on over the door was the only obvious feature.

Jeri and I looked at each other. The long summer day was drawing to an end, and the fog was steadily turning a darker shade of gray.

"Do you want to come in?" she asked.

"Yes, I would, if you don't mind." I couldn't tell by her face if she minded or not, but I didn't really feel like waiting alone in the car. Also, I was curious to see Cindy's parents, especially in light of what Bret had told me. I got out of the sheriff's car and walked with Jeri to the door, grateful that the khaki-colored blouse I was wearing didn't show the dirt that was undoubtedly on it. My jeans and boots were a little grubby, but, oh well.

Jeri knocked and we waited. After a minute, the door was opened by a man in late middle age. He had a rounded, pugnacious face with an upturned nose, like an angry pig, and tightly curled brown hair heavily flecked with gray. He was running to fat, and his polyester shirt and leisure slacks were too tight.

"Dr. Earl Ritter?" Jeri asked.

The man nodded slightly.

Jeri introduced herself and then introduced me as Dr. McCarthy, giving no further explanation.

The man listened, his small eyes wary and unfriendly. For a moment I thought he was going to shut the door in our faces, but he held it open, as if on second thought. "You'd better come in, I guess."

We walked through a front hall and down some stairs into a sunken living room. There was a grand piano in the corner, an enormous brick fireplace, and lots of ankle-deep dark brown carpet. I sat down on a gold-colored velvet couch and thought I detected signs of money. Not too difficult, Sherlock.

Jeri started to speak, but Earl Ritter held up his hand with a kind of pompous authority. "Just a minute. I have something I want to say." He paused and cleared his throat. "Cindy Whitney was not my daughter."

"You called in and said . . ." Jeri began, but the man held up his hand again. "The woman whose body is in the morgue is my daughter by birth, yes, but we disowned her from this household when she was eighteen. It was the Lord's will," he added piously.

I could feel Jeri's eyes rolling mentally, but her face stayed neutral. "Could you tell me the whole story, please?"

The man looked resentful. "There's nothing to tell. This

is a godly household. My daughter, whose God-given name was Barbara Jean Ritter, defied the Lord and her parents and came under Satan's influence. I was forced to cast her out. That would be twelve years ago."

I was trying not to stare at the man in disbelief. He looked smug and justified, to all appearances completely unmoved by his daughter's death.

"I claimed the body," he went on, "because I felt there might be legal complications if I didn't."

"Am I to understand," Jeri spoke slowly, "that you haven't seen or spoken to your daughter in twelve years?"

"That's right." Earl Ritter's eyes shifted slightly when he said that. He's lying, I thought.

Jeri watched him closely. "Your wife, does she live here?"

There was a definite hesitation now. "Yes, she does. But I don't want her bothered. Her health is very poor. I've told her Barbara's dead, but I'm not sure she's really grasped it. I can't have you questioning her."

"I'm sorry, I'll have to speak to her."

Earl Ritter started to bluster, but Jeri cut him off. "This is a murder investigation. I will be talking to anyone and everyone who might have some bearing on the case."

The man clamped his mouth with a snap and seemed to consider whether Jeri had enough clout to enforce her words. After a minute, he got up without saying anything and left the room.

Jeri and I glanced at each other briefly and then waited quietly in our respective places. When Earl Ritter came back, he had a woman with him.

She was middle-aged and overweight, with faded brown hair and vague-looking eyes. After murmuring a conventional greeting at us, she sat down in an armchair next to her husband, like an obedient child.

"Mrs. Ritter," Jeri asked gently, "are you Barbara Jean Ritter's mother?"

The woman nodded. "Barbara's dead. She's been dead a long time," she added.

"She was killed two days ago," Jeri said slowly.

The woman kept on talking as if she hadn't heard. "She was dead, but she came back. I couldn't understand it. Ask Earl. She didn't look like Barbara."

Earl shifted in his seat uncomfortably and said, "Hush, Jeannie, you don't know what you're talking about." To us, he added, "She's confused, as I said."

Jeri spoke to the woman again. "You say she came back?"

She nodded with a vague sort of enthusiasm. "She didn't look like Barbara. But she said she wanted to make peace. Earl said she was dead."

Jeri looked at Earl Ritter, whose face was turning red. "It sounds as though your daughter did come back here."

"Now you listen here." Ritter's face was suffused with color. "I told you what you need to know. My poor wife is not healthy, as I said. Why don't you just get out of here and leave us alone."

There was an edge in Jeri's voice. "Cut the crap, Dr. Ritter. If your daughter came back here, I can find out about it. Why don't you make this simple and tell the truth. You don't want to be run in as a material witness, do you?"

The threat seemed to take all the air out of Earl Ritter. He blew his breath out through pursed lips. "I didn't want to speak of this," he said heavily. Amazingly, he managed to continue to convey his air of smug righteousness, despite the fact he'd been caught out in a lie. "Barbara came to this door a week ago. I told her she was not welcome here, that as far as I was concerned, she was dead. She then left. The whole thing took about five minutes. This is a godly household," he repeated. "Barbara was under the influence of Satan."

Unexpectedly, Jean Ritter giggled. "She wanted to see us

again. She said she needed help. But Earl said she was dead. Dead to us. Now he says she's dead; I don't understand."

"Hush, Jeannie," Earl Ritter said nervously.

Jeannie giggled again. The giggle had a hysterical note. "Once upon a time, Barbara caught Earl. Earl was with his secretary. *He* was ungodly. Barbara told me and Earl threw her out. He said she was influenced by Satan." The giggles were becoming uncontrollable now, swallowing up the words. "He said . . . she was . . . dead."

Abruptly she was sobbing and laughing at the same time. Jeri stood up. "I'm sorry," she said simply. "We'll go now." She gave Earl Ritter a cold look. "We'll talk to you tomorrow. Down at the sheriff's office."

The man didn't say a word. He was staring at his wife as if he couldn't believe what she'd said, his self-satisfied dignity gone for the moment, anyway.

Jeri and I walked up the stairs and let ourselves out of the house.

When the door was shut behind us, I looked at her. "Poor thing," I said.

"Who? The mother?"

"No." I shook my head. "Cindy. That explains a lot."

FOURTEEN

What do you mean?" Jeri asked as we got back in the car.

"It's a long story." I recounted Bret's revelations as talk I had heard and ended, "I had no idea Ed Whitney sold cocaine or that Cindy used to be a hooker, but I checked with someone else, whom I promised not to mention, and he confirmed it."

Jeri's eyes moved to my face for a second, serious and unsmiling. I could feel the intensity of her mind working.

I went on. "What I meant back there is that I understand, now, what might have driven Cindy to become a whore. Shit, a father like that—a religious fanatic right out of a right-wing Bible show. And the mother—she's let her husband make all the decisions, overriding her own sense of right and wrong, until she's completely lost touch with reality. Poor Cindy. Even being a hooker looked good next to that life."

We were out of Pasatiempo now, Jeri driving slowly through the foggy darkness. She didn't say anything, so I went on talking. "Does the sheriff's department know that Ed Whitney sold cocaine?"

There was a long silence. I stared at Jeri's profile while she drove; it was as tight and emotionless as ever. She glanced at the watch on her wrist and then at me, and instead of answering my question, she asked me another. "Do you mind waiting through another visit?"

Hunger, though still present, seemed to have taken a backseat to curiosity. "Sure. What did you have in mind?"

"Dropping in on Carl Whitney."

Carl Whitney turned out to live in Scotts Valley—the town he'd almost single-handedly transformed into a city—at the top of a largish hill; he appeared to own the entire hill. His house was the only building on it—a sprawling one-story structure with lots of glass and plenty of outdoor floodlights illuminating a wide concrete drive. The house, once we were inside it—ushered in by an actual servant, for God's sake—proved as large and rambling as it appeared, and not as well lit as the driveway. I had a confused impression of brightly colored furniture that seemed oddly tasteless in a house that featured a door-opening servant, and then Jeri and I were invited to wait in a room with big windows overlooking Scotts Valley—the lights floating below us on a sea of darkness as if they'd been laid out there to improve Carl Whitney's view.

The room itself was well proportioned, with typical rich man's touches—cathedral ceiling, hardwood floors, built-in oak cabinets. The furniture, as in the rooms we'd walked past, seemed out of sync. Arranged around a gigantic TV, a mustard yellow Naugahyde couch battled with a couple of aqua-blue-flowered armchairs, a shiny cranberry-colored velour recliner, and a glass and wrought iron coffee table. None of it fit the big dramatic room; the pieces looked as though the Whitneys had moved them straight from a tract home to this mansion, their taste not having caught up with their wealth.

Carl Whitney walked into this incongruous room wearing a bright red flannel shirt tucked into baggy slacks—clothing that seemed more in harmony with the furniture than the house. He appeared to be in his seventies, and one hundred percent *there.* His eyes, under bushy brows, were bright, and the white hair that sprang off his brow was thick and abundant. He shook first Jeri's hand and then mine firmly, accepted Jeri's introduction of me as Dr. McCarthy, and invited us to have a seat.

Jeri reminded him briefly of an interview that had apparently taken place at the sheriff's department that morning and then went straight for the jugular. "Mr. Whitney, do you know of anything in your nephew's or his wife's past that might be unusual or disturbing?"

Carl Whitney stared at Jeri under and through the camouflaging screen of his brows, his eyes keenly aware. I could feel the snap decision in his mind. He knows that Jeri knows something, I thought, and he's too smart to lie.

The old man spoke without undue hesitation. "I know Cindy was once what you might call a lady of the night."

"You didn't mention this earlier when we asked for any relevant information about her." Jeri's voice was uninflected, not accusing. Would it have been different, I wondered, if the person being questioned was one of the homeless instead of possibly the richest man in the county?

"No, I didn't see that it was relevant—I still don't, for that matter—and it wasn't a thing I cared to spread around."

"How did you happen to know this?"

Again, the instantaneous calculation. The old man was very smooth; it was clear the Whitneys had not acquired their wealth solely through the luck of being in the right place at the right time. There was only a heartbeat pause before he answered. "I hired a private detective to look into her when Ed decided to get married. My brother, Ed's father, was dead, as was his wife, and Ed was always a little wild. I knew he wasn't likely to listen to my advice, so I simply checked on the girl to make sure she wasn't an out-and-out fortune hunter." He smiled without malice. "There is, after all, a considerable fortune to be hunted."

"And what did you learn?"

"That Cindy had been, and I quote, an 'out-call massage girl, advertising in the papers under the name of Diamond.' That her parents are a wealthy fundamentalist doctor and his wife who disowned her and whom she never saw. That was it, more or less. She wasn't a fortune hunter in any sense that concerned me."

"Does anyone else in the family know this?"

The shrewd old eyes watched Jeri unwaveringly. For some reason, this question was more difficult than the others; when he spoke it was slowly. "My niece, Anne, knows. My sons, Pete and Jim, don't, as far as I'm aware."

"Anne knew about Cindy?" Jeri stiffened like a pointer scenting grouse.

"Yes."

"Did you tell her?"

"No, I didn't," he said heavily. "She found out some other way, but she did let me know that she knew." There was a faint distaste in his tone.

"Did Anne imply that she was hostile to Cindy because of her past?"

The old man's face was set in careful, give-nothing-away lines. "Anne wasn't pleased about Cindy's past, as you would expect. She certainly never threatened her." There was a hint of steel in Carl Whitney's voice. "Anne did not always get along with Ed—none of us did, for that matter—but she would never, under any circumstances have considered threatening him or harming him or his wife."

Do-I-make-myself-clear was implicit in his tone.

Jeri nodded coolly, her eyes fixed on the old man. "What was your nephew's source of income before he turned twenty-five and inherited the income from his trust fund?"

She had done it perfectly, sliding the question in when he didn't expect it, and I saw the brief flash of apprehension in Carl Whitney's eyes before he answered calmly. "I have no idea."

This time he's lying, I thought. If he could hire a detective to find out about Cindy, he could certainly find out what Ed was up to. And he'd never admit it, I realized a split second later. Cindy's past was one thing, but a nephew who was a drug dealer would be something he would *not* want to come out.

Jeri was watching Carl Whitney as closely as I was. "So you have no idea where your nephew acquired his money prior to six months ago?"

"No, I do not. Presumably he worked for someone. In sales, I believe. As I told you, I did not see Ed often and we were not on friendly terms."

Jeri spoke slowly. "Would it surprise you to hear he sold cocaine?"

A long silence. When Carl Whitney spoke it was in measured phrases—a businessman discussing a controversial contract. "Detective Ward, I expect you to conduct this investigation in thorough detail; I want my nephew's murderer found." Cindy, I noticed, wasn't mentioned. He went on. "I will not, however, allow you to ruin my nephew's reputation with unfounded accusations. I have a right to put a stop to it and I will." I could hear the power, well-used, well-controlled, that this man still wielded, seventy or not.

Jeri's voice was civil but unintimidated. "We do our best to protect the rights of citizens, Mr. Whitney, particularly their right not to be murdered in their homes. That's our first priority here, as I'm sure you understand. I'll ask any questions and follow any lines I think are necessary." Do-I-make-myself-clear? was implicit in Jeri's tone this time.

They stared at each other for a second, facing off in the most civilized possible way. Neither smiled. The message passed unspoken: Stay off my turf. After a minute, Carl Whitney nodded urbanely. "If that's all, then?"

Jeri nodded back. "Yes, for the moment."

The patriarch—that was how I'd started to think of him—escorted us to the door himself, ushered us out politely. Once we were back in the car and down the driveway, I said, "Whew."

Jeri looked at me questioningly.

"He's very good. If he killed Ed and Cindy I bet you never find out about it."

"What reason would he have to kill them?"

"Who knows. Maybe Ed was trying to take over the business; maybe Carl didn't like having a hooker and a drug dealer in the family. All I can say is, there's a man who knows how to get things done; it's written all over him."

"I agree with you, but Carl Whitney doesn't have any obvious motive. Neither do his sons. His wife died two years ago. Anne Whitney is the only one who stands to gain in any way by her brother's death."

"And Anne knew about Cindy being a hooker and didn't like it."

"That was plain enough. Possibly she knew about her brother's business dealings, too. It looks as though we'll be questioning Ms. Anne Whitney some more."

I smiled. "Good luck."

She nodded grimly. "Carl Whitney has already been to see the sheriff and, guess what, Carl was one of the major contributors to his campaign last year."

"Oh."

"I'd need a watertight case against Anne Whitney or Carl

even to consider an arrest, and so far there isn't much. Their alibis are the only watertight thing in sight."

"What you need"—I glanced at Jeri speculatively—"is someone with no alibi, no connections, and some evidence linking them to the scene of the crime."

"It wouldn't hurt."

"Like Terry White."

The look Jeri gave me was not encouraging, but she said slowly, "In some ways he fits."

"I've been told you guys are questioning him tomorrow; I also heard he was the main candidate for immediate arrest."

Jeri's eyes were fixed on the road. "Who told you that?"

"A casual acquaintance with a husband in the sheriff's department." Jeri didn't say anything. I continued. "I went down to talk to Terry this morning. Mostly I wanted to find out where he was the night I was shot at. The woman, Glenda Thorne, who runs the house he lives at, said he was at home."

Jeri looked stern for a minute. "That's *our* job, Gail, to find these things out. You don't make it any easier when you get into the middle of it."

I decided not to get offended. "Has Detective Reeder already asked Glenda Thorne about that?"

We were back in Santa Cruz now, going down Ocean Street, and Jeri drove slowly, eyes on the traffic, mind abstracted. "Yes," she said slowly.

"So, either I'm making my story up, or Ed and Cindy's murder is totally unconnected to someone shooting at me that night, or Terry didn't do it."

Jeri turned into the parking lot of the county building and pulled up next to my pickup.

"Do you think Terry White killed Ed and Cindy?" I asked with my hand on the door handle.

Jeri didn't say anything for several seconds. She stared

134

straight ahead through the windshield into the dark parking lot, following some train of thought in her mind. Eventually she gave her head a slight shake, like a dog coming out of a lake.

"Terry White," she said slowly, "has a string of arrests for assaulting people. We looked into these arrests, and the situation was always the same. Suddenly, without being provoked, he'd hit someone. He's never hurt anyone badly enough to hospitalize them, but he has spent quite a lot of time in locked facilities because of this tendency to attack without warning."

I was quiet for a minute. "But did he ever try to shoot anyone?"

"No. On the other hand, I don't suppose he ever had a gun."

"Where was he supposed to have gotten this one?"

"The theory is he found it in the Whitneys' house and threw it off the cliff when he was done." Jeri looked straight at me. "I've got to admit I don't like it much, either."

"So why are you guys pursuing the angle that he did it?"

A long, slow head shake. "John Reeder likes him for it. I don't particularly. I sat in on the questioning session. Terry White seemed very confused about everything. He mumbled a lot, talking to himself. If he was asked to say yes or no, he'd say one, then the other. We never could get him to say what he'd done that night."

"Is there any reason to think he murdered the Whitneys, other than his lack of an alibi and his fingerprints in the kitchen?"

Jeri sighed. "The idea that he's crazy. That he had an obsession with Cindy. An irrational crime as they say." Her eyes met mine. "He's an easy arrest. Crazy street people have a lot less clout than the Whitneys."

Abruptly, as if she was sorry she'd spoken so frankly, she turned her head away and put the car in drive, restraining it only with her foot on the brake. It was plainly a hint. I opened the door and got out.

"Well, good luck," I said awkwardly.

She nodded, took her foot off the brake, and drove off, her eyes fixed straight ahead.

I got back in my own pickup, rubbed Blue's head, and looked at the clock: 9:00 P.M. Too late to drop in on Lonny. I decided to get dinner at Carpo's and go on home. I needed to be up early in the morning.

FIFTEEN

At 6:30 the next morning, I pulled on my cleanest, newest Wrangler jeans. Keeping in mind the cold early-morning fog and hot late-morning sun, I layered a tank top with a bulky woven-cotton turtleneck and chose my favorite jacket—gray pile covered with a soft shell. Lacing up my buckskin packer boots and twining my hair into a neat French braid—well, semineat, anyway—I clambered up my ladder stairway into the kitchen and made a pot of coffee.

I sat at the kitchen table and drank the first cup, then poured the rest into a thermos, grabbed my purse, and headed for the door. Snapping my fingers for Blue, I sneaked past Bret, snoring in his sleeping bag on the couch. I had no idea what time he'd gotten in; he certainly hadn't been home when I went to sleep. Probably at a bar, hustling women.

I pulled out of my driveway at 7:00; it took an hour to get to Salinas, and Gina had said the show started at 8:00. Rolling down the foggy highway, I began to marshal my thoughts. I often used my driving time to do this; it was frequently the only time in the day when I was left to myself.

My mind went instantly to last night, to Earl Ritter and his wife, and Carl Whitney. It would be nice to pin these murders on Earl Ritter; I'd seldom met a man I liked less. What had Cindy really said to him when she'd come to visit after an absence of twelve years? That she needed help? I wondered if Jeri Ward would be able to get the facts. Dr. Earl Ritter struck me as a man who was so deeply into denying reality he might not recognize a fact if it bit him.

Then there was Carl Whitney. Carl Whitney, who had an alibi. As did his sons and his niece, the snobbish-looking Anne Whitney, who was Ed's heir. I realized suddenly that that meant she would inherit Plumber, too. Cindy's brief will had left everything to her husband and his heirs. Anne Whitney didn't strike me as the type of person who would have any idea what to do with a horse.

It would also be satisfying to discover Ms. Whitney was the culprit, if for no other reason than she'd looked, the one time I'd seen her, as if the world existed for her convenience. On the other hand, that was hardly a motive.

I just couldn't believe Anne Whitney would have her brother and his wife bumped off because she found their lifestyle/background embarrassing. And if Ed had been putting pressure on his family for money, they should have killed him several years ago, not now, when he'd finally come into the income from his trust fund. It just didn't make sense.

No one, in fact, seemed to have any kind of a sensible motive for killing Cindy and Ed. I was on the way to this show, getting up at the crack of dawn on my one day off, in order to see if I could come up with some clues, but there was no legitimate reason for any of these horse people to have killed them, either.

I might dislike Tony Ramiro, but would he really murder somebody over a year-end award? Not likely. And what earthly reason would Gina have to wish them harm? Or

Steve? It was hardly to his advantage to lose a client. Now Amber . . . I gave a moment's thought to a fantasy in which Amber had hired someone to bump Cindy off out of jealousy and had Ed killed for convenience sake. It sounded good but was, again, unlikely.

Shit. I stared through the windshield at the foggy landscape of low, rolling hills just north of Salinas. This was ridiculous. I was a vet, for God's sake, not a detective. A vet. Jesus Christ, what was I thinking of? I'd forgotten yet again to ask Jim about those X rays on the gray horse. Gina would think I was a complete idiot.

Well, that was one problem that could be remedied. I picked up the car radio and called the office. It was only 7:45 and we weren't due to open until 9:00, but I was pretty sure Jim would be there, workaholic that he was.

Yep. His curt, "Santa Cruz Equine Practice," was unmistakable.

"Jim, it's Gail."

"Yes?"

"Did you ever look at those X rays I left on your desk?"

A moment's silence. Then: "Horse that was sound but had lousy-looking navicular bones."

"Yeah."

"Was he nerved?"

"Uh, I don't know," I muttered.

"First thing I thought of."

Damn. It should have been the first thing I'd thought of, too. Navicular is a common problem, and is often solved by nerving. A veterinarian severs the nerves that run to the horse's navicular bones and, presto, the horse feels no more pain and doesn't limp. Nerved horses looked as if they were sound, but the fact that the heels of their front feet were numb could cause problems. Also the nerves often grew back together, resulting in a once-again-lame horse. All in all a nerved horse had some major disadvantages and it was considered unethical, if not downright lawsuit-causing dishonest, to pass one off as sound.

"Don't forget, you're on call tonight," Jim added; then a click as he hung up the phone.

Good old Jim. Mister Friendly. I briefly played with a familiar daydream of some future time when I could afford to set up my own practice, and then my mind went snapping back to the gray horse.

I'd better mention the possibility of the horse being nerved to Gina when Tony wasn't around. I had an idea Gina wouldn't be up to dealing with Tony's reaction.

The Salinas Rodeo Grounds were in front of me now, the big concrete bleacher structure dark gray against the lighter gray of the fog. I parked the truck under a cypress tree, cracked the windows for Blue, and got out, carrying my thermos. I'd only gone about ten steps before I ran the zipper on my coat up to my chin. Chill and clammy, the fog seemed to seep into me instantly. I could feel little beads of moisture condensing on the tendrils of hair that curled around my face. Maybe this wasn't such a good idea after all. It looked as though I was going to freeze my butt off.

A glance at the grandstand depressed me still further. The bench seats were damp, guaranteed to soak right through my jeans. Oh well. Too late to back out now.

I chose a spot where I could watch the small arena on the track where the bridle horses were warming up and the big arena in the middle of the field where the rodeo events would be held.

Opening the thermos, I poured a cup of coffee and sipped it, surveying the scene in front of me. Horses—hundreds of horses, trotting and loping through the fog, being warmed up on the racetrack and in the infield, ridden by persons of both sexes—all wearing cowboy hats. For a second I felt I'd been transported back in history to a time when the ranchers and vaqueros from miles around had ridden into Salinas to ship their cattle and stayed to show off their talents. All the traditional events of rodeo—roping, riding the roughstock, steer wrestling—were based on skills actually needed on the ranch. And most prized was the ability to turn out a well-broke cowhorse—a stock horse or bridle horse—the event that Tony Ramiro, Gina Gianelli, and Steve Shaw were about to compete in.

Searching the crowd, I spotted Gina and Tony riding together on the track, wearing identical black felt hats. Tony rode a black-and-white paint gelding, Gina the palomino mare I'd seen her on before.

It took me longer to find Steve Shaw. He was in a little knot of people by the rail, all of them, I noticed with a grin, women. Several of the women were on horseback; Steve was standing on the ground, talking earnestly up at them. His cowboy hat was pearl gray, his coat a brilliant blue that I imagined matched his eyes perfectly. It looked as though he was coaching his nonpro clients in preparation for the show.

After a second, I saw that Amber St. Claire was standing on the fringes of the group, well away from any clumsy horse hooves, her auburn head vivid above a butter-colored jacket with a silky sheen.

Well, all the players were gathered, I thought, taking a sip of coffee and shivering. Now what?

Scratchy noises from the loudspeaker and then a voice announced the nonpro hackamore class. In the big arena, I could see the team roping had begun; men and horses dashed down the pen after cattle, ropes whirling in the air.

On the track, in the small arena, the first nonpro hackamore horse entered the ring, ridden by a woman who was middle-aged and slightly overweight. It appeared she was a client of Steve Shaw's, as he stood by the arena fence, offering instructions and encouragement whenever she rode by.

It was obvious the woman wasn't a particularly experienced rider—she looked awkward and a bit unsteady. The stocking-legged sorrel gelding she was riding was clearly gentle and willing, but she wasn't helping him any. I watched her execute a figure eight, run down and stop, spin both directions, and back up, all without any finesse, though I had the impression the horse could have done better in more expert hands. Doubtless Steve Shaw had trained him; had Steve been aboard the horse probably would have looked pretty good.

The woman almost fell off during the cow work; she'd drawn a hard-running cow, and I found myself crossing my fingers and praying she'd survive. She did—at least she stayed on—but it was clear she wasn't going to be a contender in this class.

There, I told myself, but for the grace of God, go I. Glancing at the team roping—the sport Lonny was trying to teach me—I remembered all the times I'd felt sure my horse and I were going to part company. Of course, I'd never tried to compete anywhere; I hadn't progressed beyond the stage of Lonny giving me lessons in his arena. Fortunately, too, Burt was a baby-sitter. Every time I started to fall off, he literally stopped and waited for me to pull myself back on.

Turning my attention back to the reined cowhorses, I watched the rest of the nonpro hackamore class closely and found that, despite knowing very little about it, I quickly picked up the basic ideas. Each contestant entered the ring individually and performed a reining pattern—figure eight with a flying lead change in the middle, run down to a sliding stop and then a spin in each direction, run down and stop again and back up. Horses that carried their heads in a steady, level position—nose down, mouth closed—and executed each maneuver smoothly, with speed and snap, responding immediately, alertly, and calmly to signals from the reins, were markedly superior to those that threw their heads in the air when stopped, or were sluggish, or bounced on their front ends instead of stopping and turning smoothly.

The cow work was more difficult to judge. Once the rider was done with the reining pattern, he or she nodded and a single cow was turned into the ring. Each contestant attempted to box the cow in one end of the arena, frustrating the cow's attempts to get by. Once this was accomplished to the rider's satisfaction—or the cow got away—the animal was allowed to run down the fence toward the other end and the rider dashed down after it and turned it back. This was sometimes a spectacular move, with horse and cow going full tilt at the point where the horse got his nose just far enough ahead of the cow to turn in front of it and block it.

I watched horse after horse slide deeply into the soft ground as they turned and jumped out again hard, trying to get back to the cow quickly and turn it again the other way. Some of the riders, like the first one, seemed to cling on through these turns by the skin of their teeth, clutching the saddle horn and looking scared. I could imagine how they felt, remembering my difficulty staying on Gunner when he spooked.

After the cow had been turned a few times on the fence, it was brought (hopefully) to the middle of the arena and circled up, a maneuver where the horse forced the cow to go in a small circle by maintaining a position at the cow's shoulder. This often proved difficult if the cow wasn't sufficiently tired, as the horse had to run a much larger circle than the cow, and a too-lively cow could get ahead and break out of the circle. Eventually, when the cow had been dominated to the judge's satisfaction, he blew a whistle and the contestant was dismissed.

I found that the most confusing factor when it came to

evaluating the cow work was the varying degrees of diffi-culty in the cattle. It was obvious that the goal was to con-trol the cow, but a stubborn, lively, hard-running cow was much harder to control than an easygoing, slow-moving, docile one. I had no idea how much slack the judge was sup-posed to cut a contestant who got a particularly difficult cow.

Still, when the riders came back into the ring and lined up for their awards, I found I'd correctly picked the winner—a thirtyish woman on a buckskin gelding who had completed both the dry work and cow work smoothly and compe-tently. The woman had a large cheering section composed of what looked like her entire extended family, and they yelled and clapped enthusiastically when first place was an-nounced as hers. All smiles, she patted her horse exuber-antly on the neck, trotted out of the ring, and leaned over to hug Steve Shaw, where he sat on a horse near the gate.

Another of Steve's clients, I supposed. Looking at the horse Steve was sitting on, I recognized Plumber, brushed and shiny and wearing an elaborately silver-mounted bridle and saddle. The expression on the horse's face was alert, in-terested, and calm, even when the woman and her gelding bumped up against him as she threw an arm around Steve.

Little Plumber, who was now, I supposed, owned by Anne Whitney. It seemed a shame.

After a second's hesitation, I picked up my thermos, de-scended the grandstand, and walked out through a small gate onto the track, where the bridle horses were milling around, awaiting their turn in the ring. Weaving my way between horses and people, I approached Steve Shaw and Plumber.

"Hi, Steve."

His "Gail" was illuminated by a blazing smile, blue eyes lighting up as if the sight of me had made his day.

I smiled back, reminding myself that his eyes had probably lit in a similar fashion for every other woman he'd greeted this morning. Still, it was nice to be welcomed so enthusiastically.

"You look like you're freezing," he said.

"I am." Glancing up at the thinning fog, I added, "It'll clear soon. Then I'll have to shed all these clothes."

He smiled again. *"All* of them?"

"Probably not all." I grinned up at him. Damn, he was a cute man.

Come on, Gail, be serious, I chided myself. Why do you suppose all his clients are in love with him?

I patted Plumber's neck. "How's the little guy doing?"

"Just great."

"He didn't turn out to be lame or anything, then? Those bottles of bute in Cindy's tack room made me wonder."

Steve shook his head. "No, no problems at all."

"That's good." I rubbed the quarter-sized white spot on Plumber's forehead. "Will he win this?"

Steve smiled and shrugged. "I hope so. That's my main competition over there." He jerked his chin in the direction of Tony Ramiro and the black-and-white paint gelding. "We've been running neck and neck for the year-end saddle."

"Tony's a pretty good hand, huh?"

"Damn good. And he wants that year-end championship. It's been a few years since he's had a big winner."

I glanced over at Tony, who was, to my eyes anyway, slouched on his horse like a fat toad, his paunchy belly almost touching the saddle horn, a perpetual scowl on his face. "I can't say I like the guy much," I told Steve.

Steve, ever politically savvy, merely smiled.

Out of the corner of my eye, I spotted Amber St. Claire's wedge-cut auburn hair moving toward us through the crowd. Feeling suddenly mischievous, I looked up at Steve as flirtatiously as I dared and patted him on the leg. "I hope you win," I told him, just about batting my eyelashes.

Amber came to a dead stop a few feet away and I could literally feel the steely gaze she fixed on me. Keeping my head turned toward Steve, I tilted my chin in an imitation of her adoring gaze as I listened to him talk.

"We've got a good chance," he was telling me. "I drew up last, which is a real advantage. A judge will hardly ever mark the early horses very high, since he doesn't know what he'll see later. But if you're last and you have a good run, he'll sometimes go ahead and give you the points you need to win."

"Well, good luck," I said, patting his leg again. "I'll cross my fingers for you."

"Cross them that I get a good cow. That's what it'll take."

I smiled and turned away, then stopped as if noticing Amber for the first time. "Hi, Amber."

There was no mistaking the anger in her eyes. Giving me a curt nod, she marched past in Steve's direction, flashing me one more glance as she brushed by.

No two ways about it. If looks could kill, I was a goner.

SIXTEEN

Climbing back up in the grandstand a moment later, I settled myself where I had a good view and prepared to watch the open hackamore class. I had one more cup of coffee left; I poured it and then peeled off my jacket. The sun had broken through the fog and was pouring down on the southeast-facing bleachers. There was still a slight chill in the air, but nothing my sweater couldn't deal with.

Half an hour later, I was ready to get rid of the sweater. A dozen horses had run, the sun was beating down, and I still hadn't seen Tony or Steve take his turn.

I pulled the sweater over my head, pushed some unruly tendrils of hair back into my braid, and stretched back onto the bench behind me, enjoying the sun's warmth on my bare arms.

"Next to run, Little Doc, ridden by Tony Ramiro."

Instantly I sat up, on the alert, watching for . . . watching for what, I asked myself. What exactly did I expect to learn here?

I'd learned quite a bit about bridle horses, which had been enjoyable, but I had no idea how, if at all, that might connect to the murders. Tony Ramiro was riding his pinto gelding into the ring, black felt hat pulled well down over his eyes, dark, jowly face wearing a confident look. Was I watching a man who would murder in order to win? How could I tell?

All that was apparent was that Little Doc was a very good horse and that Tony was doing a hell of a job of showing him. I wasn't crazy about his style; the black-and-white gelding looked a little too frantic to me, his eyes bugging out of his head and his mouth dripping white froth, but there was no denying he had a spectacular work. Tony rode out of the ring to an impressed silence—no applause though, I noticed.

Crackling from the loudspeaker. "Last horse to go will be Plumb Smart, ridden by Steve Shaw."

Steve was already riding into the ring. He and Tony nodded curtly at each other as they passed, and I noticed the contrast between the two horses. The paint gelding was jigging, neck arched, eyes nervous and edgy, his whole demeanor showing fear and discomfort. Plumber, on the other hand, walked quietly, his expression alert and confident, his ears flicking forward to take in the show ring, then back to his rider, in the manner of a relaxed, responsive horse. Come on, Plumber, I found myself urging him mentally. You can do it.

He could, too. His figure eight was smooth and correct, the flying change (a skip from one lead to the other) effortless. His run-downs and stops were perfect; he ran hard and got into the ground deeply when he slid to a stop, his hind feet leaving long eleven-shaped tracks in the ground. The whole crowd of bridle-horse people cheered and whistled at each stop; it was clear that Plumber, and/or Steve, was a favorite.

If Plumber had a weak spot in his dry work, I thought, it would have to be his spins—two full 360-degree turns in each direction. They were smooth and fluid, but not quite as fast or flashy as Tony's paint gelding.

Steve asked Plumber for an extralong back-up and the little horse complied willingly, acting as if he'd be happy to back the length of the arena. Steve patted him on the neck, pulled the pearl gray cowboy hat firmly down on his head, and nodded for his steer.

Right away I knew he was in trouble. The dark red steer exploded out of the chute, head and tail up, eyes wide, moving hard. I noticed that it had the long-legged, droopy-eared look of a Brahma cross, and my heart sank. This was not going to be an easy cow.

Plumber handled it, though. Head down, ears forward, he worked the steer, moving when it moved, stopping when it stopped, blocking it when it tried to run away down the arena. Steve guided him with slight, almost invisible cues on the reins, giving Plumber his head much of the time, allowing him to show off his ability to "read" the cow.

Despite the Brahma steer's best attempts to get by, Plumber and Steve held it at one end of the pen, and I yelled along with the crowd as the little brown horse crouched in front of the steer, pattering his front feet, daring the steer to make a move.

After it was clear that the steer was defeated, Steve pulled Plumber up and allowed the steer to run down the fence toward the far end of the arena, giving the animal a head start and then dashing after it.

The Brahma was a runner. Shit, I thought. He'll never catch him. But Plumber stretched out—a flat brown streak—running for all he was worth, and got enough ahead of the steer to turn in front of him. Horse and cow "buried up," dirt clods flying, and then the steer was going back the other way and Plumber was chasing it with the crowd cheering him on.

It was the second turn that did it. Like the first time, the little horse ran, stopped, and turned at top speed, and when he jumped out again after the cow it was obvious he was lame.

I gasped. Someone near the gate shouted, "Pull up," but before the words were even out, Steve was pulling on the reins, aware that something was wrong, his face apprehensive.

Lame or not, Plumber didn't want to quit the cow. He pulled against the bit a moment, trying to keep after the steer, then responded to the bridle like the well-broke horse he was and stopped. I could see that he was keeping the weight off his right front and prayed silently. Don't let it be broken. Please God, don't let it be broken.

Even as I whispered the words to myself, I was clambering down the bleachers, headed for the show ring. I told the man at the gate I was a vet and he motioned me through. Steve was standing in the middle of the ring, holding Plumber by the reins and running his fingers down the horse's leg.

I joined him, manipulating the leg to see if I could feel anything that shouldn't be there. So far so good. The leg felt normal. "Lead him a few steps," I told Steve.

Plumber walked. He limped, but he walked, bearing some weight at least on his front right.

"He's either pulled a ligament or a tendon, or he's broken one of the little bones in the foot, not a supporting bone," I told Steve. "It's probably fixable, but we ought to get ice on it right away and get him in and X-ray him."

He nodded. "I've got to show Amber's mare in the open bridle horse class, but I can have Diane—she works for me—haul him back to the clinic." He led Plumber slowly toward the exit gate as we spoke. "We can get the ice and wraps I have for that mare and put them on him."

The announcer blared over the top of us. "Plumb Smart will be drawn out due to an accident. Will the rest of the entries please come into the arena for the awards."

I glanced up to see Tony Ramiro start into the ring. I could swear he was smiling. Steve glanced in his direction briefly and looked away.

"That bastard's going to win the class," I said furiously.

Steve said nothing. His face was quiet, no chagrin or anger showing. He patted Plumber's neck and shrugged.

"You would have won," I told him.

"Maybe." He scanned the crowd and yelled "Diane!" Handing Plumber's reins to me, he said, "I'll be right back."

I stood, holding the horse and rubbing his forehead. Plumber was quiet; he kept as much weight as possible off his right front and I noticed it was starting to swell, low down, near the hoof. I hoped Steve would hurry with the ice.

In a minute he was back; with him was the young blond girl I'd seen flirting with Bret; she was carrying wraps and a couple of plastic pouches of ice.

"Diane will help you wrap this horse and haul him to the clinic," Steve said briskly. "I need to get Belle ready to show."

I noticed Amber was at his shoulder, her eyes cross. "Goddamn it, Steve, those are Belle's wraps," she was saying. "I didn't buy them for Cindy Whitney's stupid horse."

Steve barely looked at her, merely reached for the reins of the dun mare, put them over her head, and rode off. Amber stared after him angrily, then switched her gaze to Diane and me as we wrapped Plumber's leg with ice.

"I want those wraps back right away, today," she snapped at Diane, who ignored her. I kept my eyes on Plumber's leg, refusing to acknowledge her presence, and after a minute she turned and stomped off in the direction of the show ring.

When Plumber's leg was wrapped with ice packs, I told

Diane, "Walk him out to the trailer real slow. Do you know where the clinic is?"

She nodded, her blue eyes round and serious.

"I'll meet you there in an hour and a half."

She nodded again and began to lead Plumber off, watching him carefully, I noticed, and accommodating her speed to his.

I turned and searched through the crowd until I spotted Gina. She was sitting on her mare on the fringe of a little group of people who surrounded Tony, all of them talking and laughing in the flush of victory, admiring the silver belt buckle that had been presented to the winner. The owners of the paint horse, I supposed—a middle-aged man and his wife and two teenage girls.

Gina was chatting with one of the girls and I drew her quietly aside. "I talked to Jim about the gray horse," I told her. "He seems to think he may be nerved."

Gina's eyes darted to my face, then over to Tony quickly, then back to me.

"It's easy to find out," I said. "Take a screwdriver, something like that, and press on the back of the horse's heel when he isn't watching, hard enough so it ought to hurt. If he doesn't even flinch, he's probably nerved."

Gina nodded mutely.

"Also, I talked to that detective and she'll probably give you a call. I asked her to be discreet, but she wouldn't guarantee anything." I looked up at Gina, judging her reaction.

She looked unhappy—that was about all I could tell.

"Okay," she said. "I'll talk to this detective when she calls. I just hope she doesn't bother Tony."

I shrugged and, once again, bit my tongue on all the things I would like to have said. "Good luck, Gina," I told her, and headed off to my pickup.

* * *

Three hours later, I'd finished developing the X rays on Plumber and had isolated the problem. He'd broken one of his sesamoid bones, a pair of small bones in the foot.

There were two possible ways to go with an injury like this: an operation to remove the bone chips or a six-month to yearlong layup, with the hope that things would fuse back together and/or stabilize. On the whole the operation was the better choice. The horse would still have to have a several-month layoff, but the odds of him healing up and being sound and usable again were considerably greater. Of course, an operation was more expensive than no operation and a layoff.

Someone was going to have to decide, and the decision needed to be made right away. If Plumber was to be operated on, it should be in the next few days. Presumably the deciding someone was the new owner; presumably that was Anne Whitney. Anne Whitney, who was, at least in some ways, the most obvious murder suspect of the bunch. She had the classic motive; she was the person who benefited directly from Ed and Cindy's deaths. I decided it was time for me to meet Anne Whitney.

A quick perusal of the phone book revealed an A. Whitney at 72 Bayview Terrace. My map of Santa Cruz County, kept in reserve in the glove compartment for those calls where the directions proved inadequate, told me that Bayview Terrace was in Capitola, less than a mile away from Rose Avenue, where Ed and Cindy had lived. I wasn't sure what that proved, but it was interesting.

Stopping by the deli on Soquel Avenue for a turkey sandwich with Italian peppers on a sourdough French roll—my favorite lunch—I drove down to Capitola, turned onto Bayview Terrace, and started looking for number 72.

As it turned out, finding the house was no problem. Number 72 was at the very end of the street, high on a cliff overlooking fashionable Capitola, surrounded by an eight-foot stone wall as if it were the hideaway of a movie star. Inside the wall, a monster of a house towered up in a series of severe modern angles, like some kind of geometric castle. The name Whitney was carved plainly in the stone pillar that supported the mailbox.

A chocolate brown BMW sat in the driveway and the wrought-iron gate was standing open, so I walked in and knocked on the massive wooden door. Nothing ventured, nothing gained, I encouraged myself, and composed my face to a pleasant, professional doctor-is-making-a-house-call expression, rather than the avid interest of an amateur sleuth.

Anne Whitney opened her own front door. She was clearly dressed for work, though it was four o'clock on a Saturday afternoon, and her severely tailored gray business suit more or less matched her chilly eyes. Once again, I was struck by the fact that hers was a pretty face, marred by the down-turning lines between her eyes and at the sides of her mouth which gave it an autocratic cast. At close range, she was at least thirty-five, and she wore light but expert makeup.

"Anne Whitney? I'm Dr. Gail McCarthy. I'm here to talk to you about your horse." I held out my hand, smiling pleasantly.

Anne Whitney looked surprised and ignored the hand. "My horse?"

"Plumber. He belonged to your sister-in-law, Cindy. I understand he belongs to you now."

"Oh. Cindy's horse."

"Yes. I'm his vet. He's been injured, and I need to discuss what to do about him."

The once-over she gave me was cold, and I realized my tank top and jeans probably seemed a bit informal to her, but she pulled her front door open. "I guess you'd better come in."

I followed her into a flagstoned front hall, noticing a briefcase and shoulder bag on the chair in the corner, as if they'd been tossed there. Anne Whitney was just home from the office, apparently.

She led the way down her hall and I followed, wondering if this was my smartest move—sitting down alone for a chat with a potential murderer. No alarm bells were buzzing along my nerves, though, and I followed her into the living room.

"Have a seat," she said brusquely, but I was too busy gaping around to respond. The place was worth staring at, even if I *was* facing a murderer. Filled with light on this sunny afternoon, the interior of the house seemed to be one gigantic room, with half walls and angles marking the divisions between kitchen, dining room, and living room; the ceiling soared a story or two above us, and the walls facing the ocean were glass. A wide expanse of gray-blue carpet matched the water below, causing the interior of the house to stretch out to the horizon. I felt as though I were floating in some airy chamber above the bay.

Anne Whitney sat down near me and crossed her legs at the ankles. "So what's this about the horse?"

I explained about Plumber being shown today in Salinas and hurting himself, and what the options were for treating him. She listened quietly, forcefully, the impression that of a person who has learned to weigh every word. When I was through, she asked, "Was it sabotage?"

"Sabotage?" I said blankly.

"Did that other man—what did you say his name was—cripple the horse in order to win?"

"Tony Ramiro." I looked at her, surprised she'd spoken so immediately of the half-formed idea that had been rolling around in my mind. "I don't see how," I said slowly, "though I have to admit I wondered. The horse was sound when he started his performance; he appeared to hurt himself in a perfectly explainable way. It isn't abnormal, though it's certainly not common, for a horse to break that bone when he's running and turning as hard as Plumber was. I don't see how anybody could have arranged it."

She was still staring at me. "This Tony Ramiro—he had a reason to cripple the horse, though. A reason to want him out of the competition."

"Well, yes, I suppose so."

"Have the police questioned him in connection with the murders?"

I was staring at her now. It was true that all these ideas had occurred to me, but Anne Whitney seemed to be pursuing them with a single-minded vengeance that was surprising. Unless she was anxious to put everyone off some other track. I wondered if she knew the sheriffs had their eyes on Terry White and guessed that she probably didn't.

Studying the smooth dark blond waves of her hair and the carefully understated pearl earrings and necklace, I decided to try a test. "I think the sheriff's department is most interested in Ed's, uh, business dealings."

"What business dealings? Ed didn't have a business. He was strictly a leech." Her tone did not exactly sound grief-stricken.

"He sold coke," I said bluntly.

She gave a short laugh. "Is that right? It's something he would have done. If the cops want to look into that, it's fine with me. So long as they get out of my hair."

Her voice was crisp. I felt completely disconcerted. Anne Whitney was not responding in any way, shape, or form to her brother's death, other than considering the investigation a nuisance. It seemed bizarre.

My emotions must have shown on my face. Her mouth

shaped itself into a thin, hard line. "My brother was a first-class pain in the ass and his wife was a cheap little whore. I'm not going to pretend I'm sorry they're dead. They were nothing but bloodsuckers on the family business and I couldn't stand them. But all this investigation is more trouble than they were."

She tapped the toe of her black pump on the carpet. "All I want is to get the stupid cops out of my office and to get back to work. Why in the world they think I had anything to do with killing Ed, I don't know. For that trust fund? I make that much money every year. Or that house? Ed bought that house because he couldn't stand it that I live in this one. He was copying me. He was always jealous of me."

I tried not to look as nonplussed as I felt and prodded gently. "So Ed never tried to get involved in the business?"

Her lip curled. "Ed never did anything but ask me for handouts until six months ago, when he got the income from the trust fund our parents left."

"Did you know he was selling coke?"

"No. Why should I? I never had any more to do with him than I could help."

"How did you know Cindy was a hooker?"

"He told me." Disgust was plain in her voice. "He bragged about it, for God's sake." Her eyes flicked to my face. "And now you say I've got to deal with her stupid horse."

"Well, someone does. I assumed you were the owner now."

"Yes, I am. The lawyer was already after me, asking if I wanted the silly horse shown. I told him I didn't care. And now this. What's the horse worth?"

"Somewhere between five and ten thousand dollars, if he's sound and showable. He's a real good hackamore horse."

Anne Whitney seemed uninterested. "What's he worth if he's lame?"

"What he's worth by the pound."

"By the pound?"

"What the killers will pay for him," I explained. "Companies that slaughter horses for dog food buy them based on what they weigh. A horse his size would be worth about five hundred."

"And if I want this horse to be fixed so I can sell him for five thousand or so dollars, I've got to deal with him for six months at least."

"Maybe less, if you have him operated on."

Anne Whitney shrugged. "It's not worth it. Just sell him to that—what-do-you-call-its, the dog-food people."

Shock must have shown on my face, because she shrugged again. "I don't want to deal with a horse. I haven't got time."

"Would you sell him to me for five hundred?" The words just popped out of my mouth. "Knowing he'll be worth five thousand or more if I can fix him," I added quickly.

She gave me an ironic twitch of the lips that I thought was meant as a smile. "I don't care if you make a profit."

I didn't bother to explain that profit wasn't my intention; just a clear understanding that I wasn't trying to take advantage of her. I dug my checkbook out of my wallet, wondering what had gotten into me. What was I, Gail's home for crippled horses? I could barely afford Gunner, how in the hell was I going to afford another horse?

It was just that Plumber, Plumber was special. I'd work something out, I told myself.

I filled out the check for five hundred, calculating rapidly whether there was enough in my account to cover it. There was, but I'd have to stretch myself to meet this month's bills. Oh well.

Anne Whitney took the check with an amused look. "Good luck with the horse, Dr. McCarthy." She walked down her front hall and held the door open for me. "I think you're going to need it."

SEVENTEEN

After Anne Whitney shut her front door, I sat in my truck for long minutes, staring through my windshield at the village of Capitola with its apron of beach, laid out invitingly below the cliff where I was parked. A wealthy little town— Capitola. And Anne Whitney's house, prominently placed so it had arguably the best possible view, was the house of a very wealthy woman. Her lawyer had confirmed that her fortune was in good shape. She had seemed, from what little I had seen and heard of her, to be thoroughly involved in her business, competent, unemotional, pleased with her wealth and indifferent to her brother and his wife. Why would a woman in her position commit two murders that would be sure to unsettle a comfortable life? What would she have to gain? A couple of million sounded like a lot when I first heard of it, but faced with Anne Whitney's house and lifestyle, it didn't carry the weight I'd assigned to it as a motive.

I simply couldn't picture Anne Whitney having anything to do with these murders. But if she hadn't, who had? I didn't consider Terry a possibility. Tony Ramiro? It seemed ridiculous. And Gina had said he had an alibi. Carl Whitney? I could imagine him having it done, but why? Distaste for having a hooker and a drug dealer in the family would appear to be his only motive, and it didn't seem strong enough.

How about Earl Ritter? I'd disliked the man intensely; it would be satisfying to prove him guilty. However, I had trouble inventing a plausible scenario with Dr. Earl Ritter as the villain. He seemed impotent and fearful—not a man of action. His motive was doubtful at best, and I didn't know if he had an alibi.

Then who? I felt baffled. Someone had killed Ed and Cindy. I believed that the same person had shot at me. Who? And why? *Why?* I thought about that awhile. There were two "whys" really: Why had someone killed Cindy and Ed, and why had that someone thought I was dangerous to them? What did I know that I didn't know I knew?

Blue grunted and shifted his position on the floorboards, staring up at me with impatient eyes. Why are you just sitting there his expression said. It isn't like you. Don't we have things to do?

I reached down and rubbed his head absently, glancing at the dashboard clock as I did so: 4:45. Fifteen more minutes and I was officially on call.

Starting my truck and easing it out into the summertime traffic, I let my mind go back to the murders. I needed a new angle, a new idea. I'm a lot better at finding out what's wrong with a horse than figuring out a murder, I told myself. I should just stick to horses.

Horses. Horses were what connected me to this murder, after all. Cindy had been a horse person, and it was a call to see her horse that had caused me to find the bodies. Maybe horses were the angle. Gina Gianelli had said that Cindy was upset that she might not be able to show Plumber at Salinas. Could that upset, whatever it was, have to do with the something that led to her being killed? I didn't have a clue how it connected, but the first step was obviously to find out what she had been upset about.

Making the right turn onto Soquel Avenue, headed for home, I was so absorbed in this question that I jumped when my pager beeped. The clock read 5:01. Damn. I had a feeling it was going to be a busy night.

Jim and I took turns being on call on the weekend; this weekend was mine. From now until 8:00 A.M. Monday, all emergencies were my responsibility.

I stopped at the office to call the answering service; even though it was only five minutes after five, everything was shut up tight and there were no cars in the parking lot. No one was interested in staying even half a minute late on Saturday afternoon.

Plumber was in a corral in the back, munching the hay that our barn girl had fed him, his injured leg wrapped snugly to prevent swelling. I paused by his fence for a brief second to tell him he was my horse now, and smiled when he reached his nose up from his feed to bump my arm briefly before he went back to eating.

Whether I could or should afford him or not, Plumber was a sweet little guy and I felt a keen sense of happiness at the thought of owning him. Monday, when Jim was here to help me, I would operate and remove the bone chip from his leg. After that, I'd arrange somewhere to keep him and figure out how to pay his feed bill. It would all work out, I told myself.

Inside the office, a phone call informed me that Hilde Fredericks had a horse who was tying up and needed me right away. Not good.

Hilde Fredericks was a potentially difficult client. She had warm-blood dressage horses and was very particular about them. Though she and I had always gotten along well together, I had the distinct feeling that if I ever made what she considered a mistake on one of her horses there would be hell to pay.

As I drove up Empire Grade toward her elaborate setup in Bonny Doon, I fervently hoped the tied-up horse was not the new stallion that rumor had it she'd paid over a hundred thousand dollars for. Imagine doing something wrong on a horse that was worth as much as my whole house. It didn't bear thinking about.

Hilde's rage didn't bear thinking about, either. German, between fifty-five and sixty, spare and fit of body, with a bony, elegant face and well-groomed blond hair, Hilde was attractive if you didn't mind a dictatorial air. This she had in abundance, along with scads of money, which she spent in boatloads on her high-priced warm-blood horses. She was also inclined to big, fierce-looking German-type dogs . . . shepherds, Rottweilers, etc.

Thirty minutes later, when I turned in between the two stone pillars that marked her driveway and approached her formal brick, Colonial-type house with its manicured front lawn, I was greeted by a particularly large-toothed, loud-barking specimen—a Doberman in this case. I tried to remember if I had ever met this dog before; was he basically friendly or truly vicious?

Blue barked loudly back through the truck window: I'll kill you, you bastard. Just give me a chance.

"He'd kill *you,* dummy," I told the old dog, and rolled my window down a few inches, trying a "Hello, big fella" on the Doberman.

Nothing doing. He barked and snarled. Most Dobermans were chickens, though. I was trying to decide if this one would back down when Hilde saved me from what might have been a major error by appearing from the direction of her barn and calling the dog off. I got out of my truck and went to greet her.

"Gail, it has been over an hour since I called." Hilde's

blue eyes, German accent, and imperious manner hadn't dimmed a bit since I'd seen her last.

"I'm sorry, Hilde. It does take awhile to get here from Santa Cruz."

"Well." Hilde brushed off this excuse and said brusquely, "Come see Zhivago. He is getting better already," she added over her shoulder as she turned away.

I followed her, thanking my lucky stars. Zhivago was Hilde's old warm-blood gelding, not the new ultraexpensive stallion, who I believed was named Riesling. Also, if Zhivago was already better, he hadn't tied up very badly.

Tying up, technically called azoturia, is not uncommon; some horses seem far more prone to it than others. In essence, an overly large amount of lactic acid in the muscles starts to destroy the muscle fibers. Tying up can be serious if it's ignored and the horse is forced to go on working; I'd had two cases where the animal died as a result. If the problem is caught right away, however, and appropriate steps are taken, most horses recover quickly and completely.

Zhivago was tied to the arena fence, and I could see at once that the big black gelding wasn't in any acute distress.

"I stopped riding him right away," Hilde was saying, "as soon as I noticed, and I gave him some ace."

Ace-promazine was a tranquilizer and one of the better things to do for a horse whose muscles were tying up. The main thing was to stop riding the horse immediately, which Hilde had apparently done.

"He urinated a few minutes ago," Hilde said. "The urine was light brown, but afterward he seemed better."

I checked Zhivago over carefully, taking his temperature, his pulse and respiration rates, looking at his gums, and feeling him over the loins and rump to see how tight his muscles felt. This last was difficult to do, as Zhivago was all of seventeen hands high. Warm-bloods are essentially draft horses crossed on Thoroughbreds; most of them are big.

Zhivago seemed pretty normal to me. "Go ahead and lead him a few steps," I told Hilde.

She did; the horse walked out normally.

"Trot him."

Again, the horse moved out freely, no sign of resistance, discomfort, or lameness.

"I think he's over it," I said with some relief. I gave the horse a shot of vitamin E and selenium and told her, "Keep him in a stall tonight and check on him a few times; don't feed him any grain, just hay. Call me if anything changes, but he looks okay to me. You did all the right things."

Hilde took this good news with poor grace, muttering fiercely with her German accent as she led the horse away. "All the money I spend to have you up here is wasted, then."

"Now I will show you Riesling," she announced when she returned, bad humor apparently forgotten.

Riesling looked like a big gray stud to me, heavy-boned and powerful. If I hadn't known he was a hundred-thousand-dollar-plus warm-blood, imported from Germany, I would have guessed him to be half Percheron, the kind of horse a rancher might keep to breed to his grade mares. Of course, I didn't say any of this to Hilde, who would have been deeply insulted.

She watched with rapt eyes as the horse paced around his pen, the true horseman's fanatic glow on her face. "It is a shame Fred is dead," she said finally. "He would have loved this horse."

"Fred?" I asked. As far as I could remember, Hilde's husband was named Ernest, and still alive.

"Fred Johnson, my stallion manager; did you know him? He lived about a mile from here, on Pine Flat Road."

Fred Johnson, Pine Flat Road. My God.

"Not Twenty-one twenty Pine Flat Road—a little old cabin?"

"Yes. Fred was quite a character. He lived like a mountain man, in that cabin his grandfather built."

"He was your stallion manager?"

"Oh yes. Fred was wonderful with a horse. He worked most of his life for his brother-in-law, who raised Quarter Horses, but when the man died and his snooty little daughter took over, she decided Fred wasn't high-toned enough for her and she ran him off. I hired him right away." Hilde gave me a sidelong look in which amusement and malice were clearly combined. "Perhaps you know Fred's niece? Amber St. Claire."

"Amber?" I parroted blankly.

Hilde waited a moment, hoping perhaps that I would make some clever quip of my own about Amber, but my head was reeling with the implications of what I'd just learned and I said nothing.

Hilde sniffed. "Yes, Amber St. Claire is Fred Johnson's niece, although she didn't want anyone to know it. He was her mother's brother."

I was still silent and Hilde gave up on me as a source of interesting gossip. "Gail, I must feed. I will call you if Zhivago looks worse."

"Sure, Hilde."

I turned to go and she snapped after me, "Tell Jim I do not expect a full emergency charge for being told my horse is fine."

I waved good-bye to her, smiling to myself. Jim would submit the bill and Hilde would pay it. She always bitched and she always paid. It was her style.

Blue's prick-eared face peered from my truck window, scanning eagerly for the Doberman, and I jumped in quickly—no use getting eaten—and pulled out of the driveway with the truck in low gear and my mind in high.

Amber St. Claire was Fred Johnson's niece. Fred Johnson's abandoned property was the place where I had been set up to be killed. These facts were obviously crucially important; I knew they were essential to discovering the killer. The only problem was that the obvious solution—Amber had tried to kill me—wouldn't wash.

I simply could not picture Amber St. Claire hiding alone in that dark barn with a gun, stalking me. It was too dirty, for one thing. And Amber's fingernails were too long. She was just too much of a citified sissy to have the nerve for such a thing, and try as I might, I couldn't believe she'd done it.

But she must be connected somehow, I told myself. I was rolling that interesting fact around in my brain when my pager beeped once again. Double damn.

I stopped and called the answering service from a pay phone. A female voice told me that Paul Cassidy had a lame horse out on Steelhead Gulch Road. She gave me directions to the field where the horse was kept and told me the owner could meet me there in half an hour. The dashboard clock said 7:30; I sighed. It was going to be a long day. Revising my thoughts of a glass of wine and some quiet moments to think, I started trying to decipher the directions.

It took me a full twenty minutes to find Steelhead Gulch Road, which turned out to be a little one-lane dirt affair back in the hills behind Santa Cruz. Bumpy and precariously narrow, it wound down the side of a steep canyon. I crossed my fingers and drove slowly, hoping I wouldn't meet any cars coming up.

The road descended abruptly to a one-lane bridge, spanning the creek fifty feet below. A slender ramp of concrete, the bridge looked insubstantial as hell. I let the truck idle onto it at a creep, staring down at the clear water.

Once across the bridge and up a hill, the terrain opened up suddenly and I found myself in a grassy little valley—the whole thing lit with the slanting golden light of the lowering sun. The road forked left and right. I could see a couple of houses off to the left. My directions said to take the right-hand fork and follow it to the corral.

I followed the road for a half mile, maybe less. It seemed like more because I had to go slowly. The road was a road in name only; in actual fact, it was so rutted and punctured with potholes that I would probably have been better off driving across the field. I bumped along and eventually reached an old wooden corral with posts that leaned drunkenly every which way. Beyond the corral was a scrubby field, full of Scotch broom, greasewood, and poison oak, with a few grassy areas. Three horses grazed in the distance, two bays and a black. Since I didn't know which one was my patient, and the client was a stranger to me, I decided to sit and wait for him. Paul Cassidy, the girl had said. I hoped Paul Cassidy would be reasonably punctual.

He was. I had just settled myself in the cab of the truck when I noticed the black car creeping down the road behind me. It looked sufficiently out of place to make me stare. Judging by the old corral and brushy field, I'd expected Paul Cassidy to drive a battered pickup. A black Jaguar was surprising.

The Jaguar advanced up the road, slowly and purposefully; the potholes in that road were probably making the driver curse. Eventually the car reached the corral and rolled to a stop a little ways from my truck.

A man got out—a man I'd never seen before. The dark suit he was wearing looked as out of place as his long, low black car, and his eyes were hidden by sunglasses. He stood and stared around, almost as if he didn't see me standing by my pickup. I waited.

After a good long minute, he turned and faced me. I got the impression his eyes were looking me over carefully, but I couldn't really tell because of the glasses. Something about him made the hackles rise on the back of my neck. We stared at each other awhile.

"I'm Paul Cassidy," he said at last.

"Dr. McCarthy." I didn't hold my hand out or ask what was wrong with his horse. I just waited.

Paul Cassidy's name was as square and all-American as a varsity football player, but his looks didn't match his name. He was square all right, with big shoulders like a bull and a hard chin, but he looked Hispanic. I would have expected a name like Rodriguez. His skin was dark olive and his hair was black. He had a clean, polished, expensive, big-city look that was somehow ominous. I didn't like him at all.

He seemed to be waiting for me to say something, but I thought he could just wait awhile. It looked like it would do him good to learn patience.

A little more hard staring behind the sunglasses, or so I guessed, and he spoke again. His voice was flat—unemotional, unaccented, and unworried.

"I've got a message for you, Dr. McCarthy."

I noticed the gun right away. He pulled it out of his pocket casually, as if it were a pack of cigarettes, but the sight gave me a shock like a kick in the belly. This was no atypically obnoxious client. Without thinking twice, I knew Paul Cassidy was responsible for Ed and Cindy.

He kept talking steadily, as if pulling out a gun were a normal part of conversation. "I work for some people, Dr. McCarthy, whose names you don't need to know. It has come to these people's attention that you are sticking your nose in the Whitney case. They don't like it. What you need to understand"—he gestured at my stomach with the gun— "is that my people want the Whitney case let alone. They are, let's say, satisfied, with the course of the investigation."

His voice got flatter. "So this is what you do. You go on with your life as a nice little veterinarian and you don't speak to the police again. You don't call them, and if they call you, you tell them you don't know anything. Nothing at all." He moved the gun slowly so it pointed at my crotch. "If you talk to anyone about this case again, I'll come kill you." The sunglasses faced me blankly. "You can count on it."

Words came out of me without volition. "You tried once."

He shook his head. "That was bush league—not me. When I come after you, you won't be able to tell anybody about it. You understand?"

I stared at him. Though I couldn't see the eyes behind the sunglasses, I knew they were as black as his hair and as cold and implacable as glacier ice. I didn't doubt that he meant every word he said.

He spoke again. "You won't tell anybody, anywhere, anytime, that you saw me, and you won't talk to the police except to say that you don't know a thing, or I'll come kill you. And I'll kill anyone you talk to."

Silence followed that remark. I was aware in a vague way of sunshine on the brush, horses in the distance, a small lizard scuttling down the corral post closest to me—everyday life I had somehow stepped out of. The man in front of me was still, watching me, turning the world into a nightmare. He was waiting. I swallowed and nodded, not knowing what he expected. Another second of implacable silence, his mouth a quiet line, the gun held loosely pointed in my direction, then a short jerk of the chin, as if to express his confidence that he'd gotten the point across.

He turned and walked back to the Jaguar, folded himself into it carefully, and drove slowly away. No adolescent flourishes for Paul, whoever he was. I had the impression of a man who was used to power, despite the fact that he looked barely thirty. The impression of menace was convincingly real.

Sitting back down in my pickup, I stared out the window at the last sunshine on the yellow grass, my mind a shocked blank. Over and over, I repeated the Jaguar's license plate: 2ZST101. Wouldn't forget it.

In the distance, the three horses grazed peacefully, throwing long shadows. Blue snored on the floorboards, undisturbed. Loud voices would probably have aroused his protective instincts, but Paul Cassidy's quiet-voiced threat hadn't alerted him. An odd sense of unreality washed over me. Strangers who looked like sophisticated Mafia hit men did not threaten to kill you. It was impossible. It didn't happen.

I sat there for what seemed like a long time. When I finally started the truck and put it in gear, the sun had dipped behind the ridge, and the gathering dusk half-hid the horses. I drove back up Steelhead Gulch Road at a slow crawl, questions beginning to buzz in my mind like flies.

Paul Cassidy was obviously a professional killer; I felt sure he'd killed Ed and Cindy. So who had hired him? How did a person hire a professional hit man—check in the phone book under Rent-a-Thug?

Alone in the truck, I laughed shakily. Blue looked up at the odd sound and then hopped onto the seat next to me. "It's okay," I told him, trying to make my voice normal. "Not your problem." I rubbed his head.

Who would know how to find and hire a killer? Who had, in fact, hired one? Who were these people he worked for?

More buzzing questions. The same old ones: Who had wanted Ed and Cindy dead? And why me? Who was I a threat to? How?

The one person I could see that connected to things was Amber. But how in the world could Amber have known that I'd linked her with Fred Johnson? And why would Amber have killed Ed and Cindy in the first place? Out of jealousy? And why try to kill me? Jealousy again? Surely Steve Shaw wasn't worth that much trouble.

I had the license plate number. I could go to Jeri Ward

and . . . My mind shied away from that thought like a spooky horse. "You won't talk to the police," Paul Cassidy had warned me, "or I'll come kill you."

Without thinking about it, I pointed the truck's nose for home, taking the Soquel exit off the freeway, running, as a frightened animal will do, for my den.

As I passed the little cemetery outside Soquel, I saw a man digging a grave with a bright orange backhoe. Fog drifted around him, moving inland, cold white fingers on the dark pine trees. I shivered, the image printing itself on my mind. It seemed possible someone would be digging my grave with a backhoe in the near future if I didn't stay out of Paul Cassidy's business—whatever that was.

I felt queasy at the thought. I'd never encountered a professional killer before, but I recognized one when I saw him. He would shoot me; he would do it mercilessly. My guts twisted and rolled a little more at the thought, and I realized my hands were clenching the steering wheel so tightly they were getting numb. I loosened them, stretched my fingers, unlocked my jaw. Faced the fact. Paul Cassidy's threat was having the desired effect. I was scared shitless.

EIGHTEEN

I woke the next morning with the undefined sense that something was wrong. Lying there, half-asleep and half-awake, I felt as I had in college on the morning of final exams. Frightened. A knot in my stomach.

Dark and quiet and unthreatening, the bedroom was folded around me like a familiar blanket—nothing to be afraid of there. A little early-morning light filtered in through the uncurtained window, and my mind stumbled around in a confused way, like a groggy fighter. The thought of Paul Cassidy hit me like a sledgehammer.

Rolling over, I tried to go back to sleep. Tried to shut reality out of my mind. I didn't want to deal with the thought of Paul Cassidy, with the fear, with the question of what I should do.

It didn't work. Sleep was banished effectively. I rolled from one side to the other. It was Sunday. Nobody'd paged me. I didn't need to get up.

Getting up anyway, I stumbled through the litter of clothes on the floor and climbed the ladder that connected the bedroom to the kitchen. I put the water on for coffee and looked around at the chaos. Sunday was my day for housecleaning, usually, but I didn't feel very motivated right now.

When the coffee was made, I carried a cup into the living room and sat down on the couch. Bret was gone; all that remained of his presence was a note on the kitchen table that said, in his barely legible printing, "Moved in with Deb. Thanks, Bret."

Deb, my favorite of all Bret's many girlfriends, was a red-head with a somewhat thorny personality, lots of brains, and a spectacular figure. She and Bret had had an on-again, off-again relationship for the past year or so, the ons and offs fueled by Bret's flirtatious irresponsibility and Deb's quick temper. I couldn't imagine what had caused her to take him back in once again, but I was grateful to her. It would have been hard to hide my state of abject fear from Bret's sharp eye.

I sipped my coffee and stared at the house. Bret's clothes and sleeping bag were gone—an improvement—but Blue's hair was everywhere. Blue himself snored in the antique armchair, getting hair all over it. I should clean this up, I thought. I watched the steam rise out of my blue willow mug, a sight that usually cheered me. Not this morning. I should call Lonny, I thought. He'll wonder why I didn't call last night.

The truth was, I couldn't face it. Couldn't decide what to say and what not to say. In the end, I hadn't called. Hadn't eaten, either. Instead, I drank half a bottle of chardonnay and went to bed, grateful that my pager stayed quiet.

But now. Now what?

The phone sat on the counter, squat and brown and ordinary. My stomach twisted into a coil. Paul Cassidy had said he would kill me if I told anyone. I felt a stab of fear as another thought came to me. I pushed it away, but it came rolling back, as persistent as a pebble on a hillside. What if he was watching me, watching this house, tapping my phone. It seemed ridiculous, but how could I know?

I noticed that my hands were shaking and put the coffee cup down. All right, I told myself, you can handle this. Just don't tell anyone. Do what he said. A million objections jumped out at me, but I forced myself to ignore them. Clean the house, I admonished myself. Forget that license plate number. Nothing will happen to you.

I vacuumed and dusted and picked up; I washed the dishes and made a grocery list. I was just about ready to go to the store when my pager started its relentless beeping once again.

It turned out to be a wire cut—sounded bad. I clambered into the truck and headed out to Corralitos, a little community in the hills northeast of Watsonville. My mind scrambled around like a cat in a cage the whole drive—back to Paul Cassidy, back to the Whitneys. I knew there had to be some kind of fact that I was missing, something that would explain why I'd been shot at and warned off. I went over every single thing I could remember, over and over again, but nothing jumped out at me.

I got to the call in a zombielike trance and managed to stitch together the horse, which had run through a barbwire fence—an hour-long process that kept me completely absorbed while it was going on at least. The horse's chest and front legs were badly lacerated, but I thought he'd make a complete recovery given time. Just as I was putting in the last suture, my pager beeped again.

A colic that evaporated by the time I got there and a horse with an eye that was swollen nearly shut were relatively simple, stress-free calls. I managed to get the grocery shopping done and get home by five o'clock without incident, fighting to keep my mind on hold the whole time.

When the phone rang as I was shoving cans of chili beans into the cupboard, I jumped a foot.

"Gail?" It was Lonny.

"Yeah. Hi." I knew my voice sounded distant and cold. My heart was hopping in my chest like a startled rabbit.

"Where've you been?"

"Out on calls. I've been busy."

"Would you like to have dinner tonight?" Lonny's voice was hesitant, puzzled. Our relationship had evolved to the point where we expected to see each other any and every evening when neither of us was occupied. I knew my reticence was unnatural, unexpected.

Dinner. Thoughts of Paul Cassidy chased themselves rapidly through my brain. Lonny was quiet on the other end of the phone.

"Sure," I said finally. "Where do you want to meet?" A dinner date—that was safe enough. I wouldn't have to talk about Paul Cassidy; I simply wouldn't mention the murders. And, I acknowledged to myself, I longed to see Lonny, be comforted by his presence.

"How about Francesca's at six?"

"I'll be there."

"Great," he said briefly, then hung up the phone.

It was 5:15. I went into the bedroom and put on a full coat of makeup—matte-tone foundation, blush, eye shadow, eyeliner, mascara, and lip gloss—something I almost never do.

Staring into my closet, I wondered about human vanity. I was terrified of being killed and yet I still wanted to impress Lonny. Oh, well. If you feel like a pitiful, cowardly failure, all the less reason to look like one.

I chose my nicest black pants and a simple scoop-necked top in deep blue-violet silk. My freshwater pearls, silver earrings, a black belt with a silver buckle, the all-purpose black suede shoes, and I was ready. I studied my reflection in the mirror and decided to wear my hair down for once. It waved and curled, a dark lion's mane framing my face. I'd look elegant, anyway, if I faced the executioner.

Shivering, I unlocked the cupboard behind the head-board of my bed, took out the .357 pistol I kept there, and dropped it in the bottom of a deep leather bag. I'd bought the gun when I lived alone during my college years, taken a series of classes to learn to shoot it, and kept it in the "se-cret" cupboard of the old bed ever since. I wasn't sure what good it was going to be now; I certainly didn't plan to start blasting back at Paul Cassidy in some kind of western shoot-out. It was obvious enough that the only likely result of that would be to get me killed. Still, I felt better, not quite so defenseless.

Noting the fog outside the windows, I grabbed a wool coat in a black and cream herringbone tweed and threw a couple of magazines and a black suede evening purse over the holstered gun to conceal it. I toted the now fairly heavy bag up the ladder, gave Blue's head a ritual rub and told him to be a good dog and stay off the couch—to which in-struction he turned a ritual deaf ear—then blanked my mind to the possible consequences of this date. Lonny, I told myself; I'm going to see Lonny.

NINETEEN

I drove into the parking lot behind Francesca's just before six. A cheerful little shack of a place, painted dark green on the outside, with red-and-white-checked tablecloths and window curtains, Francesca's has candles in straw-covered wine bottles, an uneven wooden floor, and the best Italian food in Santa Cruz County. Pushing my way in the door, I shouldered a path to the bar. Francesca's was crowded. The atmosphere reminded me of one of Ed and Cindy Whitney's parties. The crowd was youngish, well dressed, wealthy; the parking lot was dotted with their BMWs and Porsches.

I didn't see Lonny anywhere, so I got a bottle of Chianti and two wineglasses and went out on the little deck to wait. It was cold outside, enough that I was grateful for the wool coat. Sipping the astringent red wine and watching people arrive for dinner, I could smell the wet seaweed smell of the ocean drifting inland with the fog. It would have been a pleasant moment minus the fear that was preying on my mind.

Lonny didn't keep me waiting long. He came walking

across the parking lot while I was still on my first glass of wine. I watched him hurrying, his long, rangy stride even quicker than usual, his face intent. There was an unconscious virility about him that made my heart melt a little, even under the inauspicious circumstances.

He saw me and his wide boyish smile lit up his face. "Gail." Sitting down on the bench next to me, he picked up a wineglass. "I take it this is for me. And I'm ready for it."

I smiled at him almost involuntarily. "Had a rough day?"

"You could say that. I went roping in Hollister, went three times in every pot, and never made a nickel."

I took another sip of Chianti and felt it warming me. "That doesn't sound like a major tragedy."

He grinned. "But I also never missed a steer. My partners put me out every time."

I laughed. "That's team roping for you."

Lonny hesitated a moment, then asked, "So how was your day?"

"All right."

There was a moment of quiet. Lonny drank some wine and turned the wineglass in his hand, staring at it as if it were a crystal ball. "Is something wrong, Gail?" he said at last.

I was silent, conflicting impulses screaming at me from all directions. Something was sure as hell wrong. But could I tell him? Should I tell him? It was obvious I wasn't going to be able to hide my distress. Should I make up some penny-ante problem at work and pretend I was upset about that?

"You don't have to tell me anything you don't want to." Lonny's voice was neutral, neither rebuffing nor demanding confidences. Swirling the Chianti in his glass, he tipped it back and drank. A party of diners arrived, chattering noisily as they walked across the deck and went into the restaurant. It was cold enough that no one else was interested in sitting outside.

I sat huddled in my coat, cradling my glass of wine in cupped hands, trying to decide what to do. The deck was empty, the parking lot quiet and fog-shrouded. Was Paul Cassidy out there somewhere, crouched behind a BMW, watching me, waiting? I shivered and stood up. "Let's take the wine inside and have dinner and finish this conversation there, okay?"

Back inside the restaurant, surrounded by friendly crowds of Yuppies, I felt relatively safe. We got a table in a corner and sat down. I looked across at Lonny. "Yeah, something is wrong. I'm not sure what to tell you."

"Start at the beginning and go to the end." Lonny said it lightly, but his face looked worried. Belatedly, I realized he probably thought I was upset with him, or wanted to date another man.

"It's nothing to do with us," I said quickly. "It's just that something happened, and I'm not sure if I should tell anybody."

Lonny looked puzzled, as well he might. He spoke cautiously. "Gail, I don't want to intrude on your privacy, you know that. If something's bothering you and you'd like to tell me, I'd like to hear it. If I can help, I will."

Something in the direct, sincere way he said it touched my heart, and despite my best efforts, my eyes filled up with tears. Lonny was very quiet. He reached a hand out across the table, and I took it and held it, feeling the warmth and affection pass like an electrical current between us. It was as though I were plugged into a dynamo, generating comfort. After a minute, my tears receded and I sat up straighter. Patting Lonny's hand gently, I said, "Thanks."

"Anytime."

The waitress came to take our orders and I was spared further explanations, at least for the moment. I chose clam linguini, my favorite of all Francesca's excellent choices. Lonny ordered spaghetti carbonara.

When she walked away, I took a deep breath and forestalled any questions by saying, "I bought another horse today."

"You did what?" Lonny knew my financial situation; he sounded amazed.

"I know, I know. But I couldn't help it." Briefly I told him the story of the show in Salinas, Plumber's injury, Anne Whitney's reaction, and my own decision. "I don't know what in the world I'm going to do with him," I finished up, "but I own him now."

"Gunner's about ready to be put back in training, isn't he?"

"Pretty close."

"Bring him out to my place, then, and we can get him going as a rope horse. You can bring Cindy's horse out there, too, if you want."

"I don't want to impose on you, Lonny."

"You're not imposing."

I smiled at him. "I have to admit, I was kind of hoping you'd offer."

"I figured." He smiled back at me, but then his face got serious again. "Gail, this isn't what was bothering you, is it?"

No point in lying. Lonny would know. "No, it's not."

"Do you want to tell me?"

I sighed. Looked at Lonny and wondered about trust. I trusted Lonny as much as I trusted any human being. I believed he would never knowingly choose to hurt me. But how would he react if I told him about Paul Cassidy? Would he try to take over, make my decisions for me, tell the sheriff's department whether I wanted him to or not? Could I trust him to leave me in charge of my own life, even when my life was in danger?

I thought so, but I wasn't sure. On the other hand, I hadn't come up with any solutions to the problem, other than living in fear, which wasn't very satisfactory. Maybe Lonny would have an idea; maybe he could help.

Staring at him, I tried to decide whether confiding in this kind-looking man who touched me with such tenderness and passion was the thing to do. Part of me wanted to, wanted to believe he could solve my problems and keep me safe, as well.

Yet the instinct to trust no one but myself was strong in me, almost stronger than logic. I'd become self-sufficient after my parents died, out of necessity, not choice; now it was a way of life, a habit. Getting into a relationship with Lonny had stretched my boundaries, but we seemed to have solved that problem by retaining a fair degree of autonomy and separate space in our lives. We had some real connectedness between us. Still, when danger threatened, my instinct was to pull into myself.

I had to face the facts. I was reluctant to confide in Lonny more because of my own possibly neurotic desire to remain independent—a determination not to need anyone else to survive—than because I was afraid he would tell the wrong person, or fail to respect my decisions. It was possible, I told myself grimly, that my neurotic instincts were going to get me killed.

And then again, I rationalized, what could Lonny do that I couldn't? Give the sheriff's department that license number? I cringed at the very thought. Stay with me night and day? Paul Cassidy would simply kill him, too. Cassidy had said he would kill anyone I told. I would be putting Lonny's life at risk for no good reason.

Lonny had stayed quiet through the long moments of this inner monologue, munching bread and salad, waiting for me to work things out. Concern deepened the lines of age around his mouth. I took a big swallow of wine and looked at him.

It was his eyes that decided me; I'd never known a man

with eyes as straightforward and intelligent as Lonny's.

"Somebody threatened to kill me," I said.

I recounted my meeting with Paul Cassidy over salad and dinner, leaving out only the fact that I'd memorized his license number, telling Lonny directly that the man had scared me enough to keep me from talking to anyone, including Lonny himself.

Lonny showed sympathy for that. Covering my hand with his, he squeezed gently. "I don't blame you for being scared."

"There're a couple of things I don't understand, though. Paul Cassidy implied he didn't shoot at me and miss that night in Bonny Doon." I grimaced. "And I found out from Hilde Fredericks that that cabin belonged to Amber St. Claire's uncle. I have a feeling Amber must be connected, and I can picture her hiring some hit man to bump me off if she wanted. But why? It doesn't make any sense. And I sort of believe that guy when he said he didn't do it. I have the feeling he wouldn't have missed."

We'd finished our dinner by this time and Lonny looked at me seriously over the empty plates. "Gail, I don't think the best approach to this is to go on playing detective."

"I'm not. Believe me, I'm not. It's just that I don't know what the best approach is."

"Tell the sheriff's department."

I shook my head. "That would get me killed for sure."

"They could give you protection."

"I don't trust the sheriff's department versus Paul Cassidy. I'd bet on him every time."

"So what do you want to do?"

I looked at him in frustration. "I don't know. I just don't know." As I'd realized before I told him, Lonny didn't have any answers to this situation that I didn't have myself. He also didn't know I had the Jaguar's license number. If he knew, I thought, he'd be sure I ought to go to the cops and hope they could arrest the guy. Trouble was, I just didn't believe they'd get it done.

Lonny was calling the waitress over to order coffee when my pager beeped, unpleasantly shrill in the crowded restaurant. A few diners stared at me curiously. I got up, telling Lonny, "There's a phone in the bar; I'll be right back."

It didn't take me two minutes. Back at the table I told him, "It's a horse that's been colicking off and on for a month, probably sand in the gut. It could be a problem. Horses that colic over and over like this usually need surgery in the end. I have to go up there right away."

"I'll go with you."

I studied him. The idea was appealing, but I wondered if it was smart. "I know this lady. She doesn't have anything to do with the Whitneys. She can't be involved. And if Paul Cassidy is watching me, I ought to behave normally, as if I hadn't told you a thing. And normally, you wouldn't go with me on a call."

"I still think I should go."

"I don't think so, Lonny." I put a hand on the leather bag next to me and said quietly, "I've got my gun in here. I'll be okay."

"Gail, the gun isn't going to help."

"What will help is if I behave normally," I half-snapped at him, then apologized. "I know you want to help me. I appreciate it; I really do. But I think I'd better go by myself. I don't want that guy to think I told anybody."

Lonny regarded me with obvious frustration, then shook his head. "It's your choice. Will you come to my house afterward?"

"You bet. You can comfort me."

He smiled suddenly, that surprisingly youthful smile that seemed to endow him with the zest of a teenager while the wisdom of forty-seven years was reflected in his eyes. As a combination, it was hard to beat. For a second, I forgot all about Paul Cassidy and my mind went back to three nights ago and the way my body had responded to Lonny's.

He took my hand and stood up with me. "Take care of yourself. I want a chance to do some comforting."

"I can't wait."

TWENTY

I drove up Highway 17 toward Summit Road with my mind churning like an eggbeater. Talking to Lonny had made me feel better, but it hadn't answered any questions.

The mysterious "people" Paul Cassidy worked for, the "people" who I assumed had ordered Ed and Cindy killed—were they involved with Amber St. Claire? Were "they," in fact, simply Amber St. Claire? Or was the shooting at Amber's uncle's cabin merely a bizarre coincidence, nothing to do with the Whitneys' murders and Paul Cassidy's threat? It seemed unlikely, but I supposed it was possible. Even so, Amber must be connected to that shooting, if nothing else.

I decided to give a new scenario a try. Amber either shot at me herself or had someone do it for reasons unknown; separate from that, Paul Cassidy killed the Whitneys, then warned me off because somehow or other he'd realized I was poking around the murder investigation. The "people" Paul Cassidy worked for wanted Terry White arrested for the crime and an end to the investigation. That raised certain ideas.

If I looked at things that way, it explained why Paul Cassidy had warned me off and not killed me. Killing me would only stir the investigation up again, as the connection between my finding the bodies and my being shot might be all too obvious.

Once again, that left the question, Who were these "people"?

I'd been so absorbed with Amber that the simple answer had eluded me. What had Bret's little flame Lynnie said? "Do you think it was a hit? . . . Because of what Ed sold."

Paul Cassidy certainly had the look of a man who worked for organized crime. And if Ed had offended his supplier in some way, it could explain why he'd been shot. Perhaps Cindy had been killed just because she was there. But then, who had shot at me that night and why?

I was rolling down Summit Road now, driving slowly, my mind on my problems, my eyes on the twisting curves. No fog this far inland—a high hard-white moon, half-full, shone in a blue-black sky. I could see the dark silhouettes of redwoods and firs against the silvery blanks of open fields. Houses here and there with their lights on only made the night seem blacker.

Summit Road was fairly well populated; it ran along the ridgeline of the Santa Cruz Mountains, halfway between Santa Cruz and San Jose, and was a convenient spot for those who worked in the Silicon Valley and wanted to "live in the country." Like Scotts Valley, Carl Whitney's town, which sat at the foot of the mountains, the Summit Road area had experienced a lot of growth in the last ten years.

Brenda Carrera lived on a neat one-acre plot with a house, barn, corral, and two Arabian mares. Shalimar, the older one, had colicked roughly a month ago and had never really gotten over it. She kept having recurring bouts of pain and I had advised Brenda to send her to the veterinary surgery center at Davis if she kept it up, as I had already prescribed all the medical treatments available to me.

Recurring colic of this sort was usually either caused by sand or stones or worm damage in the gut; in Shalimar's case, I suspected sand, as the Summit Road area was very sandy and I had treated many horses up here with similar problems.

Brenda was waiting for me outside her barn, her eyes big and worried in the beam of my headlights. She was at my side, talking, before I had even gotten out of the truck.

"Gail, I'm sorry to get you out, you look so nice—I must have dragged you away from a party, but she's doing it again and I think she's worse, I really do."

"No problem. I'll have a look at her."

Collecting the stuff I thought I'd need, I headed toward the barn, holding everything a little gingerly, I have to admit. I'd forgotten to throw jeans and a sweatshirt in the truck, and doing ranch calls in my good clothes was not my favorite thing. My clothing allowance wouldn't stand for the replacement costs.

Shalimar did indeed look bad. A little gray mare with a keen head, she usually had an alert, friendly expression; tonight her eyes were flat and blank, with that inward look to them that meant a horse was focused on its own pain. There were big patches of sweat on her neck and shoulders and the ground in her pen was torn up. As I watched, she began kicking at her belly with a back leg, then dropped to the ground suddenly and began to roll.

"Quick," I told Brenda, "bring a halter."

Brenda was back just as Shalimar got to her feet. I put the halter on the horse and said, "Try to make her move if she starts to roll again. I need to check her out, so as long as she'll stand there, leave her alone."

The mare's pulse and respiration were severely elevated, her gums dark and her gut sounds nonexistent. Based on her history, I was pretty sure she needed surgery.

"Brenda," I said, "I think it's time to take her to Davis, if you want to save her."

Brenda looked agonized; I knew how she felt. She held down a reasonably good job at Hewlett-Packard and could afford a big veterinary bill, but it wouldn't be easy. Still, she loved her horse.

"How good are her chances?" she asked me.

"Pretty good, I'd say, if you go now. The longer you wait, the worse the odds get."

"How expensive is it going to be?"

"At least twenty-five hundred, maybe more."

There was a moment of silence while Brenda stared at the mare. Shalimar was breathing hard but standing still, for the moment. Brenda touched the sweaty neck lightly. "All right, I'll go."

"Go ahead and hitch up your trailer; I'll call the veterinary surgery center and make arrangements," I told her.

I made the call, sedated Shalimar and gave her painkillers to get her through the trailer ride, then helped Brenda load her.

"Good luck," I said. "Call me and let me know how she does."

She nodded and pulled out of her driveway, headed for the highway, for Davis, two and a half hours away. A long, grim, lonely drive, with possible tragedy at the end of it. Poor Brenda.

I got in my own pickup and headed down Summit Road, going the other way. Summit connected with old San Jose Road several miles ahead, and I thought I'd drive back by my house and change my clothes before I went to Lonny's. I hadn't gone a mile before the pager beeped again. Damn, damn, and damn.

There was a pay phone at the Loma Prieta store. I called

the answering service. "This is Dr. McCarthy."

"Yes. An Amber St. Claire has an emergency. A horse is dying."

Amber. My God.

"Dying of what?" I tried not to sound as shaken as I felt.

"She didn't say. I asked. She said she didn't know, that it was just dying." The answering service operator sounded young, female, and nervous. I could picture Amber snapping at her questions.

"Okay," I told her, and hung up the phone.

Now what? I stared at my truck, sitting forlornly in the empty parking lot. Amber's place was, fortunately or unfortunately, only three miles from here. I could hardly justify driving down to pick up Lonny and driving back up, a process that would take a full hour. If Amber had a dying horse it would be downright criminally negligent to waste that much time.

On the other hand, Paul Cassidy was out there somewhere in the inky darkness. Was he at Amber's, waiting for me?

I drew my wool coat more closely around my body and hurried out to my pickup, locking the doors once I was inside. Now what? My mind kept repeating the question, over and over, robotically. Now what? Now what?

I didn't know. I started the truck and stared through the windshield at nothing, trying to decide what to do.

My sense of survival told me not to go to Amber's. My sense of responsibility told me I had to. After a long minute of fearful dithering, I climbed back out of the truck and ran to the telephone, looking over my shoulder as I went.

Calling Lonny, I told him I had an emergency stop to make at Amber's. I cut off his protests with a firm "I have to," trying to sound stronger than I felt as I told him, "I'll call you or be at your place in an hour. If I don't, come looking for me."

Back in the truck, I headed down Summit Road again, feeling as if I were locked onto automatic pilot. I made the turnoff to Rancho Robles and drove down the winding entry road with a sense of inevitability.

Rancho Robles, Amber's place, was spectacular in the daytime, when its many irrigated, white-board-fenced pastures stood out lush and green in the arid, brushy hills of the summit ridgeline. The house, a two-story imitation southern mansion, was blindingly white, multiporched and balconied, and had the look of a place where people drank mint juleps on the veranda. The ranch also boasted a spectacular view—miles and miles of coastal hills rolling and tumbling down to the blue curve of the Monterey Bay in the distance.

As I drove in the well-lighted driveway, it suddenly seemed ludicrous to suppose that Amber had had anything to do with these crimes. Amber St. Claire had lived in this county all of forty years and her level of wealth was right up there with Anne Whitney's. Such people didn't commit murder. Did they?

If they did, I'd find out, I told myself grimly.

I pulled my truck up to Amber's front door, as the barn was dark, grabbed the leather bag, and walked up a wide flight of steps to bang a brass knocker. Perhaps I should have been afraid, but somehow the whole situation seemed so ordinary that the thought of a killer waiting in the hall to blow my brains out was beyond belief.

Amber opened her own front door, wearing a silky, beaded, clinging trousers-and-tunic type thing that I thought was called lounging pajamas. I had to admit the autumn gold color looked good on her, but the red lips and nails and sequined silk slippers were a little much.

Still, Amber was an attractive woman if you liked that type; her figure was short and curvy with just a tiny hint of plumpness, her light olive skin and brown eyes, though obviously foreign to the dark red hair, contrasted strikingly with it, and her heavy makeup was well done. Money could buy some things, it appeared, looks being one of them.

Amber's eyes widened when she saw me, and I realized my dressed-for-dinner appearance was probably a first in her experience. Amber had never seen me out of work clothes.

She didn't look pleased. There was no "Gail, you look nice," or "I must have gotten you away from something." She simply sniffed and said, "Come this way."

Puzzled, but still not afraid, I followed her into a little side room off the main hall, a room whose fake marble floor, chilly gray walls, and stiff Victorian armchairs deceived me for a minute into thinking it was a sitting room. Then I noticed the beautiful old rolltop desk in the corner and a few framed photographs of horses, pictures I could bet had been taken by Amber's father. This was the ranch office, then, a room I suspected Amber had remodeled along her own lines after Reg St. Claire had died.

Amber sat down in an armchair and crossed one silk-clad leg over the other. She seemed to be waiting for me to sit, though she made no polite offers or gestures. What the hell. I sat, crossing my own legs at the ankle, glad for once that I wasn't facing off a dressy woman wearing my usual jeans, boots, and grubby blouse.

Somehow my clothes and demeanor seemed to discomfit Amber; instead of speaking she got out a cigarette and lit it. Oh great. Between the smoke and her perfume I was going to start choking in a minute.

"Amber, I came out here to see a dying horse," I said firmly. "What's the deal?"

"Oh, the horse is fine now." Amber waved her cigarette airily, dismissing that problem. "But I need to talk to you."

"Okay." Mentally I added that it was going to cost her

the full sixty-dollar emergency charge to talk to me under these circumstances.

"Gail, I know you don't know this"—Amber seemed to be choosing her words carefully—"but Steve and I are engaged."

"Is that so?" My eyebrows lifted as I said it, and Amber hurried on.

"It's a private thing, really. Not official."

Oh yeah? I wanted to say, but I kept my mouth shut.

"I just thought that you might like to know that we have an understanding. Steve can be very charming; I wouldn't want you to get hurt."

Oh my God. I felt like laughing out loud.

"Amber, did you get me up here on a fake emergency call to tell me this?"

"I needed to talk to you," she said defensively.

I stared at her and wondered what to think. The woman was obviously pathologically jealous. I felt sure that she was no more engaged to Steve than the man in the moon; this was just an attempt to run off someone she perceived as competition. If I'd had a kind heart, I could have reassured her that I had no real interest in Steve, that in fact I had a steady boyfriend, but Amber didn't make me feel kind.

The question was, Would her jealousy drive her to murder? I had a feeling that it could, that Amber might go to any lengths if she thought she could get away with it. Trouble was, if she'd hired Paul Cassidy to kill Cindy, killing Ed for convenience sake, and then ordered Cassidy to shoot me, too, what were we doing having this conversation? Why hadn't I simply been picked off by a bullet long ago?

I glanced at the leather bag sitting there within easy reach. It was doubtful I could get the pistol out in time to do me much good if Amber pulled a gun on me. She was smoking her cigarette with uncomfortable concentration; I had a feeling she wished I would say something.

I stood up. "If that's all, I'll be going."

Her eyes flashed to my face and she stood up hastily, her sophisticate's pose lost in the clumsy motion. "Did you understand what I said?"

"More or less."

I swung the leather bag over my shoulder and rested my hand gently on the gun, keeping my eyes on Amber as I walked toward the front door. She followed me willy-nilly, looking angry, and halted in the middle of her entry hall.

"Leave Steve alone," she hissed.

I was reminded of a spitting cat. Giving her the phoniest smile I could work up, I exited without a word, looking over my shoulder several times, I must admit.

Nothing happened. No shots whistled past my ears as I walked down her front steps. I heaved a sigh of relief as I got back in the pickup and muttered a heart-felt "bitch" to the quiet night.

I drove down the driveway with my heart thumping noisily the way it does after I've had a confrontation. Back on Summit Road, I grinned, thinking that adrenaline was surely an antidote to fear. I'd forgotten Paul Cassidy completely.

That thought brought another to mind. If Amber was Paul Cassidy's employer, surely she wouldn't have put herself through such a ridiculous scene. Or, I glanced sharply in my rearview mirror, had it all been a ploy, a way to get him on my tail? Had she lured me up to her house so he could pick me up?

No cars behind me on Summit Road—none that I could see, anyway. I kept checking my rearview mirror all the way down Old San Jose Road, but no headlights appeared.

Still, the idea of it made me nervous again and I passed my little house, sitting lightless under the redwood trees, without stopping. The notion of going through the dark doorway into the empty front room made me shiver. I'd go straight to Lonny's, dress clothes and all.

It was only when I saw Riverview Stables that I changed my plan. Lights were on in Steve's house and barn, even though it was 10:30. The place looked bright and welcoming and I suddenly realized that Steve didn't know what had become of Plumber.

Damn. I should have called him. Paul Cassidy had driven Plumber and his problems right out of my mind. Steve was far too polite to page me on an emergency call just to ask me how the horse was, but he must be wondering.

Abruptly I turned the pickup down the driveway. I had well over half an hour before I was due at Lonny's. It would only take a minute to reassure Steve, I reasoned, and maybe, just maybe, I'd congratulate him. On his engagement, naturally.

TWENTY-ONE

Yellow light spilled from Steve's big barn, and his pickup was parked in front of the house, but Steve himself was nowhere in sight. I slung the leather bag over my shoulder and got out of my truck. Deciding Steve was most likely to be in the lit-up barn, I headed in that direction, picking my way carefully. Neatly raked and sprinkled, this stable yard was an improvement over most, but my suede shoes were obviously going to be the worse for wear.

Walking down the barn aisle, I felt incongruously glamorous in black pants and a tweed coat and wished I'd stopped to change into jeans. Steve would probably think the outfit was meant to impress him.

A stall door stood open halfway down the aisle, and I peered in, expecting to find Steve, but the stall was empty. It wasn't bedded like a stall; it was more of a junk room, with broken manure carts, rakes, and odds and ends scattered everywhere. A bench along one wall seemed to be a medicine counter; I could see several bottles of bute.

In fact, I realized that the boxes stacked on the bench were also filled with bottles of bute. I picked up a bottle to study the label, an unfamiliar brand to me, and got no rattle of pills.

Curiously, I opened the jar and saw that someone had ground the stuff up. This wasn't uncommon; most people prefer not to give their horses pills; "balling" a horse is an awkward procedure that horses don't like at all. Grinding the pills up with a mortar and pestle or a coffee grinder and sprinkling them on some sweet feed is the way it's usually done.

Still, Steve must have an awful lot of horses running on bute in order to justify the bother of grinding the pills up a bottle at a time. I supposed that wasn't surprising. Bridle horses have to work hard; plenty of them had aches and pains and needed a little painkiller in order to perform at their peak.

I called Steve's name out a couple of times and got no response, walking toward the back of the barn as I did so. The huge hay shed that abutted the horse barn was dark— unlikely that Steve would be there. I stepped out a side door to peer down the driveway and my heart seemed to stop in its tracks.

There, parked in the dark behind the barn, out of sight of the casual visitor, was a black Jaguar. Even in the dim light that leaked out of the barn I could read the license plate: 2ZST101.

My God. My God. My God. I was frozen like a mouse in the eye of a snake, trying to decide what it meant, what to do. Had he followed me here, was he waiting for me here, where was he? And which way should I run?

Then I heard voices. They were coming up the driveway behind the barn, still a ways away from me, but approaching, apparently coming from the second, smaller stable a hundred feet away. I could see two figures in the orangy light from the low-intensity sodium bulbs that lit the driveway. One was Steve.

The other was Paul Cassidy. The big bulky body, the particular carriage of his head, the smooth, quiet way of moving—no energy wasted; I recognized him as instantly as if I'd known him all my life.

At that moment I suddenly understood some things that probably should have been obvious sooner. The white powder in the bute bottles, the bute bottles in Cindy's tack room. Jesus.

And Steve. Shit, Steve! Steve, who had been a part of things from the very beginning, but had no possible motive. Suddenly I could think of a motive. This barn had been neglected and dilapidated when he moved into it; it had taken lots of money to fix it up the way he'd done. So just where had he gotten the money?

Horse trainers, in general, do not get rich. I'd never questioned Steve's obvious wealth, but the thought occurred to me now. Too late.

I stepped silently, slowly backward into the overhang of the big hay barn and squeezed between two blocks of hay, willing myself to be invisible in the blackness. The men were close to me, too close for any sudden movements. If I ran they'd see me.

I held perfectly still. I could see them from where I stood frozen between the two haystacks, and I could hear them over the pounding of my heart. They were arguing. Steve's voice was raised—easy to hear; Paul Cassidy's replies were low and even, the same tone he'd used with me. I had to strain to make out his words.

"I need someone else to help distribute this stuff. I can't do it all myself." Steve.

"Your idea to take Whitney out. You take care of his contacts." Paul Cassidy.

"Don't you guys understand? We had to do something about Whitney. He threatened to blow the whistle on us if we wouldn't let him quit. He came into the money from that

damn trust fund and wanted out. We didn't have a choice."
Steve sounded resentful. Paul Cassidy said nothing.

Steve stopped and stood still, not fifty feet from the spot where I huddled. I willed my breath to stop, closed my eyes to hide their gleam, prayed to be a shadow among other shadows.

The two men stood out in the lit driveway; I was a dark spot in the dark barn. Their eyes would see only blackness, I told myself fiercely.

Steve was half-shouting, easy to hear. "Listen, you don't seem to get it. I can sell a little product out of here, and I do. I've got a guy in Watsonville and one up near the University. But I need someone to replace Ed. And I can't go around distributing. I do a lot of business for you. You don't want to jeopardize that."

Cassidy's cold voice: "Don't get the idea you're not expendable. I brought you Whitney's little book. See that you get his regular clients taken care of. Or we'll replace you with someone who will."

No answer from Steve. Just the crunch, crunch of footsteps on gravel. Footsteps moving past my hiding place. One set or two? I couldn't tell, was unwilling to risk opening my eyes until they were well past.

Crunch, crunch, moving away from me. No voices. Two sets, I thought. Slowly I opened my eyes.

The men were past me, walking toward the Jaguar, saying nothing to each other. I took a deep breath.

I needed to get out of here, right now. But they were between me and my truck. My truck. Sweet Jesus, my truck. They'd see my truck and know I was here. That truck was my death warrant.

Frantically I stared in the other direction. The driveway ran between the hay barn and the smaller horse barn and dead-ended, as I remembered, at the manure pile down by the creek. If I could get down there, I could cross Soquel

Creek, only ankle-deep this time of year, and scramble through the cottonwoods and willows on the other bank. Cherryvale Road was over there somewhere; I had a client who lived at the end of the road.

Calculating desperately, I felt sure that Julie Mobley's place was only ten minutes away from me if I started from here and sprinted. But when to start?

The men were still in easy view; if I could see them, they could spot me. As I watched, Paul Cassidy stepped up to his Jaguar and suddenly froze. Like an animal scenting danger, his head turned toward the stable yard. The stable yard where my truck sat.

He said something to Steve that I couldn't hear and Steve walked forward and looked where he was looking. I could hear Steve's comment perfectly. "It's that damn vet."

Instantly both men were moving away from me, toward my truck. I crouched to run, then hesitated. They were still in full view, but their attention was elsewhere. Should I?

They stopped, answering my question for me. There was a gun in Paul Cassidy's hand, as if it had magically appeared there. I held my breath and froze some more.

Steve made a comment to Cassidy I couldn't hear and Cassidy turned to face him, facing in my direction at the same time. I could hear him clearly.

"You listen and listen good, because I'm not going to say it again. You've been nothing but trouble from the start, you little prick, and I'm getting tired of you. We take this girlie vet out the way I say, because I don't want any loose ends screwing up the damn Whitney thing. That'd make trouble for John, and we don't need that. You"—I could taste the metal in his voice—"we can do without."

Steve didn't reply. My own mind spun wildly. John? Who was John? None of the players in this deal were named John. One of Carl Whitney's sons? Hadn't it been Pete and Jim? So who was John?

"So where would the girlie vet go? In the house?"

Steve hesitated. "No," he said finally. "She might knock on the door, but she wouldn't go in if I didn't answer. She's probably in the barn. I don't know what the hell she's doing here."

Reassuring you that Plumber is taken care of, I thought bitterly. What a stupid mistake.

"It doesn't matter what she's doing here," Paul Cassidy said flatly. "If she hasn't seen us, she doesn't know anything's up. But I'm not taking any more chances. You just go on in the barn and call her name out nice and normal, then stand there and talk to her about whatever. I'll get behind her. Then you're out of it."

"What are you going to do?"

"She can drive me up the road in her pickup. It won't take long. When they find her and her truck in the bottom of one of those canyons, it'll just be another nasty accident."

"What if she doesn't die?"

Cassidy's head moved in a slow shake. I could feel the sense of coiled power that emanated from him. "Jesus Christ. I'll kill her first. I can strangle one and never leave a mark. Then I roll her and the truck off that steep spot a couple of miles up the road. No one will suspect a thing. So get the fuck out of here and find her."

Steve turned and headed toward the front of the barn without another word.

Jesus. Now what? Should I bluff? Walk up to Steve normally and then run past him to my truck? No way in the world that would work. Once Paul Cassidy saw me I was dead.

Hide. I had to hide. Hide until they were both near the front of the barn, and then run. Across the creek, to Julie's They'd expect me to run for my truck; they'd be watching in that direction. I'd get a chance—I'd have to get a chance— to run out the back.

Paul Cassidy still stood near his Jaguar, gun held loosely in one hand. The orangy sodium lights cast an ominous glow in the air around him, as though the barn was burning. Cassidy's dark suit was black in the odd light. His head was turning toward me.

Once again I held my breath and shut my eyes. Willed myself a shadow in the shadows of the haystack. Prayed my black pants and dark jacket would disappear in the night.

He was coming. Walking toward me. I could hear the crunch of his footsteps.

Do not panic. Do not panic. I held still. He hadn't seen me. He wouldn't see me.

Crunch, crunch, crunch. More footsteps. Then silence. I held perfectly still.

Steve's voice from inside the barn: "Gail?"

I held perfectly still, eyes closed. Where was Cassidy?

"Gail?" Steve called again, louder. "Gail, are you here?"

More silence.

"She must be in the house."

I nearly jumped a foot. The voice was Cassidy's, not twenty feet from me. My eyes opened automatically.

Cassidy was standing near the back door of the barn, the door I'd walked out of when I'd seen the Jaguar. He was facing away from me, facing down the breezeway toward Steve, his back to the hay barn. He was so close the hair on the back of my neck lifted.

"Go check the house," he said to Steve. "I'll stay here."

Steve walked away in the direction of the house. Paul Cassidy stayed where he was, looking slowly around.

Move, you bastard. My mind was screaming it. Go away. Look somewhere else. Do not come back here.

As if my thoughts had pushed him, Paul Cassidy began to walk away from me. Slowly, still looking around. Every sense on the alert. Like a big cat hunting rabbits.

I kept perfectly still. I wanted to wiggle farther back into my crack, but I didn't dare. The slightest noise, I was sure, and he would have me.

He stopped when he came to the open stall door, the stall that held the bottles of bute, and stared inside.

My God, what a scam. Phenlybutazone, ground up, is a white powder. What easier, safer way for a horse person to distribute another white powder. All those bottles in Cindy's tack room—those were Ed's stash. And I'd seen them. And Steve knew I'd seen them.

Of course, I hadn't a clue what I'd seen. And I never would have guessed. But Steve panicked. That had to be it. He'd talked to me that night, after he'd discovered I'd found the bodies. He'd called me out to look at Amber's mare, when he knew she didn't have a bowed tendon. Called me out to find out if I'd seen the bute. And I had.

But why did that matter? Because, I reasoned, he'd taken it with him when he picked up Plumber. Out of greed, or to conceal Ed's link with drugs, maybe. Either way, he must have taken it, and he didn't want me to mention that I'd seen it. Didn't want it brought up at all.

It was Steve who'd tried to kill me in Bonny Doon; I was sure of it. Amber must have taken him up to her uncle's cabin at some point or other, probably for a romantic interlude, and Steve had remembered it as a good spot for an ambush. But still, what a stupid thing to do. I'd never have mentioned the bute; it never would have occurred to me.

Paul Cassidy, I thought, staring at his dark form in the lit breezeway, would not have panicked like that. Paul Cassidy was a pro. That was why he was mad at Steve. Killing me was unnecessary.

Had been unnecessary. Not anymore. Now it was vital. And Paul Cassidy wouldn't make a mistake. What could I do? What the hell could I do?

I held still. Thought about the hay barn where I stood. I'd never been inside it before, only seen it from the outside.

It looked like a typical hay barn—a pole barn—no walls, just a roof. Under the roof, the hay was stacked in separate twenty-foot-high stacks, set there by a hay squeeze, a kind of giant forklift. All big outfits handled hay this way—hand stacking was prohibitively time-consuming.

At the moment I was standing wedged between two huge blocks of hay that towered over me, their tops vanishing somewhere near the roof. If I wiggled back through the crack, more toward the center of the barn, so to speak, I could get better hidden. But I would lose my ability to see what was going on, to choose the right moment to dash for the creek. I pictured myself curled in a little ball in a crevice in the haystack, waiting silently, like a child playing hide-and-seek, for discovery.

No way. I'd stay here, take my chances on running, get shot down in action if need be.

The strap of the leather bag dug into my shoulder, reminding me that I was carrying a gun. For a second a wave of hope washed over me, but it died instantly.

I couldn't count on killing Paul Cassidy; I shot only moderately well, and I hadn't practiced since I moved back to Santa Cruz. Unless it was a point-blank situation, I'd be far more likely to miss and get myself killed. Still, it would be good to get the gun out, have it in my hand and ready.

Trouble with that was I didn't dare move. Not at all. Paul Cassidy stood in the barn aisle, looking silently and reflectively around him, quiet and relaxed. Holding perfectly still was my only prayer.

Steve's voice. He was half-running into the barn. "She's not in the house." I could see a silvery object in his hand that was probably a gun.

"She must have seen my car." Paul Cassidy's voice was flat. "She's either hiding or she ran up to the road." He looked at Steve. "Where would she hide?"

Oh shit.

I could see Steve's shoulders move. "Anywhere. She could be in any of these stalls. She wouldn't be afraid of a horse."

Cassidy's head turned slowly, scanning. Like a satellite dish finding the signal, it gradually turned in my direction and stopped. "Or in that hay barn."

Breath stopped. My heart pounded in my ears.

Cassidy again. "Turn the lights on in that barn."

"Can't. There aren't any."

Thank God.

Paul Cassidy was quiet for a long moment. "I don't want her getting up to the road," he said at last. "You"—he looked at Steve—"stand out in the driveway, where you can cover her truck and watch this barn. I'll be right back."

He turned fluidly and went out, moving with an effortless grace that belied his formal suit and bulky body. I could feel an immediate rush of relief at the removal of his physical presence.

Steve went out the front and the barn was empty. Could I run?

I didn't know. If Steve could see the side of the barn from where he watched, I didn't dare. Hastily I dug my gun out of the leather bag, took it out of its holster, and gripped the butt with a shaking hand. Then I wiggled farther back into the crack in the haystack.

Sweet dusty alfalfa in my nose, prickles of hay against my cheek. The crack narrowed. I looked up.

The crack was about two feet wide. I put my back against one stack and my feet against the other and began to chimney upward, scrabbling at small corners and holds and wishing I had a hay hook in my hand instead of a gun.

The bales were scratchy and slippery. Normally I might have said I couldn't shimmy up a crack between two twenty-foot haystacks, but, driven by fear, I found it was more than possible. I scrambled and slipped once, near the top. Caught myself by jamming my foot out, almost dropping the gun. My breath was coming in gasps as I heaved myself on top.

Lying flat on my stomach, I wiggled to the edge of the stack. I could see most of the horse barn from here, as well as a short section of the driveway that was just outside the hay barn. Because the partitions that divided the box stalls didn't reach to the roof of the big barn, I could look down into the stalls and see the horses inside: bays, browns, sorrels, an occasional palomino or gray—chomping hay, lying down, resting with one foot cocked. They looked glossy and relaxed under the lights, and I could smell their warm, familiar smell. They were everyday life, real life, the life I had somehow stepped out of. I was in a nightmare; I was prey, hunted by the predator.

The hunters were still not in sight. I gripped my gun with my hands stretched out in front of me and wiggled sideways, trying to find a low spot where my silhouette would be less obvious. When I moved the haystack wobbled.

I froze and waited for my heart to subside. If this stack tipped over, I was dead. The fall could kill me, let alone being smashed by a 140-plus-pound bale. And if that didn't happen, Paul Cassidy would take care of things.

Cassidy. My heart beat harder and I fought desperately to stay calm. I had to think of a plan, some way to defeat Cassidy. He would come back; he would search the hay barn. What could I do?

I could shoot him. From up above, I would have the advantage. He didn't know I was carrying a gun; he wouldn't be afraid of me. I would wait until he approached the haystack I was on top of, then shoot him.

And if I missed him, he'd kill me. There was absolutely no doubt in my mind that he would shoot me and kill me. And if by some miracle I killed him with the first shot, Steve would shoot at me. I had no idea how well Steve shot; it could be very well.

I simply could not see how I could shoot and not get shot myself.

He would be back soon. I lay on my stomach, with the side of my face pressed into the scratchy, dusty hay and thought, I will not be killed like this; I will not. I will beat these bastards.

I wiggled a little, very gingerly, trying to flatten myself still further, and felt the shudder go through the haystack. The bales I was lying on were balanced precariously. I held my breath. Thought about haystacks.

The twenty-foot-high stacks were actually two blocks set on top of each other by a hay squeeze; each block was seven bales high and eight bales to a layer—fifty-six bales to a block. The way they were constructed, the third and sixth layers had a "tie" bale—that is, a bale turned lengthwise instead of laid side by side with the rest. This kept the stack joined together and made it stable. But occasionally the tie bales got forgotten.

By the feel of things I was lying on a stack that was minus a tie bale, a dangerous situation. It was fully twenty feet to the ground, and each bale weighed about one hundred and forty pounds. Falling bales had killed more than one person, which was why ranchers and truckers got angry when the tie bales were forgotten. It would be an ironic twist of fate if I was killed by a haystack before Cassidy could get to me.

Cassidy. Cassidy was coming. The hair seemed to rise on the back of my neck as I heard his voice.

He was in the breezeway. My face was pressed flat against the hay, so I couldn't see him, but I could tell by the sound where he was.

"Check these box stalls. Then the hay barn."

The hay barn. I had a few minutes at most. I could hear

the sound of bolts being slid back, the squeak of stall doors opening, then the slam of the bolts shot home. Praying that both men were occupied by their search, I wiggled gently, delicately backward on my haystack, away from the edge.

One careful shift at a time, I moved my weight until I was lying on the half of the block that was closest to the interior of the barn. Stretching out a foot and hand together, I touched the two bales I had been lying on and felt them move away from me, ever so slightly. The whole other half of the haystack wobbled.

I held my breath and lifted my head. I couldn't see much from my position, just a small section of the breezeway, which was empty at the moment. Slamming stall doors sounded from the other side of the barn.

I waited. Dry mouth. Pounding heart. No voices. Suddenly Cassidy appeared, striding down the lit breezeway toward the hay barn. He had a gun in one hand and a flashlight in the other and he moved with sinewy confidence. The flashlight clicked on, pointed straight at me.

My heart seemed to stop, but he kept walking. The flashlight beam moved erratically, pointed, I realized, merely in the general direction of the hay barn. He was coming to search it.

He would be out of my sight in a minute, so close to the haystack that it would block my view. I could hear the soft scrape of his footsteps, see the top of his dark head moving slowly from side to side; then he vanished beneath me. The diffused light of the flashlight beam filtered upward to my hiding spot; he was pointing the beam itself lower, searching the cracks between the stacks. His footsteps paused. I imagined the flashlight pointed at the crevice where I had hidden. My leather bag was there, abandoned when I began to climb.

Now. *Now.* My heart thudded in my ears. I took a breath, gripped the gun in my right hand, and shoved as hard as I could with my left hand and foot. The stack lurched and wobbled, and in a sudden tumble of falling bales the darkness dissolved into chaos.

Whump. Whump. Whump. Clinging to my half of the stack as it shuddered, tipped, and leaned to rest on the stack next to it, I heard and felt the thuds of bales falling, tumbling, bouncing down twenty feet to the ground. I thought I heard a muffled shout, a sound of shock and reaction, but couldn't be sure. Too much noise and motion, choking clouds of hay dust in the darkness. Fully half the block had fallen—roughly two dozen bales.

Over everything, Steve's shout: "What the hell!"

From the horse barn, I thought. Nowhere near the avalanche of hay. Steve was out there still.

My ears strained for any sound, any response from beneath me, but there was none. It was almost too much to hope for.

Steve's voice: "Cassidy?"

A horse neighed, hooves clattering against box-stall walls. Nothing else.

"Cassidy!"

Steve sounded half-panicked, and hope rose in me. Cassidy was dead or incapacitated and there was only Steve out there to deal with.

Steve. Rage choked my throat, more powerful than fear. Cassidy, dead or alive, was inhuman, a frightening force of nature; I felt nothing about him other than the urge to survive.

But Steve. Steve had smiled his blue-eyed smile at me and tried to kill me. I had liked Steve; I had never imagined such treachery from him.

I tightened my grip on the .357. Steve had a gun. He would come after me. But he didn't know that I had a gun, too. I'll kill you, you bastard. I repeated the words like an incantation.

Flattening myself on the haystack, I pointed my gun in the direction of the breezeway, at the spot where Cassidy had appeared. All my senses seemed to focus; the disorienting rush of events narrowed like a telescope on that one point. I waited.

Nothing. Only silence. No Steve. A minute passed. I counted the seconds slowly. Where was he? What was he doing?

His voice, when it came, was so unexpected I almost jumped.

"I know you're up there, Gail."

Light, pleasant, his everyday voice.

"You might as well give up now. I've got a gun. If you come down, I'll let you go."

Right you will. I held my own gun steadily in front of me. His voice came from the arena, very close to the haystack. I wiggled a little and peered over in that direction.

He was walking toward the gate that led out of the arena into the breezeway, moving slowly, looking up at the haystack. He held a gun in one hand and a flashlight, unlit, in the other. There was nothing of Cassidy's confidence in his movements; despite his casual tone, he looked tense and worried.

Could I shoot him now? Too far away for my limited abilities. I would probably miss him and succeed only in revealing my hiding place. Wait. Wait.

He was in the breezeway now; I could see him clearly. Still too far away, but coming closer. He clicked the flashlight on and the beam sprang out in a white rush of light.

Belatedly, I realized it was moving up, moving straight at me. Steve wouldn't waste time searching crevices; he would guess I was on top of the stack.

No time. I sighted the gun as the light touched me, dazzling my eyes. Aiming at the blinding white spot, I pulled the trigger.

TWENTY-TWO

Deafening noise and what felt like a fist driven into my shoulder. Crashing volleys echoed off the tin roof. My shot and another, I thought disjointedly as I lurched backward. I didn't know if I was hit or merely thrown off balance by the recoil from my own gun.

Horses neighed, clattering in their stalls, frightened by the gunshots. My ears rang. I had no idea if I'd hit Steve.

Long moments before violent sound and motion were replaced by the thought that the flashlight beam was gone. Steve was no longer standing in the barn aisle. I raised my head cautiously. I couldn't see him.

Gently, I twitched my shoulder, then moved my arm. It worked. I couldn't see any blood. Not hit, then. It was another second before I registered the moaning. Low, inarticulate animal sounds underneath the restless noise of upset horses. My first thought was that some stray bullet had injured a horse.

My mind rejected that idea instantly, replacing it with Steve. I craned over the edge of the haystack and saw his feet sticking out in the breezeway.

For a second I was filled with pure elation; I had hit him, then; he was down. Unadulterated relief washed over me in a wave, feeling like the sudden cessation of intolerable pain. I was alive. No one was hunting me anymore.

Like a mouse which scampers free, having seen the cat struck dead by a vagrant bolt of lightning, I slithered down the unstable haystack without thinking, clutching my gun, wanting only away from that barn, when the moans escalated into a cry. "Gail."

I pressed myself against the haystack. Steve lay flat on his back where the breezeway emptied its lit corridor into the darkness of the hay shed. In the spilled light, I could see his prostrate form but no details.

Where was the gun? I knew he had one. He wasn't pointing it at me at the moment, but that didn't mean he wouldn't.

"Gail." It sounded like a croak, so distorted I hardly recognized his voice. "Help me."

I stood frozen, suddenly torn. A minute ago I had tried to kill this man, had wanted him dead with all my heart. Now I felt an inescapable need to help him, despite my fear. I'd been trained to save life, not to take it.

No point in being a fool. "Throw the gun out where I can see it," I ordered, pointing my own gun at him.

"I can't. I can't move my arm."

I stared at him, fearing a trick, finally discerning the black puddle near his right shoulder, seeing the metallic gleam of the gun near his right hand but not in it. Moving carefully, keeping my own gun pointed squarely at his body, I approached him and kicked the gun away.

Standing well back from him, I aimed my gun trained in his direction, and tried to decide what to do.

He found my eyes with his. "Help me. Don't let me bleed to death."

"Why did you kill Cindy?" I hadn't planned to say that;

the words seemed to come of their own accord.

"I didn't." It was a bleated protest. "He did. All I did was call my supplier and tell him we had to deal with Ed. Ed wanted to quit. He was threatening to turn me in if I wouldn't let him quit."

"You knew they would kill him."

"No, I didn't. They sent Cassidy and he just took over. He told me to call Ed and tell him I was coming by to talk about things, then arrange an alibi for myself. That's all I knew."

"What else could it mean? You killed them." I stared down at him, helpless as he was, and felt the volcanic tide of rage bubbling up. "You killed Cindy and you tried to kill me. Because I saw the bute. You can't shoot for shit, or I'd be dead."

He said nothing. The eyes that fixed themselves on mine looked frightened. I pointed my gun directly between the eyes. "Admit it."

"My God, Gail." He seemed to choke. "I didn't want to. I always liked you. I was afraid you'd find out."

"About your dirty little coke racket." Abruptly I felt sick. It seemed to me I could smell Steve's blood over the familiar horsey smell of the barn, and I had a sudden vision of the hay bales behind me shifting and Cassidy emerging, gun in hand.

"I'll call an ambulance," I muttered, and turned away from those pleading eyes, eyes that had had no mercy for anyone else.

Stumbling in my efforts to hurry, I ran down the breeze-way and across the stable yard to the house. The front door stood open and I found a phone on the hall counter. Dialing 911, I requested police and ambulance and hung up as quickly as I could.

Somehow the picture of Paul Cassidy rising from the hay bales like some evil prehistoric monster out of the primordial slime wouldn't leave me. I shivered and my fingers tightened on the gun butt. I needed somebody, anybody; I needed help. Automatically, it seemed, my mind pictured Lonny.

Lonny! I had told him to come looking for me in an hour. I grabbed the phone and dialed Amber St. Claire.

Amber answered on the second ring, her voice sounding edgier than usual. "Yes?"

"Amber, this is Gail."

The voice verged on stridency. "Gail, where the hell are you? There's a man here, and he seems to think I know where you are, which I don't, and he's threatening me."

"Put him on."

Lonny's voice came on the line, sharp with urgency. "Gail, where are you? Are you all right?"

"I'm all right, but I'm in trouble. Don't say anything to Amber, just come straight to Steve Shaw's place."

"I'll be right there."

There was a click as he hung up the phone, and I smiled, reassured, even at this moment, by the empathic certainty in his voice. Glancing up, I caught my smile in the mirror over Steve's hall table, and I almost dropped the phone.

My God, was that me? I was unrecognizable, even to myself, some sort of battered human remnant dug out of a landslide. My whole body was covered with cobwebs, dirt, and bits of hay, my tweed coat was a mottled gray-brown, likewise my pants, which had several long, gaping tears. My face was smudged with dust and my hair was filthy and tangled—a cartoon witch. I raised a hand to wipe some of the grime off my chin, succeeded only in blackening my face still further, and felt sudden tears rise.

Shit. Don't cry now. I sucked in a deep breath and took a firm grip on the gun. Cassidy might be out there, hunting me still. Don't weaken, Gail.

To my relief, I heard the distant whine of a siren growing

rapidly louder. Two minutes later it came down the driveway, proving to be a fire truck. It disgorged several people,
some of whom identified themselves to me as paramedics. I
warned them that the injured men had guns and could be
dangerous, and they milled around uncertainly until a
Highway Patrol car pulled in a moment later. After a quick
conference, they all moved off in the direction of the barn,
the cops with their guns drawn. I stayed where I was,
thoughts and questions turning themselves over in my
mind. I replayed the conversation between Cassidy and
Steve, over and over.

Eventually, a dark green sheriff's car pulled into the stable yard and Detective Ward and a younger male deputy
got out. Jeri Ward's dark blue suit looked as pressed and
immaculate as if it were nine in the morning rather than
midnight, and her always-composed face wore a cool, aloof
expression, but I virtually ran to meet her.

"I need to talk to you. Alone." I was almost babbling in
my urgency, and I felt her recoil; no doubt my appearance
and expression were that of a lunatic. I tried to sound
calmer. "There are two injured men in the barn. The paramedics and cops went after them. They both have guns."

Detective Ward and her colleague turned in that direction, but I grabbed her arm. "I need to talk to you. It's important."

A split second of indecision and then she nodded at the
deputy. "Go on. I'll just be a minute." After he left, she
looked back at me. "Make it quick, Gail."

"What's Detective Reeder's first name?"

Jeri's face went blank. "John."

"I think he's involved in this."

TWENTY-THREE

The next half hour was one long confusion of cops and red lights and sirens and questions. I ended up in Steve's living room, huddled at one end of a leather-covered couch, guarded by a young deputy. Various people asked me things and I answered as best I could; shock and fatigue were beginning to catch up with me.

I was feeling particularly lifeless when I heard Lonny's voice in the hall, raised in no uncertain tones against my guard. A minute later he was beside me on the couch, one arm around my shoulders. "Are you okay?"

"I'm okay. I'm dirty."

My answer must have sounded as weak as I felt, because he took in my obviously drooping spirits and asked only a couple of questions, settling for a brief gist of the story. We sat together on the couch for what seemed a long time, until Detective Ward reappeared with an older, very senior-looking man she introduced as Lieutenant Delgado.

"Would you please tell the lieutenant what happened this

evening and explain what led you to make the statement you made to me earlier." Jeri's voice was impersonal, but I had the sense there was some sort of unspoken conflict going on between her and Lieutenant Delgado.

Once again, I told my story as well as I could and finished up with, "The only John I could think of that had had anything to do with this whole thing was Detective Reeder. I remembered his first name was John. And it made sense that an organized coke racket might have police connections. The idea that I might would 'make trouble for John' fit into that context, too. And Detective Reeder was way too anxious to arrest Terry White. So I told Detective Ward here, whom I trust, my suspicions. That's all."

Lieutenant Delgado and Jeri Ward faced me with equally blank faces, betraying not the slightest reaction to what I'd said. Yet I had a feeling there was a lot going on behind those wooden expressions.

When they didn't speak, I asked, "What happened to the two men?"

There was a long silence, but Jeri finally answered me. "The one you called Paul Cassidy is dead. His neck was broken, presumably by a hay bale.

"He killed Ed and Cindy; I'm sure of it."

"We'll be checking to see if the bullets from his gun match."

"What about Steve?"

"They took him off to the hospital. He's lost some blood and his shoulder's shattered, but he'll heal."

Now it was my turn to be silent. That almost inaudible shout I'd heard, that had been the last sound Paul Cassidy ever made. The sound of life going out of him. And Steve's shattered shoulder—I had broken that shoulder with my bullet. I felt dazed, but not guilty or remorseful. Not yet, anyway. Mostly, I felt tired.

"We'll need you to come down to the department and answer some more questions and sign a statement," Jeri Ward was saying.

"I need to go home." My words were almost drowned out by Lonny's firm, "She needs to rest."

"Tomorrow morning will be fine," Lieutenant Delgado said calmly. "You can go now."

I remember nothing of the drive home. Lonny must have put me in my own bed, because that's where I woke up the next morning. The clock on the table said 10:30. I stared at the footboard of my bed and tried to remember what had happened. Lonny had slept with me, I knew that, but he was gone now. He must have left without waking me.

Sounds of footsteps upstairs stirred me further, so I got up and threw some jeans and a sweatshirt on and went to investigate. Bret was making coffee in the kitchen.

He grinned when he saw me. "How's the heroine?"

I shook my head. Bret's hair was sun-streaked, his brown skin tanned, his green eyes laughing. Next to him, I felt like a faded, pallid ghost of a human being.

"The heroine's ready for a cup of coffee," I told him.

Walking into the living room, I collapsed on one end of the couch. Blue was curled up on the seat of my good armchair. He got down stiffly when he saw me, wagged his stump of a tail ferociously, put his chin on my knee, and licked my hand. I patted his rough hair and breathed his smelly old-dog breath and was glad to see him, too.

Lonny'd left a note on the big wooden power company spool I used for a coffee table. In his usual hasty scrawl, it said merely that he'd gone down to the sheriff's department and would tell them not to bother me, that I'd be in later. "Come by my place around six, I'll cook you dinner," it closed.

"So how'd you get here?" I asked Bret.

"I went down to Steve Shaw's place this morning to finish shoeing the last couple of horses he had for me. There were cops everywhere and the horses hadn't been fed. Your boyfriend was there"—Bret gave me a grin—"and he was talking the cops into letting him feed. I helped him and he told me the story and sent me up here to see how you were doing. So here I am."

He fixed me with a solemn stare, solemn for Bret, anyway. "So how the hell did you get involved in that shit?"

"Beats me," I said wearily. "As far as I knew, I was just doing my job when I stumbled on two dead bodies. Then I get shot at and warned off. But the funny thing is, I had no idea Steve was behind it all. I dropped by his place last night entirely by accident; I was going to tell him about Plumber. I didn't even figure it out when I first saw the bute bottles in his barn." I shook my head, feeling stupid.

"Steve." Bret looked as confused as I felt. "I mean, I never liked the guy and I've got no problems believing he was dealing coke and having Ed sell it for him, but . . . killing Ed and Cindy? That's hard to believe."

"I'm pretty sure he didn't actually murder them. He just basically set it up for that hit man to do. Told Ed he was coming over to discuss things." I looked at Bret. "That's why Ed wanted you out of there that evening." Bret nodded blankly, no doubt thinking about what might have happened if he hadn't left in time.

"Steve probably had a nice little alibi." I had to smile. "In fact, I bet he stayed with Amber. I wouldn't be surprised if that's what all her hoopla was about."

"What hoopla?"

"Oh, Amber called me up to her place last night to warn me off Steve. Said they were engaged or had an understanding or something. I imagine he spent that one night with her and she was trying to build it into a lifetime commitment."

Amber. Amber would find out about Steve today, through the papers, if no other way. For a minute I felt sorry for her. All her fantasies would be torn to shreds. Because of me.

I put my coffee cup down and got up abruptly. "Guess I'd better get dressed and get down to the sheriff's department."

"Okay." Bret grinned again, irrepressible as always. "Hope you don't mind riding in Big Red. Your truck's still down at Steve's place; Lonny drove you home last night. I'll take you down there if you want."

"Let's go."

TWENTY-FOUR

At six o'clock that evening, I was on my way to Lonny's. I'd signed my statement at the sheriff's office and learned that the bullets recovered from Ed and Cindy Whitney's bodies had undoubtedly come from Paul Cassidy's gun. I'd also heard that Steve Shaw was still in the hospital, saying nothing to anyone except his lawyer. That was the extent of the information Jeri Ward would give me.

When I asked about Detective Reeder, her face closed up. "We're investigating," and "He's on a paid leave right now," was all she would say. Still, I had the notion there was satisfaction in her voice. She would probably never tell me a thing, but I felt sure that Jeri had been unhappy with John Reeder's conduct for a long time and was resolutely pushing this investigation into his dealings, possibly against the lieutenant's wishes.

At any rate, I'd learned nothing more from her, merely spent an hour rehashing the story I'd told them last night. After that, I'd paid a couple of visits.

The summer afternoon had been in its full glory when I'd driven down toward the harbor. Blue-green water glittered in front of me, sparkling with little points of dancing white light. A soft breeze came off the bay, smelling of seaweed and wet sand, and a sailboat moved through the channel, brightly colored sails billowing in the sunshine like a scene off a Santa Cruz postcard.

Glenda Thorne met me at the door of the Start house, wearing another swirling skirt, her frizzy hair hidden by an ethnic-looking bandanna. Her eyes were friendly this time, though, and she remembered my name. "Gail, isn't it? Detective Ward called this morning to let us know that Terry was cleared."

I smiled back at her. "I just wanted to find out how he was doing."

"I'm not sure how much he's really taken in yet. Come say hi to him."

I followed her up the stairs to Terry's room. He was sitting in the same chair he'd been in before, but it faced the window this time, and the window was open. The warm salt smell of the beach filled the room; I could see the boats down at their docks, hear the screech of the seagulls. Terry turned to look at me as I walked in his door.

"Hi." I still found it difficult to talk to him. "I'm Gail. I saw you in Cindy's garage, remember?"

Terry mumbled some words, none of them intelligible to me.

"I just wanted you to know it's okay. We caught the man who killed Cindy. Everybody knows it wasn't you."

Another mumble, and then he looked straight in my eyes and gave me a sudden surprisingly sweet smile. "I miss her." Another mumble. "She was nice."

"She *was* nice." A picture of Cindy had emerged, it struck me, since I'd been involved with her death, that was much more complete than the one I'd had of her when she was alive. In some ways her life must have been very difficult, yet she remained the friendly, happy extrovert I'd known, the woman who'd loved Plumber and had taken the time and energy to befriend Terry. A woman, I thought, with a positive attitude.

"Is the horse okay?" The words were barely articulated.

"Yeah. He's hurt himself, but he'll be all right."

Terry looked down, talking to his private voices, his stores of concentration apparently running out, and Glenda touched my arm. As we left, she said, "Things are much better, as you can see. I think he'll recover."

"I hope so."

We said our good-byes and I'd paid my second call. On Plumber.

Standing in the pen with him, I rubbed the light brown neck, straightened his mane so it hung neatly on the left side, and pulled his forelock gently. Plumber bumped me with his nose, his eyes bright and friendly despite the fact that he was keeping his weight off his right front leg. The injured ankle was still neatly wrapped and I patted his shoulder gently.

"You'll be all right, fella," I told him. "I'll take care of you."

Jim was at the office, busying himself with some paperwork, and I made arrangements with him to help me operate on Plumber the next morning and talked him into taking my appointments for that afternoon—no mean feat. Nothing less than a shoot-out with a killer would have convinced him.

Now, driving up the road toward Lonny's, my heart lifted a little, for the first time in what seemed like years, but was really only days. Glancing down at my legs, I smiled. They were light brown, sticking out of fashionably faded and cuffed denim shorts. I hoped Lonny would admire them. Hoped the evening would stay warm and the fog would remain out on the ocean where it belonged.

Lonny's house looked as cheerfully iconoclastic as ever.

Lonny himself was sitting in a chair on the small brick patio outside the kitchen. There was a fire in the barbecue pit in front of him and a bottle of chardonnay in a bucket of ice on the table next to him. He smiled when he saw me.

"Hey, Gail." He gestured at an empty chair. "Have a seat. How about a glass of wine?"

"That would be great." I settled myself into the chair and watched Lonny open the wine. His garden rambled around us, loose and colorful, blue pansies rioting over and through bright red geraniums, salmon-colored climbing roses festooning the brick walls.

Sam was chasing Lonny's young gray cat, Gandalf, around the patio, their two tails fluffed out like bottle-brushes, their eyes big and black. Suddenly Sam stopped, leapt up in the air, and reversed, letting Gandalf chase him. I laughed out loud.

"I like your shorts." Lonny smiled at my legs approvingly as he handed me a glass of wine.

"Nothing like a bottled tan."

His mouth twitched. "Save yourself the skin cancer."

"That's right."

His eyes looked into mine, suddenly serious. "So, how are you doing?"

I looked back at him and we studied each other assessingly. "I'm okay," I said.

"That's good."

"I still feel a little lost, like I don't understand how this all happened to happen to me, if you know what I mean. I didn't suspect Steve of anything; I never thought he had any possible reason to want Ed and Cindy dead. I'm still in shock, I guess."

"He was dealing cocaine in a big way," Lonny said reflectively. "Making lots of money. He probably couldn't stand to see that threatened."

"And it wasn't as if he had to kill anybody himself," I

added. "He just turned the problem over to his 'supplier.' He could always pretend that he had no idea they'd be murdered."

"So why the hell did he ball things up by shooting at you?"

"Stupidity. Panic, maybe. Steve might have been comfortable selling cocaine, but he was out of his league when it came to killing people, I think. I remember he brought up the subject of the bute in Cindy's barn in this roundabout way—that night he called me out to see a horse that he knew was no emergency. When he found out I'd seen the bute bottles, wondered about them, even, he panicked. If he'd just sat tight, everything would have been fine—for him, anyhow. Poor Terry White would have been in jail."

"Thanks to your buddy, old Detective Reeder."

"I suppose so. I couldn't imagine any other John that Cassidy could have meant. I never liked Reeder, anyway. I think he was trying to pin those murders on Terry, and the reason Cassidy didn't want me to look like a murder victim was because the connection between my finding the bodies and my being killed would be too obvious. That would make trouble for John. But Cassidy did have to kill me, at that point, because I'd made the connection between him and Steve."

Lonny was quiet for a minute. "You know, there's one thing I don't understand. Why did they kill the woman, too?"

"Cindy." I sighed. "I think because she knew all about what was going on. From what I picked up, she was upset during the last few days before they were killed. Maybe Ed told her that Steve was threatening them. At any rate, she called Gina Gianelli and told her that she might have to back out of showing Plumber at Salinas. I'd guess that was because she didn't want to be around Steve. And apparently she went to see her parents and told them she was in trouble and needed help. She just knew too much."

We sat together in silence for a while. I could hear bees buzzing on the flowers. A blue jay squawked in an oak tree and flashed between the branches, a bright streak of blue, vivid as the sky. The long, low slant of the evening sunshine lit the equally brilliant blues of delphiniums and lobelias, the sharp crimson of geraniums.

Lonny brought his eyes to rest on mine. "How do you feel about killing Cassidy?"

I'd have to talk about this sometime. "He would have killed me if he could," I said slowly, "and I know now that he killed Ed and Cindy. It's better that he's dead. If he were still alive, I think I'd always be afraid. I can still hear that sound he made, though."

Lonny held out his hand. "You did what you had to do."

I took the hand, and it was warm and comforting, as his body had felt when he held me last night. "I know," I said. "Sometimes it doesn't seem good enough."

Lonny squeezed my hand. "It's good enough. Good enough for me. I love you." There was a smile in his voice, but . . . he'd never said those words before.

"I love you, too," I said after a moment. It sounded right, felt true. I wondered where it would lead.

Lonny squeezed my hand again. "Finish that wine and let's go inside."

I should have guessed.